Sinking

Coming Soon:

Drifting
Book Two of the Sinking Trilogy

Rising
Book Three of the Sinking Trilogy

Standalone Novel:

Autumn in Neverland

Sinking

Sarah Armstrong-Garner

Love2ReadLove2Write Publishing, LLC

Indianapolis, Indiana

© 2015 Sarah Armstrong-Garner

Published by Love2ReadLove2Write Publishing, LLC
Indianapolis, Indiana
www.love2readlove2writepublishing.com

Library of Congress Cataloging-in-Publication Data is on file at the Library of Congress, Washington, DC.

ISBN: 1-943788-04-9
ISBN-13: 978-1-943788-04-0
Library of Congress Control Number: 2015960166

This is a work of fiction. Names, characters, incidents, and dialogues are products of the author's imagination and are not to be construed as real. Any resemblance to actual events or persons, living or dead, is entirely coincidental.

Cover Design by Sara Helwe (www.sara-helwe.com)
Stock Model and Photography by Gemma Wright

For Dad and Josh,
both of you never stopped believing

Prologue ⚛

Remember.

This single word struck through her, seized her even as the sickening maelstrom replaced air with water and reduced her body to convulsing panic.

Remember.

She clawed her fingers into the pulsating sea as it pushed her deeper into the abyss, the dark water clutching tight to its captive. Gasping, she inhaled a throat full of burning saltwater. In desperation she tried to kick, her legs limp, useless.

A storm raged over the ocean; lightning bolts streaked the black sky above her. She struggled to push herself toward the surface. Blinking to keep her heavy eyelids open, she clenched her tingling fingers into fists, driving fingernails into her flesh and something solid. Her fingernail peeled back. She welcomed the pain that might keep her awake, but the stinging quickly dulled. Lifting her arm, she pulled her right palm open, discovering a delicate intertwined knot of coral.

Do not let go, an anxious old woman's voice ordered from deep within her mind. She caged the medallion with her fingers, protecting the fragile coral from the invasive pull of the surrounding water.

Her heart pounding against air-starved lungs, she lunged with every fiber of her body, demanding freedom. But her oppressor held fast, and she only spiraled deeper. The never-ending blackness danced, guiding her into its eternal embrace. Refusing surrender to the angry sea, she used her last bit of strength to pierce the water's surface. She gripped the medallion, fanned her arms wide, and glided forward. The darkness suddenly dissipated, giving way to a starry night now peeking through the black clouds atop the rocking sea. Her hands free of the water, the cold air bit at her skin. One more push and freedom would be hers.

Remember.

But the raging ocean had made its promise to claim her. A fierce wave rolled up and over, driving her weak body to the suffocating crucible below.

Chapter One ⚛

Lady Edith pulled her well-worn shawl closer as she strolled down the beach. The previous night's storm had left debris strewn across the cold, dark sand. Lifting the golden-threaded hem of her dress, the gray-haired matron stepped over a large piece of driftwood and stopped to admire the calm sea. A glimmer in the sand diverted her attention from the rolling waves. Edith prodded the wet earth, stopped, and pulled free an undamaged shell, spiraling radiant orange and cream from the inside out.

Knowing it held no true value other than to collect dust on one of her shelves, Edith nonetheless wrapped her crooked fingers around it and dropped the shell into the pocket of her faded blue overcoat.

Her eyes darted around for any other treasures she might claim. She then turned her gaze toward home: a structure of gray rock and narrow glass windows that forever stared at the sea, separated by flat wooden supports and cement mud. Three protruding chimneys spat dark smoke toward the heavens. Sprouts of grass and clover pushed through the roof shingles. The once beautiful home had become a prison since her husband passed away. She hadn't enough money to maintain the property or go back to her homeland of Norwich, England.

Bantry, Ireland, had claimed her years ago and still would not let her leave.

Servants roamed the grounds, performing the daily duties of the household. Lady Edith spotted a maid teaching a child how to swat a rug. Her smile widened at the thought of the next generation already preparing to serve her.

Dusting grains of sand from her rumpled dress, she walked on until her feet sank into wet sand and she stumbled. Straightening, she saw slim, pale legs encircled with seaweed, protruding from behind a clump of driftwood. A low gasp escaped her thin lips. Edith cried out for help and ran ahead. Stopping short of the ghostly spectacle, she bowed her head, a wizened hand over her fast-beating heart. She whispered a prayer.

"Please, Lord Almighty, let it be no more than I can handle."

She crept to the other side and steadied herself. Her mouth dropped. At her feet lay a naked young maiden, with hair that glistened like brown silk, covering her breasts and part of her face. The old mistress leaned closer. The body was untouched by bruises, but a long cut with dried blood ran from the young woman's right foot up her leg and the discoloring of a fading burn covered part of the woman's left forearm.

"What happened to you, young one?" Edith breathed.

The lass had the appearance of a divine messenger. Her skin glowed like the moon. Her cheeks bore the tint of a fresh red rose. At every curve, her figure was flawless.

"You would have been a prize," Edith mused, sweeping the *cailín's* hair from the porcelain face. "'Tis a pity the ocean took you so young."

A glint of brilliant pink tore Edith's stare from the beautiful face to the dead young woman's hand. The white knuckles of the maiden gripped a fragile skeleton of coral. Edith pried open the hand and held the exquisite display to the sunlight, squinting at its unique design. The cream coral twisted together, three slender branches individually curled toward one another, knotting in the center to form a small triangle. Thin lines of metal copper weaved through the external skeleton holding the design into the place. Small gears linked together inside of the protective core of coral. Edith's fingers traced the outline of the ornament, exploring tiny cavities and pointy edges. An aureole glowed around the seaborne jewelry.

"Are ye all right, Milady?" a stodgy, middle-aged servant shouted, running toward Edith, the breeze ruffling his sandy blond hair.

With the speed of a trained magician, Edith hid the coral in her coat with the shell. The trinkets from the sea clinked together as Edith shifted to answer her servant.

"Yes, William, I'm fine," Edith said. "This poor soul washed up on shore from the storm..."

She stopped mid-sentence as the stranger's eyes opened. Edith dropped to her knees.

"Oh, my holy saints!" she exclaimed. "The child lives."

Edith's fingers briskly touched her own forehead, chest, and shoulders in the sign of the cross.

"My dear, are you all right?"

She stared into the maiden's unfocused eyes, waiting for an answer. Startled, Edith leaned forward in near disbelief. Shades of blue spiraled around dark pupils as the lass frantically surveyed her surroundings. Edith took hold of her arm, propping her up.

"Where do you hail from?" she asked, her voice betraying her eagerness as her mind spun with ideas of nobility and possible reward.

The damsel looked at the roaring waves then back at Edith. Her eyelids fluttered shut. Edith braced the stranger's head before it hit the sand. William reached her side. He stared spellbound at the motionless creature who lay at his feet.

"Don't be improper!" she barked. "Hand me your coat."

He unbuttoned it and handed it to her. Edith laid the coat across the young woman's body and brushed her long, soft hair to the side.

"Carry the lass."

William knelt down, closed his eyes, and inhaled.

"Where could you have come from?" he asked in a trance-like state.

"Get her to the manor!" Edith scolded. "Do not waste my time by asking such silly questions. She cannot answer you. She will only be speaking to the Lord Almighty if you don't move. William. William!"

Edith watched as William reluctantly tore his gaze away from the helpless cailín.

"Pick her up now," she ordered.

He nodded. Lifting the limp body into his arms, he followed Edith to the manor.

Whispers of the mysterious damsel traveled through the ranks of the servants. Only a few had a chance to see her in the long hours that followed her arrival. A young servant, Helen, was assigned to be her sole attendant.

Dew slid down the rock walls of the naturally lit room. Red curtains, faded with age but not a cobweb or a speck of dust on them, swayed over the open window. A seagull perched on the windowsill, crying out to its fellow fliers.

Helen covered the cailín's forehead with a warm, damp rag as Edith paced the room. The maiden, clad in a long, white nightgown, pushed the rag away.

"Do you recognize her?" Edith asked, praying Helen would answer yes, and she could reap an award for the young woman's safe return.

The seagull turned its attention to the room, turning its back to the ocean below.

"No, Milady," Helen said without making eye contact with her employer.

Being in the same room with her mistress turned Helen's stomach with nerves. No more than three months had passed since she was assigned to help Karen, the underweight cook, in the kitchen. Helen was hidden down there, and she liked it that way. Gossip was her window to the world above. Now a part of that world, she felt uneasy.

She grabbed a jar and pulled the cork from the glass lid, releasing the sweet scent of honey. A white ointment gathered at the bottom of the container infused with German Chamomile flowers. Pushing three fingers into the cream, Helen lifted a lump of it on her fingertips. As gently as her callused hands would allow, she rubbed the ointment into the young woman's left arm, covering the healing burn. Infection was something Helen had no desire to deal with, and all precautions were taken, even if it was unnecessary. Lifting the blanket, she lathered the long gash on the woman's leg.

Tapping her fingers on her starched skirt, Edith stopped at the window and pushed the seagull off the ledge. Helen watched the bird spread its wings and sail on the wind. The gull turned its head and squawked at the old woman for displacing him before flying over the crashing waves, skimming the sand of the shore as the dimming afternoon sky bled into the navy blue waters.

Helen turned back to the cold body, and open, alert eyes beamed out at her. She was amazed at how much the cailín's eyes glimmered; deep blues danced with white swirls, intertwined with a bright gold. Helen gazed at the sun setting over the endless ocean and then back at those eyes. It was as if the two were painted from the same canvas of pure beauty, yet somehow lacked human warmth.

"Milady, she be awakened," Helen whispered, putting the young woman's leg down and pulling the covers over her.

Edith hastened to the bed. Frantic, the wide-eyed lass tugged at the blankets. Edith leaned forward, but the young woman dodged the old woman's advance, as a rabbit would a fox.

"You are safe here," Edith reassured her.

The maiden shifted her stare to Helen's eyes with an unnerving focus that chilled the servant's bones. She had the strongest feeling the cailín could see into her soul.

Without taking her eyes away from Edith and Helen, the stranger sat up in bed.

"What is your name?" Edith prodded.

Where am I?

The question repeated itself over and over in the maiden's head.

What is going on? This isn't right!

A plump face with deep-set lines and dried-out lips, breathing out strange words, moved closer to her. A fire lit in her lungs, sending her heart racing.

Stay away from me!

The old creature continued to mouth her words, again with

13

the same pronouncement.

Name? I know that word.

Focusing, she watched the pale lips spit out letters and tongue out syllables.

"Why are her lips turning blue? Helen!"

The old woman's screech sent a chill down the cailín's spine.

"She's not breathing."

Who said that?

The maiden turned to stare into the young servant's face, one she remembered seeing upon waking.

"Oh, for heaven's sakes, girl, breathe!" the old woman screeched again.

Stop making that sound.

The room blurred with every blink. She shook her head, trying to make the pain in her head disappear.

The young servant reached behind her and patted her back.

"It be all right, miss," she said. "There, there."

Bending forward to avoid contact, the cailín felt stale oxygen rush up her windpipe. The taste of blood rested on her tongue for a moment before her lungs reflexively inflated, pulling in heavy dry air and sending her into a coughing frenzy.

"You need to be calm," Helen soothed as she tried to touch her.

Coughing harder, she pushed the servant girl away with more force than she anticipated. Helen flew back but kept her balance.

"What is the matter with her?" the old one said.

"I don't know, Milady." Helen stood fast, rubbing her side.

The lass' throat burned, but her lungs rejoiced with the

invisible necessity of life. She swallowed spit, attempting to stop her coughing fit.

The old woman's lurking, cloudy eyes formed a question, but she waited before saying the words.

"What is your name?" finally issued from the tired mouth. "I'm Edith Donnell, and this is my servant, Helen. Where are you from?"

Breathing in deeply, the maiden looked from the old woman to the young servant girl.

"Did you hear me, my dear? Where are you from?" Edith asked again in a stern voice.

From. Where am I from?

Nothing came to mind of her home, no images or names. Only darkness filled the space where the memories should have been.

Where am I? she tried to ask, but the old one's eyes just bored into her as she realized not a sound came out of her own mouth.

Moving her lips, she tried to mimic her observers.

"Frrromm," she breathed, matching Edith's dry tone.

"Yes, 'from.'" The old one tapped her foot. "Do you understand me?"

Of course I understand you.

She slowly nodded, running her fingers over the stitching of the blankets around her.

"Helen, get her water. Are you thirsty?" Edith asked. "Of course you are."

Helen tipped a glass pitcher. The maiden watched the clear water cling to the spout of the pitcher, growing until its weight sent it falling into the unknown, the goblet.

"Cailín, do you know your name?" Edith asked.

She pulled her eyes away from the cup.

I have a name. God, what is it? Why can't I remember?

Avoiding eye contact, she shook her head, scanning the cold, unfamiliar room.

"Do you remember anything?" Helen blurted.

Edith shot a glance at Helen.

"Retie your hair," Edith ordered.

The stranger took in the strawberry-blond curls that spilled from the messy bun on top of the servant's head.

"Sorry, Milady," Helen whispered.

She liked the sound of Helen's fresh voice. The old woman's voice was raspy and dry.

The servant girl looked down and fumbled with her matted, oily hair.

"Water. I only remember water," she answered, noticing the two women staring at her. "I was sinking to the bottom, and everything around me glowed."

She straightened her sore back.

"Glowed?" Edith asked.

"It could be the lightnin', Milady," Helen whispered.

Helen walked over, holding out the cup for her to take. The cailín glanced at the cup and then up to Helen.

"It be for you, miss. Just fresh water," Helen encouraged, pushing the cup forward.

The cailín wrapped her fingers around the cold glass, pulled it toward her chest, and peered down at the water.

"You need to drink."

Helen pretended to lift a cup to her mouth. The maiden mimicked, sniffing the cool refreshment. A stubby hand grazed her forehead.

Don't touch me!

Quickly, she scooted away from the servant's touch, a rush of anxiety reddening her cheeks. She dropped the cup onto the blanket.

"I'm sorry," Helen said. "I just need to check if you carry a fever."

Helen swiftly picked up the cup and pressed the bottom of her apron over the damp blanket.

The old woman smoothed the wrinkles from her dress before walking to the bed, trapping the maiden between her and the servant. The wary lass shifted sideways, but Edith grabbed her hand and sat next to her. The old woman smiled, displaying a set of crooked yellow teeth, and stroked her hand. The touch felt unnaturally warm. The maiden glanced down at the rough, wrinkled hand that covered hers, unsure if she should pull away.

"My dear, we're not going to hurt you," Edith said. "Helen needs to see if you have a fever, and to do that, she needs to feel your forehead."

"Fever?"

"We need to see if your body carries any sickness, Milady," Helen answered.

The maiden slid her hand away from Edith's, fingertips tingling.

Helen placed the cup back onto the washstand and walked to Edith's side of the bed. She leaned down to look in the stranger's eyes before touching her forehead. The servant's touch burned. The maiden shook her head, and the invading hand moved away.

"You do not have a fever, and you be moving fine. The only thing seeming to be out of place is your memory," Helen said.

Edith smiled again. "Don't worry. I love mysteries. We'll figure out your past, and, if we don't, we'll just make one up. The past is not as important as the future. For now I will call you..."

The old woman held her stare; a cloud of sadness drifted over the faraway brown eyes.

"Jocelyn," she said finally.

Edith stood and proceeded to the heavy door.

"Are you hungry?"

"No," Jocelyn replied, but her tongue was dry, her body ached, and her memories were gone. "Where am I?"

"In my home. Why not try to get some sleep? You have been through a lot and need to rest."

Edith twisted the door's great brass knob.

"Where is your home?"

One foot out of the room, the old woman stopped, irritated. She exhaled before answering.

"In Bantry, Ireland, my dear."

Where the hell is that? Camedia!

Helen rushed to close the threadbare curtains as the sun disappeared into the ocean.

"Goodnight," Edith said, taking her leave.

Helen followed her mistress, leaving Jocelyn alone in the dark room.

Chapter Two ⚛

Edith sat on her large, empty bed and observed Helen
going through her nightly routine: gathering clothes,
approaching the burled wood armoire, throwing open the
doors. Delicately, the maid laid the garments on a burgundy-
upholstered stool, then picked up Edith's dress and looked it
over for stains. None found, she hung the dress with the
others. Helen picked up the blue overcoat and shook the heavy
fabric, sending a sprinkling of dust and the hidden shell and
coral treasure across the hardwood floor.

Edith watched as the fragile shell shattered and the coral
bounced and skittered, waiting for it to break into pieces also.

"Be careful, girl," Edith hissed.

She reached for it, but Helen's fingers were faster.

"I am so sorry, Milady."

The girl cradled the gift from the sea, searching it with
nail-bitten fingers. She was young—a little too young for a
ladies' maid, but healthy and strong. Most were bone-thin,
starving little things, but Helen was plump, quick, and quiet,
virtues of a good maid.

Isabel, Edith's first and only ladies' maid since she was
fifteen, came to Ireland with her many years ago. Edith's older

sister, Jane, had been the wife of the unimaginably wealthy
Baron Christopher Corwin, owner of the Corwin Trading
Company. Jane had convinced their parents a marriage to
Christopher's cousin would be best for Edith. Shortly after, the
marriage was arranged, and Edith was shipped off to marry a
man ten years her senior, whom she had only spoken to once
before.

Her heart quickened as she remembered how scared she
was of her new world. She had clung to Isabel, never allowing
the woman to leave her side, except for the dark hours. Edith's
new husband was kind, but still a stranger who stole her away
from her childhood home.

In the beginning, she would cry into her pillow after he left
her alone in the shifting darkness of her foreign chamber,
begging God to take her home. But it didn't matter how much
she pleaded. Her fate was written in a marriage contract,
signed and sealed, never to be broken.

"Here, child." Edith reached for the coral.

Helen obliged with shaking hands and turned to clean up
the shattered shell.

Edith examined the design for cracks but found none.
What if this would help her guest's memory return? She rolled
the coral in her finger to examine the back. The surface was
flat and smooth as glass, a polar opposite to the rugged front
that protruded to fight away the curious. It was beautiful.
Unlike any jewelry Edith had seen. If she gave it back to
Jocelyn, it would no longer be hers, and the idea of losing
something so unique and alluring without some type of
payment pained Edith's stomach. No, Jocelyn would have to
find another way to remember her past.

"Be there anything else you need, Milady?"

Edith looked up. She handed Helen the coral.

"Put this safely away," she said.

Helen nodded, holding the coral gingerly as she turned to leave.

Where is a safe place to put this? Helen thought as she walked through the manor. She should have asked Lady Edith, but to disturb the mistress now would surely put her out of a job. Helen poked her head into the game room and spotted the bookshelf stacked with books and knickknacks. Their only job was to collect dust—the perfect safe place.

Helen tiptoed, even though she was alone, through the dark room to the tall shelves. She didn't make a sound, afraid to wake the ghosts rumored to sleep in the walls, as she pulled out the coral medallion from a hidden pocket in her dress and looked at it.

It must be new from London, Helen thought, touching the polished copper. A small electrical charge zapped her fingertip. She jerked back, almost dropping the coral.

"What was that?" Helen gasped, watching the lifeless ornament in her palm. She touched it again. The copper was warm as if placed near a fire, but the coral was cold as frost. A pit dropped in Helen's stomach—a warning not to play with the trinket anymore.

Pushing aside a crystal bell, Helen gently put the trinket onto the pine shelf and stepped back. The small coral design was out of place in the room. It was meant to be in the sea, not surrounded by books and man-made knickknacks.

Helen stepped out of the room, delighted with her choice of a safe place to display this unique trophy.

※

The next morning, Jocelyn woke to an insistent pounding on the heavy wooden door of her room. Her heart raced, screaming at her to flee.

Helen poked her head into the dim chamber with a warm smile.

"Good. You be awake."

She closed the door behind her and marched over to the window, opening the curtains. A burst of light flooded the room.

Jocelyn blinked against the burning light. She'd escape if she could, but she didn't know where.

"The mistress asked me to help you get dressed this morn.' She also wishes for you to have breakfast with her."

Breakfast, why?

She nodded, staying silent, watching the young servant's every movement.

Helen stepped to the armoire and pulled out a yellow dress decorated with flowered lace. She held it up to show Jocelyn.

"This one is me favorite. We might have to pin it a wee bit, but I think it will work until we fit it to your size."

Helen smiled as she stroked the material.

"What is that for?" Jocelyn beheld the slightly faded dress.

"You wear it," Helen said, a giggle in her voice. "But you have to get out of bed to put it on."

She placed the dress on a chest at the foot of the mattress and pulled the blanket back, revealing Jocelyn's legs.

"Slide to the edge, and I'll help you up. You must be sore from the beating the ocean gave you."

Jocelyn glared at the closed door. *What's behind it?*

"Is something wrong?"

She shook her head, again debating escape.

"Good. That darn door be the heaviest one in this place. We all have a wager on when the hinges will give way."

Jocelyn swung her legs over the bedside. Helen reached out to take her arm, but Jocelyn shoved Helen away with as much force she could muster and leapt for freedom—only to plummet to the cold, stone floor. Her elbows hit first, knocking hard, then her chin, snapping her head back.

Helen dropped down next to the dazed Jocelyn and pulled her into her arms. Jocelyn reached for the closed door.

"Milady, I have you."

Helen guided Jocelyn to her feet, holding tight to her waist.

"Spread your feet."

Helen stepped between Jocelyn's feet and moved them in line with her shoulders.

"That should help," she said.

Helen stood away from the wobbling Jocelyn, still clutching her waist for security.

"Do your legs hurt?"

Jocelyn stepped forward. Her knees gave way, driving her into Helen's plump arms.

This isn't right. Why don't they work?

She swallowed a knot in her throat, sending it to her stomach, which protested with mad force.

"There be no rush." Helen balanced Jocelyn again. "You'll be running soon enough. Just step with me."

Helen stepped back. Jocelyn slid her foot on the floor.

"Very good," Helen encouraged. "Again."

Helen walked backward around the room until Jocelyn

was able to keep herself off the ground.

"I think you have it, miss," Helen said, guiding Jocelyn to a bedpost.

She clung to it while the servant retrieved the dress.

"My cousin fell off a horse once. Hit his head real hard. It took him three days to remember his own name. His da' had to carry him around the house till he remembered how to walk. Funny what a little bump on the head can do."

With controlled steps, Jocelyn released her grip on the post and inched toward the door.

"One would think you be trying to escape." Helen laughed. "First ye might want to get dressed. The mistress would have me rear end if you leave this room in your chemise."

Jocelyn turned. Helen's joyous laughter radiated kindness. Jocelyn's shoulders relaxed as she took in the sound. No harm would come from this young girl. Still, a tendril of fear crept toward her heart as she thought of what lay beyond her room. What if there were no other Helens?

With the warm dress on her arm, Helen lifted the nightgown over Jocelyn's head and draped the heavy yellow fabric over her naked body. The servant girl pulled at the dress to make it fit and began alterations.

"It definitely be out of fashion, but it is still very beautiful. Isabel will take it in more when you have a proper corset on. There."

Helen stood and turned Jocelyn to look in the tall mirror. They both looked at the scar on Jocelyn's arm.

"Do you remember how you got it?" Helen asked.

Jocelyn shook her head no. Yards of fabric hung from her shoulders, weighing her down.

"How am I to move?"

She tilted her head to admire the way the yellow silk

glittered in the light.

"What a silly question. Just walk. You be doing it all morn.'"

A loud knock on the door startled Jocelyn.

"Comin,'" Helen called. "It be only a servant," she reassured Jocelyn. "The mistress never knocks."

Helen opened the door to William. He whispered to Helen before stealing a glimpse of Jocelyn in the oversized dress. She shrank from his gaze. Though enveloped in fabric, she still felt naked.

"She be ready. Tell her we need only a moment to tie her hair," Helen said.

William nodded and left. When he was gone, Jocelyn stumbled over to Helen.

"Who is he?"

"Oh, that's William. He was with the mistress when she found you. He carried you all the way up here. Now, sit. We need to do something with your hair—and quickly. The mistress does not like to wait."

Moments later, they made their way down to the dining room with Jocelyn holding tight to Helen, fearful of tripping over her own feet. She could feel eyes lurking in the dark corners of the manor and heard whispers moving among the shadows.

She entered the large dining hall, looking for a way out if needed. An imposing wooden table sat in the middle of the room with Edith seated at the far end.

Edith eyed the servant and her guest.

"That took quite a long time."

"Sorry, Milady," Helen said. "We had to size the dress to fit."

"Very well. But tomorrow I expect my guest to be on time

when asked to eat with me."

Helen nodded and turned to leave, but Jocelyn held tight.

Don't leave me, she begged with her eyes.

"You will be fine, Milady. I'll be right in there, in the kitchen."

Helen tilted her chin toward a door. Gently, Helen lifted Jocelyn's fingers from her arm and walked away.

Jocelyn stood stock-still as her only ally left her in the unfriendly room. Edith waved to a young boy standing in the corner. He pranced out into the room, one skinny leg after the other. Jocelyn watched the nimble boy with envy.

"Breakfast will be here soon. I hope you are hungry," Edith said.

Jocelyn, wobbling now, looked around the room. A magnificent tapestry cascaded down the far wall. At first no more than beautiful, colored threads, Jocelyn saw a forest emerge with wild animals that stared back at her. She stood entranced.

I know you.

She leaned in to follow the lines of a deer drinking from a stream. Jocelyn locked eyes with the threaded beast.

"That's a deer from the family *Cervidae*, correct?" she asked.

"That is silly, my child. Deer do not come from families." Edith sniffed.

Her wooden chair groaned as Edith shifted uncomfortably in her seat.

"They are beautiful," Jocelyn whispered.

Edith regarded the tapestry with disdain.

"My husband bought that old thing when he was no older than you. I don't have the heart to throw it out now, with him gone."

"What is it?" Jocelyn asked, still transfixed.

A long silence came and went. Edith cleared her throat.

"A tapestry."

Jocelyn pulled her stare from the tapestry to Edith.

"Where did he go, your husband?"

"He died," Edith said calmly.

"Is he coming back?"

"Dear God no, child. Death is the end for now."

Edith drew a long breath and looked at the woven art.

"Sit down, my dear." Edith waved to a seat on her right. "You cannot eat standing. It's unhealthy."

Jocelyn glared at the chair. *What am I suppose to do with that?*

"It's for sitting."

With irritation, Edith demonstrated by lifting from her own chair and plopping back down.

Jocelyn jerked her way toward the table, struggling with every step. Finally, she grabbed hold of the chair and bent to sit. Her feet thanked her, pulsating from the release of the weight.

A young servant filled her cup with water. She gulped the refreshment, trying to wash away the fusty taste of the room.

Edith watched Jocelyn keenly. "Thirsty?"

Jocelyn put the cup down and wiped her mouth with her palm. The old woman cringed.

"Don't do that, my dear. Use your napkin."

Edith lifted her cloth napkin and patted the sides of her mouth. Jocelyn mimicked.

"Did you sleep well?" Edith asked.

"I believe so."

As she answered, servants marched in with plates of food and placed them in front of the two women. A pleasant aroma filled the room.

"Did your dreams stir memories of whom you may be?"

Edith asked, cutting into a piece of ham.

"Edith?"

Edith swallowed. "My proper title is Mrs. Donnell. What is it, my dear?"

"What is a dream?"

Edith cocked her head, mulling the odd inquiry.

"It is what you see when you are asleep."

Jocelyn looked at the tapestry once more.

"Darkness is all I see."

She turned her plate to angle the ham in front of her. The sweet smell tickled her nose.

Edith observed Jocelyn as she gingerly poked at her food.

How dreadful it must be not to remember your past.

Years ago, Edith would have sold her soul for just that. Her husband, Mr. Gearoid Donnell, wanted for nothing—he had property, a handsome income, and a young wife. He had everything except an heir to carry on his name. Edith was to provide him with a son, no questions asked. For years they tried to no avail—until an October evening, when Edith knew her body was no longer hers alone.

When Gearoid heard the grand news, he began showering her with affection and protection. In the nine months to follow they slept in the same room, ate together, and talked of the coming baby almost constantly. The abandonment she'd felt before her pregnancy now ebbed a little more each day. Her husband had always been good-natured to her, but now he loved her. She was home.

On a warm summer night, their baby was born. The pain tore at her body in waves, crushing her with each blow, but with her final push a joyous cry belted from the lungs of the tiny infant. After hours of pacing the halls listening to his wife's screams, Gearoid burst into the room to welcome his son to the world. But there was no son.

The nurse handed him a daughter, whose gray eyes demanded love. Tears dripped from his cheeks onto the tiny newborn in his hands. Uncontrolled laughter rang from him as he covered the child with kisses. If they could have one, they could have more, and an heir would come eventually, Gearoid announced. He did not care if the firstborn was a girl.

Sitting in bloodstained sheets, a rush of jealousy flooded Edith as she watched her jubilant husband and her new daughter.

What kind of mother am I to feel this way?

She turned her gaze to the ruined bedclothes and inhaled the bitter sweetness of the room, unwittingly locking the painful moment in her heart forever.

They never had another child.

After Gearoid passed away, the property and her fortunes went to the next male heir, Gearoid's cousin — Baron Christopher Corwin, Edith's sister's husband. He was kind enough to allow her to stay, as well as pay for her housing and provide a small stipend. Before he passed away, he demanded his son, Thomas, do the same. Thomas would visit once a year with enough money to keep her afloat until the next year.

But Edith was sick of merely surviving. She wanted new curtains, new furniture, new tapestries. She wanted to be surrounded by glamorous guests at a ravishing ball, and she as hostess.

Edith examined Jocelyn — the fair skin, the uncommon beauty. Perhaps even a regal elegance.

A grinding of glass pierced Edith's daydreaming. She grimaced as Jocelyn pinned her ham to the china with her fork, then sawed with the wrong end of the knife. Edith gestured for a servant to attend Jocelyn as she continued to eat.

Jocelyn chewed with interest. It tasted salty, like the sea.

The young woman, now flanked by a female servant, continued her assault. Edith withdrew quietly from the room and retired to her study to write her nephew a letter.

My dear, sweet Thomas,

I hope all is well in London. I know it is four months' time until you come to visit your aging aunt, but I write you to come sooner. During the last visit I was blessed with, you mentioned you longed to escape the tiring world of a bachelor to enter into a life as a husband and father but have not yet found a bride. I believe I have found a wife for you.

She is truly not from our lands, for she is not like any ordinary woman. She is one who makes men's hearts stop, with eyes that seem to hold the ocean within, and hair softer than feathers from a swan. Her youth of Seventeen is older than most of the brides, but she is no old maid, I assure you. She is of fine breeding, even though we do not discuss such matters, for such a creature to exist without fortune would be a cruel joke from the Lord himself.

I urge you to travel with all speed, for I fear she might not be with me long. Word of her beauty is traveling fast, and the townsmen have already begun to bring gifts to win her heart. I cannot stop her from choosing one of them. I do pray this gets to you before it is too late.

Sincerely, your aunt,

Edith Donnell

Edith glowed with delight. She hurriedly closed the letter with red wax and her husband's seal then handed it to her servant to post to London.

Chapter Three ༄

After two days of stumbling around the manor, Jocelyn walked along the beach with no aid, tripping only a few times. The cold wind coursed through her hair as she gazed at the ocean, and a longing to be held by it crept into her.

Come back to me, the wind whispered.

Peering over her shoulder at Helen, who sat on the sand watching the rolling waves, Jocelyn slipped off her shoes, pulled her dress up, and walked into the low tide. A sudden rush of energy sprang from her toes and sparked through every inch of her. Her lips shivered with the burst. Trembling, she crept further into the sea.

Come back to me, it whispered again in a man's voice that quickened her already racing heart. Her toes pushed into the sand, moving her forward in the strong current. She knew that voice.

Where are you, Mli?

The voice danced though the wind to Jocelyn's eternal thoughts. The memory of a kiss brushing her lips warmed her cheeks.

"Who are you?" Jocelyn exhaled, answering the wind.

Where are you? The voice asked again.

Jocelyn's feet pressed forward. The surrounding world of sand and stone faded away with each slow movement, each step toward the unknown.

"What you are doing?"

A hand grabbed her shoulder. She turned to see Helen, her short legs wiggling in the cold water. Jocelyn turned toward the deep blue of the ocean.

"Don't you hear that?"

"I only be hearing the ocean, Milady."

Helen took her by the waist and led her out of the sea.

"Is that what it is?"

"Yes. It always be sounding like that. Calming, you agree?"

Jocelyn nodded. Humming reverberated from the rocking waves.

"You're shivering. You can't be tromping in the waters," Helen said. "You'll catch your death. Both of our dresses are soaked. Let's go back to the house."

Jocelyn looked at the hem of her dress clinging to her wet legs.

"Come on, Milady."

Helen guided her back to the manor, the ocean's pleas fading in the whipping winds. Jocelyn looked back as the slam of the manor's thick door sealed her into her somber new home once more, quieting the only familiar voice she'd heard since her arrival.

The day passed with no excitement. Jocelyn wandered the halls, looking for a way out of her caged box, but nothing in the floral wallpapered rooms unlocked her memories. Rewinding the few moments she remembered, she focused on the ocean's voice. A butterfly fluttered to her heart, tickling it to beat faster with every word residing in her mind. The deep, orotund voice penetrated with lost remembrance of fear and love.

Jocelyn sat down on a velvet-lined bench, cornered at the end of the long hallway. Closing her eyes, she whispered, "Mli."

What is that? A place? A person? Am I Mli? Jocelyn thought. If she were, then the ocean wanted her back. The salty aftertaste of drowning filled her senses as her eyes sprang open. She would not sink back into the darkness. She stood and walked to her room. If the ocean wanted her, it would have to wait until she knew how to survive the fall into oblivion.

Day after day she stood guard on the dunes overlooking the ocean—when she wasn't occupied by Edith's never-ending gossip—waiting for the voice, but it never came. She was gaining new memories, but her past stayed hidden deep within.

She stood on the edge of the grass-covered dune, wrapped in a blue wool shawl that blocked the biting wind. The ocean was dancing with the air currents. It stroked the sand, daring Jocelyn to step closer. Boredom forced her to swallow her fear. She pulled the shawl closer, covering her exposed neck. If she could hear the voice again, maybe she would get answers. Her feet slid down the dune's edge, landing on wet sand. She pulled off her shoes and stockings, burrowing her naked feet into the warmth. If the ocean wanted her, it would have to come to her.

She watched the ocean's gentle pattern of waves press into the land, daring it with her eyes to stretch out and grab her.

Where are you, Ocean? Jocelyn thought.

You're alive!

The relieved voice boomed over the sea into Jocelyn's mind.

"Who are you?" Jocelyn asked. She waited for the voice to answer, but nothing came. Disappointment flooded her veins. *Come back!* she demanded inwardly.

The ocean swelled, birthing a massive wave that rushed toward her anchored body. The water pounded the beach, swallowing her body, forcing her back into the never-ending blue. Jocelyn struggled to breath as the water flowed into her mouth and lungs, but a welcoming energy shot through her.

Let me go, she ordered the ocean, clawing and kicking the water.

What is happening, Mli?

The voice was back, stronger than before. Fear washed through her, but it was not hers.

Swim to me, the voice demanded.

The wave pulled into another wave, shoving Jocelyn into the sand. She dug her heel into the collapsing sand, struggling to get her head above water. She inhaled deep as another wave crashed down. The sand gave way.

Calm down, the soothing voice whispered into Jocelyn's mind.

Jocelyn's eyes widened. He was near. She could feel him without seeing him. His aura washed over her, urging a blush to paint her cheeks as she waited for his arms to wrap around her.

Calm down, my Mli. Don't struggle.

Jocelyn pounded her fists against the ocean, struggling to gain control again, but it held tight, dragging her further into the sea. She closed her eyes.

Calm down! the voice said again.

Going limp, Jocelyn allowed the ocean to take hold. If she

were going to die, it would be to the sound of this voice. She trusted it. Her body floated to the surface of the calming wate pushing her face through the barrier into the cold air. Where was he? She gulped the oxygen and filled her lungs.

Swim to me, the voice urged again.

Jocelyn looked around, at the ocean pushed against the blue sky and the beach, searching for the owner of the voice. Seagulls pecked the surface of the sea and flew to land, but that was all the life Jocelyn could see.

"Where are you?" she shouted.

Only the gentle pat of the ocean echoed back to her. She had nowhere to swim but to the welcoming, still land. Her fe kicked as a wave took hold of her and pushed her into the beach. The weight of her garments imprinted into the sand as she crawled out of the sea.

The energy of the sea lingered in her, injecting her with adrenaline. She sat up, dripping with water and sand, searching the open sea. The presence of the owner of the voic had been near, lingering somewhere in the deep blue, but nov he had vanished with the changing waters. A man she knew and trusted, leaving her alone and cold.

"Why didn't you save me, damn it!" she cried out, tears dripping onto her drenched dress.

Jocelyn sat shivering in the sand, waiting for the disembodied voice to answer. The sun shifted over the cloudless sky, eating away the hours and drying the unwante tears off Jocelyn's cheeks. The stiffened fabric cracked as she pulled herself from the beach, giving up the war of waiting. She would be back, but she would play it safe and bring Hel with her. The sea would give her what she needed. She lifted her dress and climbed over the dune. The ocean could only have her shoes and stockings for now.

A month passed as Edith waited for her nephew's
sponse. Eager for action, she had written other letters only to
scard them, afraid of sounding too desperate. A storm blew
o the bay, and she had no hope of receiving Thomas's letter
til the storm broke. What ship would dare sail in such
ather? When William placed the damp envelope addressed
m Thomas Corwin on her desk, she let out a small squeal of
before tearing open the letter to reveal fine penmanship.
e read hungrily as rain pelted the roof.

My Dearest Aunt,

*I was quite worried when I received your letter. I feared the worst
til I understood your purpose. Your words are true. The bachelor life
es me, and I do long to settle and produce my heirs. But first I must
d a bride.*

*If this woman is as lovely as you describe, then I must lay my eyes
n her. I will travel at the end of the next week, for I cannot escape
or business arrangements. Please sway her mind from marriage with
y other until my visit.*

Your Loving Nephew,
Thomas

After reading the letter, Edith wasted no time. She called
celyn to the study to begin her training for high society. Day
er day, Edith taught Jocelyn how to use the right
verware, start a conversation, and what not to do or say. She
ked on and on, never noticing Jocelyn's glazed-over eyes
ering out the window toward the imploring ocean.

Chapter Four ✆

Jocelyn gazed at her reflection in a dark walnut-framed mirror. A navy blue satin dress with white ruffles lining the sleeves and bottom flared off her hips. The sleeves puffed up to display her slender arms.

"The dress be fitting ye well. Isabel did a fine job. 'Tis the only thing she be good at these days," Helen remarked as she tidied up the room. "Did ye know she was making the mistress' dresses before the mistress came here to be married? They say she was pretty then, the mistress."

Helen folded Jocelyn's nightgown and placed it under the pillow.

"Is she not pretty now?" Jocelyn rubbed her hands over her face, blinking away the urge to fall asleep.

"I suppose so, but she be warn down. Hold still."

Helen loosened the lace on the back of Jocelyn's dress and began to retie it with a vengeance. Jocelyn gasped for air. Most of the other dresses were loose-fitting and barely hung from her frame. The only repercussions from these were sore shoulders and occasional bruising from the weight of yards of fabric. But this dress hugged tight to her, squeezing her lungs closed.

"Sorry, Milady. The ribbon 'tisn't tied properly, and the mistress wants ye to be looking your best today."

"Why?" Jocelyn grabbed the boned bodice, pulling it away from her crushed ribs.

"You heard her nephew sent word he be coming early this year, and this morn' there was word his ship was spotted off port. The mistress is in a frenzy, not having enough time to prepare and all. She sent William to the dock to keep watch."

"How long until he returns?"

"It be depending on how far out the ship be and how long t takes to dock. The mistress believes the young master should be here before dusk."

"Will her nephew live here after his arrival?" *Breathe. In, out. In, out.* Jocelyn reminded herself.

"Lordy no. He only stays a couple of days and then ventures to Scotland to do business. I heard he be coming early to see ye." Helen tied off the top of the lace as Jocelyn tried to breathe. "You'll be fine; it just takes a while to get used to."

"How can anyone get used to this?"

"Proper ladies do," Helen said. "It be the fashion."

Jocelyn closed her eyes, taking in the small puffs of air the corset would allow.

"Helen, why would he come early to see me? I don't think e has ever met me before."

"I don't know, but we be finding out soon enough."

Helen left the room, leaving Jocelyn alone with her reflection.

She still couldn't remember who she was or where she had been before her arrival two months ago, but she was starting to et used to Edith's home. Helen had helped her become accustomed to Edith's rules of dining, and the other servants ried to explain the ways of their land. She learned quickly, but

39

there was still more knowledge to acquire. Yet she knew things they didn't. She could read, write, and do arithmetic without a second thought. She knew every flower and plant's name that inhabited the area but didn't know why.

Even though Jocelyn was fond of her new home, the ocean still beckoned to her. At night, the waves sang for her to join them in a dance with the stars. But her visits to the sea became less and less frequent. Edith wanted Jocelyn by her side to show her the etiquette of society and to teach her embroidery and needlework. Jocelyn was fascinated with needlework until she poked herself and drew blood. She dropped the needle and refused to touch it again. Edith sighed in resignation and sent Jocelyn to be fitted for her secondhand dresses.

The old ladies' maid, Isabel, sat on a short stool, her back hunched from years of hard work, when Jocelyn came to her. Tufts of gray hair draped the old woman's face, drooping with loose skin, and her body looked little more than a skeleton. When she saw Isabel, Jocelyn's heart dropped to her stomach.

Death was coming. She could smell it lingering around the woman. With two long strides, Jocelyn stood in front of Isabel and knelt down. She peered into Isabel's childhood-blue eyes.

"Good Lord, child. What are you doing?" Isabel asked.

"Do you hurt?"

She placed her hand on Isabel's.

"What a kind soul you have. I hurt no more than I should at this age." Isabel stood, straightening her spine. "Now turn, child, so I can see how the dress hangs."

Jocelyn shook her head. "You hurt more than you are telling me, *merina*."

"What did you say?" Isabel sat down, winded.

"*Merina*. Old one."

"What language is that? Gaelic?"

"No." *Where is it from?*

Standing, Jocelyn hoped more would come to her mind, but only images of dark waters remained.

Who am I? The question stung. She had been down to the ocean searching for answers, but the voice was gone. Only a sweet melody from the ocean's movement serenaded her. The pull to step into the cold waters was becoming too much to bear even with Helen watching over her. Jocelyn started with her toes, dipping them in. Energy sprang to her body, waking dormant cells. The need for this shock of vitality was becoming a daily fix for her.

Jocelyn yawned, yearning for the waters that jolted her to life.

"I may be old, but this the only job I have left, and I will not allow it to be taken away from me. Did you hear me, child?" Isabel twirled her finger. "Let me see that dress."

Jocelyn smiled at the strength in the old woman's voice. She turned, holding tight to the hanging fabric.

"We have a lot of work to do."

Hours passed as Isabel and hundreds of pins redesigned each dress to fit Jocelyn's body. She watched the old woman's fragile fingers expertly work the small needle and thread with perfection. The old woman crackled with energy at times, talking of England and her life experiences.

"If I were to stop working, I might as well die."

"You soon will."

Isabel stopped and stared up at Jocelyn.

"Do you always speak so freely?"

I shouldn't have said that.

"The mistress must be soft in her old age," Isabel said, squinting. "Or your pretty face is keeping you safe. I heard her nephew is gracing us early this year."

Why would my face matter?

"I am told he is on his way," Jocelyn said carefully.

"Jocelyn!" Edith called.

Jocelyn scurried down the stairs from her room, hurrying to Edith's side.

"William just arrived with news from the village. My nephew's ship is no more than an hour from dock. He will be my guest for the next week or so. He is always such a delight to have. Do you, child, remember everything I've taught you?"

She wished she'd paid closer attention to Edith's lectures.

"Yes, Milady."

Edith smiled and took Jocelyn's arm. They walked to the sitting room.

"Good. Under no circumstance must you sway from my words."

Edith patted Jocelyn's hand.

"Mrs. Donnell?"

"Yes."

"Your nephew..."

"Mr. Corwin, my dear, from the Corwin trading company," Edith bragged.

Jocelyn's brow creased.

"It's only the largest trading company in England. He is very wealthy. It is very good for whomever he decides to marry —very good for her indeed," Edith said.

"Good for him," Jocelyn said quietly. She fiddled with the seam of her bodice. "He will not be here for an hour. Is there anything you wish for me to attend to before he arrives?"

"No, my dear, the servants are already attending to everything and you should not get dirty, not today. You may do as you wish until his ship arrives, but do mind the time. I will not tolerate tardiness."

The old woman brushed the back of her hand down Jocelyn's sleeve. "It fits you well. The years have been kind to this old thing, unlike me."

Jocelyn lightly touched Edith's elbow. "What do you mean?"

"Never you mind. The future is bright, my child, for the both of us."

A yawn managed to escape from within Jocelyn's constrictive corset.

"You should rest," Edith said. "Go back to your room. I will call you when he is here."

Sleep would be delightful, but the ocean's cry was too much to bear. She had to be a part of the sea. Somehow, she knew it was dangerous to keep the waters waiting much longer.

Jocelyn didn't wait for Helen to accompany her. There was no time to waste. She ran down the hill to the sandy beaches, her lungs arguing the entire mile. If anyone caught her, they would scold her on how improper it was for a young lady to run.

By the time she reached her sanctuary, her heart pounded with excitement. She slipped off her shoes and stockings, pulled her dress to her knees, and stepped into the cold water. A burst of energy ran through her. Her eyes began to dance. She closed them, focusing on the sound of the waves. Lost in the moving water, she took no notice as a stranger walked up behind her.

Chapter Five ⚛

Aidan docked his ship and gruffly gave orders to Gregory, his first mate, to supervise the crew. He had to get off the boat before he strangled his passenger, Thomas Corwin.

Aidan had begun his employment with Thomas's father, Christopher Corwin, as a ship hand at the Corwin Trading Company. After five years, Christopher approached Aidan with a proposal to captain a new ship. He jumped at the opportunity; he'd always respected and enjoyed the elder Mr. Corwin's company. Soon after, following a four-month voyage to India, Aidan was devastated to hear of his mentor's death.

Christopher had confided to Aidan that Thomas was pushing him to expand his operations. The family had a noble name and an income that would never cease, in spite of the spending sprees of his wife and son. Christopher knew Thomas would never be satisfied until he controlled the entire trading market of England. Power was what Thomas wanted, and when word got to Aidan that Thomas planned to travel to India to explore the possibility of furthering his father's trading business, he was not surprised.

Aidan had only seen Thomas venture onto a boat once—a short voyage to his aunt's home in Ireland. The idea of Thomas on a trading ship for longer than a week made Aidan laugh—until he was informed by Thomas's steward, Mr. Marklee, that his ship had been chosen for the trip. Aidan tried to think of ways to slip the dreadful arrangement but could find nothing other than unemployment. He hated taking on extra passengers, especially those born to privilege, but could not turn down his employer. The day they set sail, Aidan displayed a cold smile as he helped Thomas board his ship.

Aidan was familiar with Bantry and most of the other small port towns of Ireland. The pubs and the inns were the first places his crew would visit, but Aidan didn't like to go inland. He went when his ship was under repair or when they docked at his homeport. Otherwise, he stayed close to the ocean.

Now safely landed in Bantry and free of his loathsome payload, he sauntered along the shore, imagining how it would feel to throw Thomas overboard. The man barked more orders than the king himself. Every time Thomas opened his mouth, it meant another long night for Aidan, talking his crew out of a murderous or otherwise injurious plot to rid themselves of the odious tycoon.

A strong gust ruffled Aidan's dark hair as he quickened his pace. He finally stopped and sat down on a large log. Closing his eyes, he listened to the ocean. When he opened them, he saw a barelegged woman gliding into the ocean. He sprang to his feet, expecting the maiden to dive into the freezing waters, but she stopped and stood calf-deep in the bitter sea. With open palms, she reached out. Aidan stepped closer, trying to catch sight of what she saw in the swell. He could see nothing except the sun's rays glistening off the sapphire surface. She stepped farther, her skirt draped over the waves.

What is she doing?

It appeared she was waiting for an invitation to submerge

herself, but from whom? Aidan hated to get involved, but he didn't want her death on his conscience. Taking large, heavy steps, he approached; but the maiden was oblivious, lost to the ocean. He began whistling, hoping not to startle the desperate soul. She turned toward him but stopped, trance-like, focused on the unseen. In all his travels, he had never seen such a creature. A golden halo from the sea-reflected sun surrounded her perfectly sculpted body. Her chest rose and fell, matching the pace of the long waves that hit the shore. If he were not a reasonable man, he would have thought her to be of a higher power. But Aidan was a very reasonable man.

"Lass?" Aidan yelled, trying to get the woman's attention.

She only stared deeper into the brilliant sea. Reluctantly, he forced himself to trudge into the freezing ocean, shivering and wondering how this woman could stand the temperature of the water for so long. A strong wave pushed him back, refusing him passage.

Determined, he yelled again.

"Lass!"

She stood like a statue, the rough waves having no effect on her. He forced his way to her.

When he neared her, a sweet perfume of broom, honeysuckle, and rain engulfed his nostrils, leaving him momentarily breathless. He touched her shoulder, and a rush of energy sprang through his body. The woman jumped and turned to look at him. He stood speechless when her eyes met his.

Jocelyn's gaze locked with that of the tall stranger. She quickly memorized his face and noted a large scar on his well-defined chin.

"Lass, I saw you in the water and wanted to make sure everything is all right," he said.

He reached out his hand to her.

Don't touch me.

The weight of the water stopped her from moving quickly, making it hard to evade him. A wave rammed the back of her knees, pushing her down into the bone-chilling sea.

With hawk-like reflexes, the man grabbed her before she completely submerged and pulled her into his arms.

She paused against him, inhaling his scent—a bold musk of wood, brandy, and salt that somehow culminated with satisfying effect. The man held onto her with only their breathing interrupting the silence, until he let a shiver escape. Jocelyn pushed away from him, gathered her soaked dress, and marched toward the shore.

"Here—let me help you."

The man slid an arm under her and lifted her to him, tromping to the sandy beach.

"What are you doing?" Jocelyn squirmed. "Let go of me."

"I'm just trying to help."

With a swift jab, Jocelyn's elbow stabbed his ribs.

"Damn!" he exclaimed as he recoiled, dropping her in the shallow water near the shore.

Jocelyn crawled to her feet as water dripped from her chin and stomped to land. The man stumbled forward but quickly regained himself before springing after her.

"I was just trying to help you," he yelled out.

Once her feet were on dry sand, she wheeled to face him.

"You grabbed me," she yelled back.

"No, I lifted you," he corrected. "The next time you want to jump into freezing waters, make sure no one is around."

"No one was!"

"Apparently not."

He turned and walked away.

"Fine."

Her cheeks flushed hot despite the brisk winds.

The man stopped and turned back.

"Let me at least ask you this," he said. "What in God's name were you doing in the water?"

She shrugged. She couldn't tell him about the hunger she had for the sea; he would think her a fool.

"If it is that bad, run away—but don't go drowning yourself."

He brushed his hair away from his eyes. Jocelyn thought she detected a look of concern.

"I wasn't drowning myself, sir," she said, embarrassed at the idea.

The ocean called to her every waking moment, but the only memory she had was it dragging her, killing her. The thought of sinking brought chills to her skin.

The man took off his coat and wrapped it around Jocelyn's shoulders.

"Here."

As he moved closer, a strong wind pressed his shirt flat to his skin, outlining his thickly muscled arms. Jocelyn tried not to notice as she pulled the coat close to her neck. She hadn't felt the coldness when she was in the ocean, but now she was freezing, and the saturated dress weighed her down.

"What were you doing out there, other than killing yourself?"

Jocelyn's eyes widened. She tried to think of something to say. Her mind filled with his presence. Even the ocean seemed a blur to her.

"I was..."

Jocelyn stumbled on her words.

"You were what?"

"I was washing my feet."

"In freezing waters." The man let out a loud laugh. "Are you mad?"

"How dare you!" she shot back.

She wanted to turn and leave, but his smiling eyes held her in place.

"I did not mean to offend you," he said graciously, "but you must admit it is a bad answer. No lady would say 'wash' and 'feet' at the same time. You are a lady, I assume?"

"Of course I am a lady, just as you are a man."

"My name is Aidan Boyd." He extended his hand.

Jocelyn looked down at it, then at him with questioning eyes. He shrugged and withdrew his hand.

"What is your name?" he asked.

"Jocelyn!" Helen yelled from a mound of sand. "What happened to you?"

The servant rushed toward the two, stopping when she noticed Aidan standing next to her ward. Without hesitation, Helen placed herself in front of Jocelyn.

"What do ye think ye be doing?" she demanded.

Aidan raised his hands and stepped back.

"Not what you think, miss."

"It sure in hell better not be," Helen said hotly.

"I fell," Jocelyn said. Her dress now ruined, she thought of how hard Isabel had worked on it and felt sick with guilt. "Aidan—he helped me."

He smiled and nodded at her in gratitude.

Turning her back to Aidan, Helen examined Jocelyn.

"Jocelyn, you know better than to be in the water—and today of all days! What were ye thinkin'? The mistress will have both our necks."

"She told me I could go out," Jocelyn defended.

"The mistress' nephew—he arrived early."

"Oh, no!"

Helen nodded as Jocelyn pulled her dress up to relieve the weight from her shoulders.

"We'll fix the dress. First, ye must get to the house." Helen turned to Aidan. "You best be on your way."

Aidan gave a little bow to the distressed maid, who huffed and stomped back the way she came.

"It was nice to meet you, Aidan Boyd," Jocelyn said.

"And you. Try to stay out of the water, lass."

An urge for him to know her name swept through her.

"Jocelyn."

"What?"

"My name is Jocelyn, not lass."

"Jocelyn, she doesn't like to be kept waiting!" Helen yelled into the wind.

Jocelyn picked up her shoes and stockings and ran toward Helen and the great stone house beyond.

"I will remember you, Jocelyn, and I hope our paths cross again," Aidan called.

Jocelyn stopped, a thrill in her heart. In weeks past, she had heard her new name spoken hundreds of times, but not this way. This was different. Heat rushed to her cheeks, and she turned to look at him one more time. He watched her still, solid as a ship's mast despite the now-howling wind and rising tide.

Come to me, the ocean begged her.

"No," she whispered. "Have him come to me."

Aidan's heart thudded in his chest.

Go to her. Do not let her leave.

From the short distance, he could see her eyes shining. In an instant, he would have run to claim her, but the servant broke their gaze as she grabbed Jocelyn's hand and turned her away. He watched the two women run toward the manor.

She is not of your world, you fool, his conscience retorted. *Let her go.*

Jocelyn got to the door of the manor before Helen did, holding the skirt of her dress above her knees. She began to walk in, but Helen grabbed her shoulder.

"Wait," Helen said, pointing to Aidan's sea-worn, brown leather coat. Jocelyn pulled it off and handed it to the servant. Helen wrapped the coat over her arm. Jocelyn held up her stockings and shoes.

"Put your shoes on and hand me your stockings. No one will notice," Helen said, reaching for the soaked undergarments.

Dropping the shoes to the ground, Jocelyn found the inside of one with her bare foot and slipped it in. Once she got the other shoe on, she opened the door with a gentle hand and slipped inside.

The slow creak of the door divulged that Thomas and Edith were no longer alone. He turned to the door as the two women tiptoed into the foyer.

"There you are!" Edith said.

Thomas stared at Jocelyn, fascinated. Water dripped onto the wood floor, surrounding the soaked beauty. He could tell she was afraid, but of what he wasn't sure. Thomas didn't care. He followed his aunt to her.

"Mr. Corwin, may I introduce you to Jocelyn, my guest."

He extended his arm, waiting for her to offer her hand for

him to kiss. She just stared at him. Disappointed, he let his arm drop.

Her eyes flickered. He leaned toward her to make sure what he saw was not a trick of light. Slowly, her bright eyes darkened.

Beautiful.

His aunt was right. She was no ordinary woman; she was hypnotizing. Her sweet perfume rose to his nostrils, filling his lungs.

Jocelyn didn't like the way the man gaped at her. She felt like an animal stalked by a predator. When she suddenly found herself face to face with him, she froze. She couldn't help peering into his dark eyes, and her pulse quickened. The kindness she saw in the eyes of the servants and sometimes in Edith's was missing. Her stomach lurched, warning her not to gaze too deeply. But he smelled sweet, even tasteful.

"Jocelyn, this is my nephew, Thomas Corwin. He sailed from Bristol," Edith proclaimed proudly.

Jocelyn curtsied the way Edith had taught her. When she rose, Thomas took her hand. The ruffle from his white shirt grazed her wrist.

"I thought my aunt was exaggerating when she wrote of your beauty, but I now know I was the one mistaken," he flattered.

He kissed her hand without taking his eyes from her face.

Her skin crawled when his lips touched her. Grinding her teeth, she fought back the urge to pull away. Instead, she searched for Helen to help her deal with Thomas in a more civilized way.

Helen saw Jocelyn bristle but couldn't understand why. Thomas was a handsome man, tall and strong and of superior breeding. Being younger than three decades and having a large fortune would lure any other woman to try to win him over—even with his irksome habits. But Helen knew Jocelyn was far from any common woman. Helen quickly whispered in Edith's ear while hiding Aidan's coat behind her back.

"Her dress be drenched. Should I take her to her chambers to change, Milady?"

Edith nodded to Helen. "Make it quick," Edith whispered. She smiled pleasantly at Thomas. "I'm sorry to interrupt, but Jocelyn must change. The weather is getting damper by the minute, and I fear the chill could make her ill."

Thomas, still smitten, released Jocelyn's hand as Helen ushered the young woman away. He watched the maiden skip up the stairs.

"Wherever did you find such a creature? I have never met anyone like her. Those eyes!"

Edith smiled, her trap neatly laid.

"The ocean washed her up during a horrible storm, and I found her on my shore the next morning. I was quite amazed she was not dead, and I knew God had sent her so that I may bring her back to health. These last few months I've grown quite fond of her. She is such a sweet girl. I think of her as my own."

"Own what?" Thomas asked.

"Daughter."

Thomas snickered. "I did not think you had a motherly bone in your old body."

Edith's shoulders slumped. "It is not something that goes away."

After the door had fastened, Jocelyn lay on her bed, staring at the ceiling.

"I'm glad Edith's nephew will not be staying long," she mused.

Helen walked to the armoire and stuffed the coat out of sight. She then ran her fingers over the row of dresses until she came upon a creation of aqua-blue flowers. She tenderly laid it on the bed near Jocelyn, noticing a growing pool of moisture spreading over the bed cover.

"Get up, cailín!" she shooed, pulling the damp blanket off the dry sheets.

"What is it?"

"Other than more work for me, you'll catch your death being dressed still in them clothes. Hurry, undress."

Jocelyn peeled the wet fabric from her body, dropping the burden to the ground with a splat. Toes pointed, she stepped out of the sodden cloth.

"How damp are your undergarments?"

Helen did not wait for an answer. She grabbed hold of the white lace and squeezed. Droplets hit her shoe.

"Good Lord, you should have froze out there! What be the matter with ye, walking into those rough waters this time of year? If you are not careful, it will get you, mark my words." Helen stopped and looked up at Jocelyn. "I mean no disrespect, Milady, none at all."

"Why would you say that?" Jocelyn asked, hands on her hips, eyes locked onto Helen's.

"I spoke too freely," Helen offered. "I know I do it a lot, but me mind, it just won't be quiet most of the time. I didn't mean to bring up your mishap or tell ye what ye should do. It be not my place, Milady."

"I like that you speak freely," Jocelyn said. She bent down

and peered into the servant's face. "Please don't stop. You did nothing wrong."

"I just don't want to be disrespectful," Helen said humbly.

"You were not."

A creak echoed from a warped board behind the door. Without skipping a beat, Helen unlaced Jocelyn. Her pale skin glowed orange in the light of the weak fire spitting in the rock pit.

"Aren't you chilled?" she asked.

Jocelyn shook her head.

"My da,' he says these waters have to be extra cold for them mermaids."

Helen enveloped Jocelyn with the warm dress.

"What is a mermaid?"

Helen pulled the lace tight, strangling the maiden's chest.

"They be nothing but stories from drunken simpletons." She chuckled. "Once he brought home a dead seal's skin, sayin' he captured one and the creature would stay and love him no matter what became of him."

"Why would he do that?" Jocelyn crinkled her nose.

"He be a halfwit, that's why. Broken-hearted halfwit." Tears welled in Helen's eyes. "He was a fool, but he still was my father," she whispered.

Jocelyn swiveled to face Helen.

"What are you doing?"

Helen wiped her eyes with her sleeve.

"I can't stop them once they start."

"What are they?"

Jocelyn ran her finger over Helen's cheek, lifting a teardrop for closer examination.

"Nothing more than a tear."

"It's beautiful."

"It's just a tear." Helen wiped the droplet from Jocelyn's hand. "There be hundreds more where that one come from. Now, we need to retie your hair."

She stroked the bristles of the sliver-plated brush through Jocelyn's locks without catching on a single strand of knotted hair. Pulling tight, she tied a bun and pinned it down.

"There, the mistress should be pleased," she said. "And Master Corwin, with the way he be looking at ye, might never leave."

Delighted with the quick costume change, Helen caught herself focusing on Jocelyn's eyes. The once-luminous gold melted away, leaving behind a blinding white raging within dark blues. Dumbfounded, Helen stumbled forward, squinting.

"I hope not," Jocelyn said.

"What?" Helen asked, still transfixed.

"I hope that he doesn't stay here longer than planned."

"Do ye not care for him, Milady?"

"I do not know him," Jocelyn said, moving toward the window. "But there is something strange about his eyes."

Helen raised an eyebrow. "I found his eyes quite pleasant."

Jocelyn opened the curtains, bringing rays of sunlight into the room. The cold ocean breeze rushed in as well, overwhelming the scant warmth from the dying fire.

"He has bad in him," she said, turning to the servant. "I don't know what it is, but I can taste his demons."

She quickly stepped forward and grasped Helen's hand.

"Don't ever be alone with him," Jocelyn insisted. "Do you hear me, Helen?"

Helen nodded. The worry in Jocelyn's eyes frightened her. In past visits, she had heard Thomas yelling and thrashing about when the servants in the household did not serve him to his high standards. But that was to be expected. There were rumors, though, of his other habits. This wasn't the first time she had been warned never to be alone with him. He was known to take what he wanted, and "no" was a word he simply would not hear. Helen counted herself lucky she was never assigned to be his chambermaid.

Helen smoothed out Jocelyn's dress.

"We have to go down," she said.

"What if we didn't?" Jocelyn mused.

"I would be out of employment before nightfall, and I fear you would be out of a home," Helen answered.

The ocean's song reached Jocelyn's ears again, carrying on the steady wind.

"You do not want to keep the mistress waiting," Helen warned.

Jocelyn descended the staircase and entered the parlor, finding Edith and Thomas talking over a porcelain tea set. Helen followed behind her.

Edith looked at Jocelyn and then down at the steam rising from her flowered teacup.

"Helen, you may go," Edith said.

Helen curtsied and quietly exited.

Relieved Helen was out of harm's way, Jocelyn stood taller, determined not to show nervousness. The minutes stretched on as she waited for an invitation to sit. Edith had been extremely strict about her rule: never sit if not invited to do so. Jocelyn once waited for nearly an hour for Edith's invitation, having previously sat to take tea before Edith waved her to an empty chair.

Edith gestured to a seat close to Thomas. Jocelyn's heart dropped as she glided toward him. Avoiding eye contact, she focused on a tapestry of two quails perched on a rock, hanging on the wall behind Thomas, who was sitting ramrod-straight.

"How is my sister, the baroness?" Edith asked, bringing her small cup to her lips.

"She is up to her devices, but she sends her love."

Thomas stared at Jocelyn.

"I'm sorry, but what is a baroness?" Jocelyn asked, watching Edith.

Thomas took the question before Edith could answer.

"It is a title, my dear, that members of upper society receive from the King because of their loyalty. My father was a baron and so was my grandfather, allowing me to inherit my position at birth."

Curious, Jocelyn turned her gaze to Thomas.

"By being born, you were placed above all others — due to your family's place?" she asked, barely masking the contempt in her voice.

Edith coughed.

Thomas rallied. "I'm not above everyone, I assure you. The King is superior to all besides God, though even he might argue." Thomas smiled, amused at his own joke. "I am in a class above servants and peasants."

Arrogant, pampered junicorn.

Jocelyn bit her tongue.

"Truly, Miss Jocelyn, they know their place just as you should know yours," Thomas said.

She tightened her jaw, trying to control her rising anger.

"You, sir, have no place to judge me or anyone else," she said, her voice cracking.

A tense silence intervened, broken finally by Edith's voice. "Thomas?" she ventured.

Thomas hesitatingly turned from Jocelyn. Never before had anyone spoken so liberally to him—especially a woman. He admired her spirit, improper though it may be for a lady. An outburst of this nature would laugh her out of court, or worse, have her in a noose. Someone had to break her.

"How long will you be with us?" Edith asked her nephew.

"I depart Friday," he replied.

Jocelyn's mouth twitched.

Was that a smile? wondered Thomas.

"My dear nephew, only three days? I was hoping for a longer visit."

"I have business in India I must attend to in order to secure my father's fortune. Otherwise, I would spend a longer holiday with you, my dear aunt, and your guest."

After an hour of awkward conversation, Jocelyn finally escaped Edith and Thomas. She climbed the stairs, not noticing Edith's presence until the elderly matron hissed her name from below.

"Jocelyn! I do not wish to sit through another of your outbursts! I will not tolerate it," Edith said, firm but quiet. "Dinner will be served promptly."

Jocelyn nodded and continued to ascend the stairs.

Once safe in her room, exhaustion took over. The energy of disliking Thomas was taking its toll. She lay down on her bed, allowing sleep to take over.

A blue light surrounded her. Her body floated in air freely. Her mind followed the blue light and nothing else. Water began to rise around her. Her feet tingled as the water lapped them.

Where are you, my love? a voice called.

She knew she should be afraid of what was to come, but she was drained of emotion and had no desire to feel anything.

Jocelyn sat up abruptly, searching the room. The image from her dream burned itself into her memory. She didn't understand what had just happened. Edith had explained dreams, but Jocelyn could never remember having one. She stood and paced. The feeling of water at her feet lingered. At that moment, she knew the only way she would get answers would be from the ocean. She ran to the door and swung it open. Helen stood, hand in the air, ready to knock.

"You be up, Milady," Helen said, guiding Jocelyn back into the room. "I checked on ye earlier, but you be lost in sleep."

"Helen, I think I had a dream!"

She gripped the servant's hand.

"That is grand! Did it help your memory?"

Jocelyn told Helen every detail of her dream.

"This dream of yours be from earlier today. Dreams are silly things. Retelling your day in a different way."

Jocelyn shook her head. *No, this was different. I felt different.*

"More than likely it be a dream of you putting your feet in icy water and soaking your dress. Oh my, remember the mistress's face when we came sneaking in? I be surprised I wasn't scolded," Helen giggled.

"Why would you be scolded and not I? It was my doing," Jocelyn said.

Helen patted Jocelyn's shoulder and pointed to the vanity. Jocelyn sat, waiting for an answer.

"It be my job to watch over ye. I'm your maid, and that's what I'm required to do. Dinner will be served in less than an hour."

Jocelyn looked down at her own fingers. They were

absent-mindedly locked together, almost as if knotted. A whisper sailed in through the open window.

Where are you, my love? I will find you, Mli!

She perched on the edge of her chair and shifted toward the voice—the voice from the ocean.

"Did you hear him?" Jocelyn asked.

"Who, Milady?"

Helen stroked the bristles through Jocelyn's hair. Jocelyn peered at her.

"I don't know. It was a man's voice."

"I only be hearing the ocean and those God-forsaken gulls." Helen leaned over and placed the silver brush on the vanity. "It could have been a servant below the window. The wind can carry voices."

Jocelyn rubbed her hands over her nose and down to her chin.

"Perhaps you are right. He spoke of a Mli."

"An Emily? I know an Emily."

"I swear he said 'Mli.'"

Jocelyn turned back to the world in the mirror.

Chapter Six ⚇

Jocelyn drifted into the dining hall with her hair hanging loose. The room was unoccupied, but she had no desire for company. After taking a seat in a corner chair, she closed her eyes and listened to the waves crashing outside an open window, engulfing the room with the salt air. Seagulls flew by, squawking.

The name Mli echoed in her head.

Why does it sound so familiar? What is the matter with me?

A deep longing for the memories of her past rushed over her. Her eyes fluttered open; an inner clock began ticking. She didn't know where to start. She knew Edith would be no help, but she had to find answers. She could not go through life without knowing her true name.

The sound of footsteps stirred her from her musings. She glanced in the direction of the interlopers, plastering a thin smile on her face.

I could leave. Run—someone out there must know me.

Edith strolled in first, wearing a fine green silk gown with lace trimming. She had never seen the old woman dressed so elegantly—and so uncomfortably. Jocelyn assumed with family you could be the most familiar, but she had yet to see the elderly matron behave with any intimacy.

Thomas followed his aunt while talking to someone behind him. When his eyes met Jocelyn's, he smiled and gave her a small bow. In response, she stood and curtsied. As she raised her head, she saw Aidan standing in the doorway. He was dressed in black breeches and a white shirt covered with a navy blue, sleeveless waistcoat—much finer garments than during their first encounter. Jocelyn stared, speechless.

You!

Aidan had not wanted to go to dinner with Thomas, but the invitation was non-negotiable. When he arrived at his ship to check his crew's progress before venturing into the small village of Bantry, Mr. Marklee, Thomas's steward, was waiting for him.

"You are formally requested to dine with Mr. Corwin this evening at his aunt's establishment," Mr. Marklee stated.

"I can't."

Aidan pushed past him.

"It is not a request, Mr. Boyd. It is custom for the captain to dine with Master Corwin. He believes it keeps life civil at sea to have a relationship on land, and you want this voyage to be civil."

Aidan tightened his jaw.

"Of course."

"I will collect you at five o'clock," Mr. Marklee declared before stalking away.

"Damn it," Aidan growled, walking toward the belly of the ship.

A cabin boy rushed past Aidan.

"You," Aidan called to the lad.

The boy stopped.

"Yes, Captain?"

"Inform Mr. Gregory that I need to have a word with him in my cabin."

The boy nodded and ran toward the bow of the ship. Aidan trekked toward the stairs leading to his cabin.

As Aidan sorted through his tiny closet of threadbare clothes, a sharp tap sounded at the door.

"Come in," Aidan groused.

The door had barely closed before Aidan began complaining to his first mate, Gregory.

"What the bloody hell? The only job I ask is to sail from one port to another without the inconvenience of entertaining the wealthy."

Gregory shook his head in agreement as Aidan went over all that needed to be accomplished in his absence.

Aidan found a clean shirt and shrugged it on. Another sharp tap sounded at the door, and a crewmember announced that a footman had arrived at the pier to collect him. Aidan rolled his eyes at the thought of getting in one of those flimsy carriages to be tossed in every direction. He preferred the rocking of his ship to any bumpy, four-wheeled contraption.

After the uneven, winding ride, Aidan, now a little nauseated, stood in front of the stone manor with its high windows.

It looks like a prison.

With a sigh, he walked to the tall door, smoothing the wrinkles from his waistcoat. Before he could knock, a small, older woman opened the door. She avoided eye contact as he smiled at her and walked into the cold foyer. She afforded him a slight nod.

"They be waiting for you. Please follow me," she said before turning and walking down a hallway lined with portraits.

"Are these of the family?" he inquired.

"They're the master's ancestors," she said with a hint of sadness.

"Will he be dining with us tonight?" Aidan asked, locking eyes on a painting of an overweight man in a white wig.

"Oh, no, sir. The master be dead for almost a decade now," the woman said, turning her head to look at him.

Aidan glanced from the painting to her eyes and had the feeling when the master had walked these halls, the manor was not the tomb it was now.

They came to a smaller door, slightly ajar. The woman shuffled in to announce his arrival, leaving him waiting in the hall. After a few moments, she came back out and waved him toward the room. Aidan walked in as quietly as possible.

Here we go.

Thomas stood in the middle of the fire-lit room, clad in red breeches and a floral waistcoat. He motioned for Aidan to join him and the elderly woman seated close to the dancing flames.

"Aunt, this is the captain of my ship, Mr. Boyd," Thomas announced. "And this is my dearest aunt, Mrs. Edith Donnell."

Edith curtsied and smiled, displaying her yellowed teeth.

"Mr. Boyd, my nephew told me of your mastery of sailing. He described you as young, but with the skills of a wise captain," she flattered.

"I believe your nephew has mistaken me for someone else. I am truly blessed I am able to keep the ship afloat."

Edith and Thomas chuckled.

"Your modesty, sir, is deceiving," Thomas said. "My father

had big plans for you, and I wish to honor them if you impress me as you impressed him." He patted Aidan on the back. "Now, Aunt, when will dinner be served? Aidan here has had only potatoes and biscuits to fill his stomach these last few weeks, and I imagine he is as hungry as I."

Edith grinned and guided the two men into the dining room.

Aidan was surprised to see Jocelyn standing at the table — and much worse for wear since their last meeting. Her shoulders slumped forward, and dark circles collected under her eyes.

He bowed.

What could have drained her so?

"Jocelyn, may I introduce Mr. Aidan Boyd, my captain," Thomas said, staring at Jocelyn. "Mr. Boyd, this is Miss Jocelyn, my aunt's guest."

Jocelyn's genial smile made the blood in Aidan's cheeks warm. Edith walked to the head of the table and took her seat, then waved for Jocelyn to sit. He watched Jocelyn diligently oblige the old woman.

Thomas sauntered to the seat next to Edith with his chin lifted high. Aidan sat in the empty seat next to his employer. Shifting forward, he caught a glimpse of Thomas watching Jocelyn. Aidan quickly turned and glanced at her. Fidgeting with a fork, she examined the dry, chipping table.

Look at me.

As if commanded, she lifted her eyes, but they settled on Thomas. Heat rose to Aidan's face.

She is not of your world, just let it be, you fool! His stomach turned. *What am I doing?*

He wanted to take his leave, return to the ship, and sail away. How could this woman have such a grip on him in so little time? Her perfume lingered in the air. He drew the scent in with a long, deep breath, closing his eyes. When he opened them, she was staring at him. The corners of her mouth betrayed a smile—a smile for him—even while she nodded at Thomas and Edith's inquiries. Aidan leaned in closer.

Who are you?

A cough from the hostess returned his attention to the room. He sat back in his chair, Jocelyn's sweet aroma momentarily clearing from his mind. He breathed in deeply once more.

"May I ask what a captain does?" Jocelyn asked, still fiddling with her fork.

Aidan didn't know where to start. Everyone he knew understood sailing; he'd never had to explain it before. He mulled over her question.

"I travel from one port to the next, dropping off or picking up trade for the Corwin family," he said finally.

"How do you do that?" she asked, wide-eyed.

"I travel on a ship with a crew of 30 men who keep the boat afloat," Aidan said, watching her absorb the information.

"I see. What is trade?" Jocelyn quickly asked.

"That's enough about business, my dear," Edith interrupted. "I believe Mr. Boyd would rather talk about something a little more proper."

"I don't mind," he offered, his eyes fixed on Jocelyn.

"That's nice," Edith said, politely mechanical. "Do you play cards, Mr. Boyd?"

Aidan found himself irked by the shift in conversation. He wanted to continue talking to the enigmatic Jocelyn regardless of the subject, but he knew he couldn't be rude without losing his livelihood.

"I do," he answered Edith.

"Good. We should have a game after dinner." Edith gestured to a servant girl. "Wine?"

Everyone nodded. The young servant filled the four glasses and quietly returned to her place in the corner of the large room.

"Will the ship be ready by Friday for our departure?" Thomas asked as Aidan sipped his wine.

Aidan nodded and swallowed. "Saturday morning, by the latest. We have to restock supplies and livestock before the journey."

"How long is the trip to India?" Jocelyn asked.

"How did you know we are traveling to India?" Aidan asked, taken back by her knowledge.

"It was mentioned in a conversation earlier," Jocelyn said.

"You have a fine memory, I see. The voyage is a six-month journey," Thomas broke in.

Aidan knew it was only four and a half months at the most, but he wasn't going to correct his employer.

The ocean cried out to Jocelyn at the thought of spending six months at sea. She longed to journey with them, even though Thomas would be there.

Is my memory out there?

"Jocelyn, will you be joining us for our game?" Thomas asked.

She had only played with Edith once, and the old woman had gotten frustrated with her for not understanding gin and asking too many questions about the game. Edith was so angry she had left Jocelyn without a word. She did not understand why Edith was upset but knew not to ask to play cards again.

"I don't know how to play," she said, embarrassed.

"How could you not know how to play cards?" Thomas chuckled.

"I assume it was something I was never taught as a child," she snapped. *Just let me be!*

The room suddenly grew stuffy and warm. She pulled her dress to her knees under the table, but it didn't help.

"I don't care for cards, so I will sit out also," Aidan said, playing with his glass.

Thankful for an ally, Jocelyn smiled at him. She let her eyes play over his face, stopping at last on his lips. She wanted to touch them, to see if they felt as soft as they looked. Butterflies raced around her stomach.

"Why is it you do not like cards, Mr. Boyd?" Edith asked.

"I never played particularly well, and I learned I would rather spend my time reading or playing billiards than sit around a table looking at numbers on small pieces of paper," Aidan said with good humor.

"Aunt, I fear the game will consist only of the two of us. You both will accompany us to the game room? There are other forms of entertainment," Thomas offered.

Jocelyn nodded.

"Good," Thomas said as servants entered with the evening's meal.

After dinner, the four of them made their way to the game room. Edith prepared the card table for gin. The men stole glimpses of Jocelyn while admiring the books that lined the shelves around the room.

"Do you have a favorite?" Thomas asked.

"I...don't remember," Jocelyn said, picking up a leather-bound book and gently opening the cover. "The design of the page and the flow of the words are familiar and easy to read, but I don't remember these stories."

"Thomas, are you ready to play?" Edith asked, taking her seat.

He ignored her and walked closer to Jocelyn.

"In my home I have hundreds of books in my library," he bragged, sitting on the sofa near her.

She inched toward the armrest, away from him.

"Have you read all of them?" she asked, beginning to read.

"Good God, no. That would take a lifetime," Thomas laughed.

"Then why do you own them?" she asked without looking at him.

Thomas's smile faded.

Aidan tried to hide his grin while examining the small collection of books. A small coral knot rested in front of a battered book. He picked it up and turned it over in his hand, examining the copper metal that intertwined with the coral. His ship had brought up its share of broken coral, but he had never seen anything like this.

"Mrs. Donnell," he said, turning toward Edith, "may I inquire about your artifact?"

Edith looked up from the table and squinted at Aidan.

"In London, the jewelry fashion is indescribable," Thomas gushed.

Not like this, Aidan thought.

"Is this from London?" Aidan asked, looking closer at the interworking of the device. "It seems to be mechanical with the same gearing system as a watch."

Jocelyn stared at the coral, eyes flashing blue and gold, instantly obsessed with holding the talisman in her hands.

Aidan noticed, wishing she would look at him with the

same intensity. He imagined giving the treasure to her, her look of gratitude as she averted her eyes, her cheeks flushed with color.

Edith watched him. "It's been in the family for ages, but if you are interested, I might sell it for a fair price."

Aidan detected a hint of artifice in the old woman's voice. She would not let it go without a hefty price—one he could not pay. He set the trinket down carefully. Selecting a small book, he moved to a chair across from Jocelyn.

She quickly glanced up at Aidan.

"Tell me. Do you have such a collection as Thomas does?" she asked in a low whisper.

Aidan leaned toward her. He smiled and shook his head no.

"I only own the books my mother left me," he said, "and I fear they won't last another season out on the salty sea."

Jocelyn smiled at him and went back to her reading. Aidan couldn't help feeling a pang of inadequacy. His small collection of books was an embarrassment compared to the hundreds Thomas owned. He took one more look at Jocelyn before he lowered his eyes to the tome on his lap. He tried to read, but could not get past the first sentence. All he could see was Jocelyn standing barefoot in the cold water.

Chapter Seven ෯

Jocelyn woke to Helen's knock on the door.

"After you had retired, Master Corwin insisted Mr. Boyd stay here in one of the guest rooms," Helen said, entering the room.

Jocelyn's voice leapt in her throat.

"He is still here?"

Helen nodded as she bustled around the room.

"The mistress wants you dressed and ready for breakfast. Today, she wants you to show Master Corwin our village of Bantry."

Helen inspected a grass-green dress from the armoire, draped it on the chest, and wandered over to the window.

"Why, he has more knowledge than I do about this place! I've only seen the ocean and the house."

"Then I guess you be showing him the ocean," Helen joked, pulling back the curtains to the sun and the sea.

Jocelyn slid out of bed, stepped lightly to the window, and looked down at the roaring tide. The cry from the ocean that was so strong yesterday had faded today—but not her desire to somehow be a part of it.

"Do you think Aidan will be going with us?" Jocelyn

asked without taking her eyes from the water.

"I reckon so. It sounds as if the mistress will also be attending," Helen said, scooping up Jocelyn's dress once more. "Milady, we must hurry."

Aidan woke to the sun shining through the thin curtains. It hadn't been his wish to stay in the dank manor, but he felt it would offend Thomas if he refused. Two days on land with his employer was better than having to find a way home. Aidan stretched and strode to the window. He threw open the draperies, and the sunshine engulfed his room. He unlatched the window and pushed it outward. The salty breeze swept through his hair—filled his lungs. He grasped the windowsill and leaned into the sun, his eyes closed. One more day and he would be back on the ocean, closer to home.

A knock sounded outside his door. Aidan shook himself from his reverie and crossed the room. He opened the door to a male servant.

"The mistress invites you to attend breakfast with her and her other guests," the man intoned without a hint of emotion.

Aidan nodded. He was grateful to have a chance to spend more time with Jocelyn if Edith and Thomas permitted it.

"Tell her I am delighted."

"Yes, sir. Breakfast will be ready within the hour. I will send up a servant to attend you."

"That won't be necessary," Aidan said. "I will be in the dining hall on time. Thank you...?"

He couldn't remember if the man had mentioned his name.

"William, sir."

"Thank you, William."

Aidan closed the door and looked for a clean shirt.

Jocelyn walked into the dining hall. Aidan stood at the far end of the table, gazing at the great tapestry. Hearing her footfalls, he turned toward her and broke into a grin.

"So this is where you live?" he asked.

"For now," she replied.

Hands behind his back, he slowly walked toward her. Jocelyn's pulse quickened. He stopped in front of her.

"Do you have another home somewhere else?"

"I believe so," she answered, looking at the window. "Will you be accompanying us on a walk along the shore?"

"I didn't know there would be any exercise today. But nothing can keep me from the ocean. I assume you feel the same from your display yesterday," Aidan said, tilting his head to the side, locking his dark brown eyes onto hers. His lips pulled apart as he smiled, showing a hint of his white teeth.

Jocelyn was fascinated with him. She wanted to spend the day watching Aidan. As she thought it, Thomas walked into the room.

"Am I late?" Thomas inquired.

"No. I believe we are early," Aidan replied grudgingly.

Thomas approached Jocelyn.

"I hope you slept well?"

"I did," she said politely. "Thank you for asking."

She innocently stepped away from Thomas to admire the tapestry. Thomas grabbed her hand.

"I was wondering if you would do me the honor of

accompanying me to town?" Thomas requested, his hand wrapped around hers.

Jocelyn stood fast, coiled and alert.

"I have plans, but you may join us for a stroll along the shore," she offered.

"I'm not accustomed to changing my plans, Milady," Thomas countered, tightening his grip.

Jocelyn wiggled her hand free and faced him.

"I'm sorry, sir, but neither am I," she replied, dark eyes piercing his.

Thomas seethed. He would have slapped Jocelyn if Aidan had not been present. He stepped forward but stopped when Aidan did the same. Instead, he clenched his teeth and held his ground—for now. This woman would be a fine addition to his property, but preparing her to be properly shown off would take a lot of work. Before he could train her, he must first own her. He began hatching a plan to convince Edith to give him Jocelyn's hand in marriage.

She turned away from him and settled her attention on Aidan.

"Aidan, were you born a captain?"

"Don't be daft," Thomas laughed loudly.

Aidan shook his head. "No, I was born without a title, just a name," he said.

Edith bustled into the room, wrapped in her shawl.

"My, all of you must have been starving to arrive before me!" she exclaimed. She waved over a young servant girl already in the room. "Go see what is taking Christina so long with breakfast!"

"Yes, Milady."

The young girl rushed out of the room.

"Thomas—you look ill," Edith said, looking with concern

at her nephew.

"I'm fine," he said. "I just...found Miss Jocelyn amusing."

Edith followed her nephew and sat down at the head of the table.

"Come and join us," Edith insisted.

Aidan watched Jocelyn sit in front of Thomas. Without hesitation, Aidan took the seat beside her. The young servant girl ran out of the kitchen, slowing her steps as she approached Edith.

"What is it, child?" Edith asked without looking at the nervous girl.

"Breakfast is late due to the wood bein' wet. It took longer to get the fire started in the oven. Christina says it be out shortly," she blurted.

Edith sighed. "Very well."

The young girl scurried back to her corner, waiting for her next order.

"Mr. Boyd, will we have the pleasure of your company on our trip to town?" Edith asked.

"I'm sorry, but I have other arrangements I cannot escape," he replied.

"Oh well. You will be missing out," Edith said, fingering her necklace. "Bantry has the finest markets in Ireland. Isn't that right, Thomas?"

Thomas looked at his aunt, then at Aidan.

"I fear it will only be the two of us to Bantry."

"Jocelyn?" Edith asked, turning her gaze to her prized houseguest.

"I was to understand a stroll on the shore was planned for the day," Jocelyn replied.

"And who told you this? I know I did not," Edith reprimanded.

"I thought you said...?" Jocelyn quickly responded.

Aidan could see by the way her lips quivered that Jocelyn was hiding something.

"You thought wrong," Edith said sharply.

Aidan bristled at Edith's tone. He wanted to rebuke the old woman and walk out of the cold room with Jocelyn by his side, but he knew it was not his place.

Thomas scanned Jocelyn's chastened face. If he wanted to win her over, this was his chance.

"I believe Jocelyn may be right," he said with a smile.

Edith shot Thomas a questioning glance.

"I'm sorry—I do not understand..."

Jocelyn raised her eyebrows and looked at Thomas hopefully. He smiled at her. She reluctantly returned the gesture.

"Today is too fine of a day to waste in a market," he said. "A stroll sounds delightful."

Aidan noticed the change in Thomas and knew he had more than just a stroll in mind. The thought of Thomas wooing Jocelyn turned his stomach. He had to do something. He didn't know what, but it would have to be fast.

The doors to the kitchen opened as the servants carried in their breakfast.

Storm clouds in the distance held watch over the choppy sea. Mist kissed Aidan's face as he followed Jocelyn along the beach. She picked up her dress as she moved swiftly over the wet rocks, her cream-colored stockings drawing Aidan's gaze. Her feet danced over the rigid surfaces as his own slipped and scrabbled for purchase.

"Are you in a hurry?" he laughed, stumbling.

"No."

Hands on hips, she stopped atop a cluster of moss-covered earth and glanced back.

Breath taken, Aidan watched the wind blow against her. She let go of her dress, freeing it to sway with the playful current of air.

What beauty I lay my eyes upon?

Strands of her hair waved him to her. Balancing, he stood tall and tiptoed over the loose rocks, insensate of the cold waters lapping his boots.

"Good God, Mrs. Donnell is taking her *inele*."

Jocelyn picked up her dress again and bounded to the neighboring rugged rocks protruding from the water.

Aidan turned to watch Edith, arm linked in Thomas,' stroll over the safe, flat sand.

"Her what?" he asked.

"*Inele*," Jocelyn said into the wind.

"I've never heard that word before."

He admired her blushing cheeks.

"It means time," she whispered.

"Miss Jocelyn, where are you from?"

She let a long breath come and go, then looked at him.

"I do not know."

A wave rolled over the uneven path, washing into his boots.

"Should we go back?" Aidan asked, looking out at the dark clouds drifting closer. "Rain will soon be upon us. It will bring the tides."

"No—we are almost there."

Jocelyn placed her hand on the wall of the cliff and

stepped down.

Not again.

Aidan steeled himself for the icy water, but when he stood on the edge of the rocks, he looked down at an open cove of damp sand. Jocelyn moved down the beach.

Aidan looked back at his fellow travelers. Edith would never set foot on such dangerous terrain, and he hoped Thomas would not leave the old woman. Aidan jumped to the sand and grinned. Alone at last.

He sprinted to Jocelyn, his boots swooshing with salt water. She stood facing the giant bay of water.

Pulling off his boots and dripping wet wool stockings, Aidan's toes pressed into the sand. He emptied his boots and wrung out his stockings before hiding them in his pocket. His fingers brushed against the coral trinket he'd inquired about the night before. It had cost him a week's salary, which Edith happily took, but after breakfast he would have spent every last coin he had to win Jocelyn's favor. He began to fantasize about the moment he would bestow it upon her, but the thought was quickly erased by the very real woman before him, luminous as she drifted over the sand, windswept hair framing her flawless face.

Aidan was amazed at the transformation in her eyes the closer she got to the ocean. They weren't dancing as they were the morning before, but there was a change. They were darker, even more alluring. Her scent whirled into his cold lungs. Then and there he knew he wanted to follow her, no matter the cost.

"How do you not know where you are from? Were you abandoned as a lass?"

"Not that I know of," Jocelyn said softly. She bent down, picked up a flat rock, and sent it skipping over the restless waves. Aidan watched the rock flit over the water. "The only thing I remember is sinking to the ocean depths and then waking up here."

"Sinking? Were you drowning?"

She nodded.

His heart sank. He imagined her floundering in the limitless water, struggling to get to the surface. The torment she must have endured. Aidan drew closer to her.

"Mrs. Donnell found you?"

"Yes. She was kind enough to take me in."

"You have no relations with her?"

"No. She was nothing more than a stranger."

Jocelyn peered out to sea, making out a swift-moving storm.

Drops of rain began to pat the sand around them. Aidan watched as the crystalline beads caught jewel-like in Jocelyn's hair. Soon they would be drenched, but he would not abandon the opportunity to be alone with her. If she protested the coming downpour, he would lead them to shelter.

She opened her hands to the multiplying droplets. Aidan followed the water running down her arm over a long scar.

Jocelyn followed his stare.

"It's the only thing I have from my past."

"Do you remember how you acquired it?"

She shook her head no.

"I imagine it hurt."

She smiled at him.

More rain released from the sky.

"Do you wish to go?" Aidan asked, though he already knew the answer.

"No." She turned to him. She inhaled the water, cooling her dry throat. She gazed into his eyes—a dark brown ring spread out from his pupil, bleeding into a dark green. "Will you stay with me?"

Aidan's heart leapt against his chest. Without thinking, he pulled her close and kissed her.

The ocean's song faded when his lips covered hers. Jocelyn closed her eyes and melted into Aidan's arms. His breath was warm on her skin, and the hair at the nape of her neck tingled, sending shivers down her spine. The earth began to swirl beneath her. She didn't know what to do other than surrender.

Gusts of wind blew the now-heavy rain hard against them, the cold water coursing in tiny rivulets. Jocelyn leaned her body into his as the surf rushed up the shore and pounded against their legs. Aidan pulled her in closer, squeezing the trinket between their bodies. The object lit up, glowing through his pocket.

A spark zapped through the water, up Jocelyn's leg to her head.

No! the ocean screamed.

Her eyes flew open, storming with every shade of blue.

Her body stiffened in his arms. Aidan let go as quickly as he had grabbed her. She seemed to be lost in some kind of trance.

"Jocelyn, can you hear me?" he called out.

She steadied her gaze on him.

"Who am I?" she murmured as her legs gave way.

Aidan caught her before she collapsed into the rushing waters.

Chapter Eight ❧

Aidan sprinted up the stairs, carrying Jocelyn's motionless body. Her head pressed against his beating chest. His arms wrapped around her back and under her legs. To be so close to her made Aidan's mind race with desire. He glanced down at her face. Her eyes were closed, and her breathing was shallow.

Helen emerged from a room at the end of the hallway, carrying a washbasin. Aidan locked eyes with her.

"Where is her chamber?" Aidan demanded.

"Is she all right?" Helen asked, putting down the basin and rushing to the second door in the hallway.

"She fainted."

Aidan heard the front door bang against the wall as Thomas marched into the foyer.

"Where is she?" Thomas yelled.

Aidan jogged into the room without answering, his footsteps weighed down with the extra weight. Helen ran past him to the bed, pulling back the covers.

"Why did she faint?" Helen asked.

Because I kissed her, Aidan thought. He looked up at Helen, unable to give a response. His eyes betrayed his guilt.

"I see," Helen said. "Lay her down."

Aidan relinquished Jocelyn to the mattress. Strands of her hair masked her face. Aidan brushed his fingers through them, pushing them to the side. She moved toward his touch, placing her cheek in his palm. Aidan caressed her face, inhaling her intoxicating scent. He leaned toward her, ready to kiss her once more—certain it would wake her from her slumber.

"Sir!" Helen exclaimed.

Aidan shifted from the bed, away from Jocelyn. What was happening to him? He lost all self-control around Jocelyn even when she was not awake. He ached for her even though he knew he could never have her. She was of nobility and high society when he was without title.

He watched as Helen slipped drenched shoes off of Jocelyn's feet. Helen peered up at Aidan.

"You need to leave the room, sir."

Aidan did as he was told.

Thomas swung up the stairs as Aidan walked out of the room, shutting the door behind him.

"What happened, man?" Thomas asked, advancing toward him.

"She fainted," Aidan mustered, still feeling the kiss upon his lips.

"Was a doctor fetched?"

"Not yet. The chambermaid is removing her wet attire. A rogue wave hit her from behind."

"No wonder she fainted. That water is deadly cold."

Aidan could not help laughing to himself. The temperature of the water seemed to be the last thing to make Jocelyn faint. She was accustomed to the cold, seemed to welcome it. But his kiss did something to her, making her faint. Aidan's smile disappeared. She had kissed him back. Her arms wrapped around his shoulders, clinging tight to him. She had surprised him with her passion. Yet, she had stiffened in his arms and passed out.

Aidan stood up tall. In the past, other finely bred young ladies vied for his attentions—until they learned the value of his pocketbook. They would then flutter like the butterflies they were—beautiful yet without substance—back to the wealthy suitors who could sustain their lifestyles.

Aidan stared at Thomas. Aidan would never have his money or title. Maybe swooning was her way of distancing herself from Aidan. A way to let him know he was not up to her standards.

He pushed away from the wall and leaned over the rail, watching Edith enter through the doorway, panting.

"Is she all right?" Edith asked, looking up at Aidan.

"She fainted," Thomas answered.

"Was a doctor fetched?" Edith asked, ascending the stairs.

"Not at the moment. Her chambermaid is with her," Aidan answered.

"A doctor should be sent for," Edith said, eyeing Thomas.

"Of course, Aunt. Send word for the best physician, no expense spared."

Edith smiled at her nephew before making her way down the stairs in search of a servant.

Aidan spun at the light squeak from Jocelyn's door. Helen stood in the doorway, and Jocelyn lay unconscious in the bed. He took a step forward, but Thomas blocked him. His employer pushed past Helen and strutted to Jocelyn's side.

Aidan cringed as Thomas took hold of Jocelyn's hand. Helen looked up at him.

"You can stay if you wish."

Aidan shook his head as he eyed Thomas sitting on the edge of the bed, inches away from Jocelyn's body.

"I am not needed anymore," Aidan said. He tore his stare away from Jocelyn. "Take care of her."

"Of course, sir," Helen assured him.

Aidan walked out of the room, down the stairs, and out of the manor. The outside air forced his hands into his coat pockets, where the trinket hid. A dull stinging grew on his upper right thigh with every step he made toward the pier where his boat anchored. He rubbed his leg, hoping to stop the pain, but it burned more, forcing him to grind his teeth to ignore it.

The pain spiked, and, with a yelp, he ducked into a growth of trees and pulled his breeches down to his knees. His upper leg was welted bright red as if pressed by a fire rod. Aidan gently traced the burn, cringing at the throbbing sear. It was the same symbol as the coral medallion.

A fingertip traced Jocelyn's lips. A man's eyes, dark as the night, held hers.

Who are you?

He pulled her tight to him, begging her not to go.

Don't do this, Mli. It will kill you if you don't come back, he whispered before sleep disappeared.

Jocelyn woke alone in her moonlit room. The heavy covers were suffocating. She pulled them back, got out of bed, and paced the room, remembering the man's face, hands, smile— but not his name.

"Why can't I remember?" She pressed her hands to her face, blocking the light of the full moon.

Come back, his intoxicating voice repeated.

"How?"

A seagull pecked at the window. Jocelyn dropped her hands and faced the creature of the sky. It wanted in, and she wanted out.

"What are you doing up this late?" she asked.

She approached the window and opened it. The bird took flight.

"Come in if you wish," Jocelyn offered, leaving the window wide. A gentle breeze swept in, playing with the dying flames in the hearth.

Come back to me, the ocean called.

Jocelyn turned on her heels and thrust her head out the window. The light of the moon gave view to the white-capped waves crashing from the black sea.

"Why?" she yelled.

Come back.

Jocelyn's heart skipped as she turned and ran out of her room. The man in her dreams was down there, and answers waited with him.

Downstairs, Thomas emerged from the kitchen with a glass of red wine in one hand and a chamber stick in the other. A small flame dimly lit the foyer as he made his way to his room. His body ached for sleep, but his mind fought against it, dwelling on the superior comforts of his own home. Spirits were the only remedy that seemed to speed the hours of insomnia, other than the company of a good chambermaid.

He gulped the wine, savoring the sweet first pass, the bitter aftertaste. Stopping against the staircase rail, he looked up at the hallway leading to the second-floor landing. The scent of broom, honeysuckle, and rain enveloped him. He sniffed at the wine but found no similarities, only bold alcohol and red grapes. He took another sip and put the wine down. The smell was stronger than before.

Where is that coming from?

The sound of soft, pitter-patter feet drew his gaze upstairs. The moonlight spilled through the windows, lining the hall, washing onto a white nightdress and slender figure rushing toward him. Thomas backed away, watching the creature glide down the stairs.

The nightgown molded to Jocelyn's body, outlining her legs. Curls from her free hair cascaded down her back and bounced with each step. The blue light shone on her porcelain face. Thomas drank the last of his wine and abandoned the glass on top of a demi-lune table.

She lifted her nightdress, exposing her calves and bare feet. He struggled with his desire to claim her. It would be easy. But she was different than the rest. He would do it properly this time. He stepped out of his hiding place.

"Miss Jocelyn."

Jocelyn jumped, tripping on the last step. Her hands absorbed most of the impact, but her hip landed on a sharp edge. The pain dulled the shock of Thomas's sudden appearance.

"Are you all right, my dear?"

Thomas extended his hand to her.

"It stings a little."

Jocelyn took his help and stood, rubbing her hip.

"What are you doing out of bed? You should be resting."

Thomas stroked the top of her hand with his thumb, scratching her skin.

"I should ask you the same thing," Jocelyn snapped.

She jerked her hand away, looking past him at the large door.

"I am not the person having fainting fits today. And of all places—Mr. Boyd had to carry you over the rocks. My poor aunt thought you had died."

Jocelyn touched her lips. She could still fill the warmth of Aidan's touch. Her heart fluttered.

"Is he still here?"

She turned to face Thomas's questioning eyes.

"No," he said. "He left before the doctor clarified you had only fainted and your health was fine."

"Where did he go?" she asked. She paused when his face flushed red. "I need to thank him," she added.

"To man the ship, I assume," Thomas said curtly. "It needs its captain, you know. We should get you back into bed. Rest is beneficial to recovery."

"I am not tired, but thank you," Jocelyn said.

She walked past him and turned into the library. The front door was so near, but she could not flee without him following her. And if she did leave, would she ever see Aidan again? His kiss burned on her lips. She wanted one more.

"My dear," Thomas said.

Jocelyn focused on him with reluctance, wishing he would just stop talking.

"If we are both going to occupy this room, shall we have a fire made?" Thomas asked.

He crossed the threshold and walked to her side.

What are you doing? I don't have inele for this.

"No, I do not think it necessary," she said.

Thomas held the chamber candle before her.

"Are you not cold?"

She shook her head.

"I feel fine."

"I am glad to hear."

Thomas sat on a sofa.

It was going to be a long night with him on watch.

"I was talking to Mrs. Donnell, and she said you do not remember your past. She has asked around town, and it seems you are not from these parts."

"No, I am not from here," Jocelyn said, distracted. "But I do remember a face."

The man in her dream—was he still down there?

What did he mean? Why would it kill me if I don't come back?

"How intriguing—whose face?" asked Thomas.

"A man's," she said.

Thomas jumped up from the sofa. Jocelyn stared at him. His brow creased, and his jaw clenched. She felt like prey once again. Her stomach urged her to go, but she stood her ground.

"A man? A brother maybe?" Thomas's voice wavered uncertainly.

"I do not know." *Why would he care?*

The air of the old house felt stale in her mouth as she tried to devise her flight to the shore.

"I set sail tomorrow." Thomas took her hand. "I could help you."

"Help me how?"

"Search for your family," Thomas said, moving closer. "From port to port we can inquire about a lost girl. Someone is bound to recognize you."

His grip on her hand tightened.

"You would take me?" she asked.

"Of course."

The corners of her mouth turned up hopefully. She would

be on the open sea with Aidan and possibly closer to finding out who she was.

"Then it's settled. I will arrange the rest with my aunt, and you shall need to pack. We will depart Ireland by noon."

Jocelyn, escorted to her room by Thomas, closed the door behind her and entered her cold room. Mist drifted in from the open window. She went to it and looked down at the waters. The world was quiet and peaceful under the observant moon.

Should I go?

Find me, the ocean answered.

Chapter Nine ☙

Edith walked into her study and came upon Thomas looking over the small shelf of books.

"What are you doing here this early in the morning?" she asked. "You never rise until a few hours after the sun."

"Aunt, what are your relations with Miss Jocelyn?"

He cracked open a dusty book.

Edith watched her nephew skim the words on the page. She knew he would never disturb his daily routine unless it had to do with business, and this was business.

"I consider her as my own," Edith said, folding her hands primly before her. "I would never be able to part from her."

Thomas closed the book with a loud clap.

"Never. Not even for a dowry of 10,000 pounds?"

Edith's eyes widened. "That is very generous." *And out of practice for a man to pay for a bride.*

She had hoped for a larger allowance, but a lump sum of this multitude was beyond her daydreaming.

"She is not like the others. She will be the talk of London. Especially if she is brought back as my wife."

"10,000 pounds." Edith smiled. "Are you going to extend your visit for a wedding, then?"

"No, I will depart at noon today with Jocelyn at my side."

"Unmarried!"

"I will marry her in India and announce her as my bride on our return to London," Thomas said confidently.

Edith saw her carefully constructed plans fading before her.

"That is improper. Society will—"

Thomas interrupted his aunt. "Blast society. The woman has captivated me, body and soul. From the moment I walked into this drafty house, she has been my light. I don't care if she has no money or title. She is flawless, and that, my dear Aunt, makes her priceless."

"She hasn't agreed, has she?" Edith sat on the baroque couch covered in damask.

"She does not know. I want her to come to the realization she cannot survive without me. Only then will she truly be mine. What I want from you is to help her pack. Tell her nothing of the dowry, only of the chance her family might be out there, at a distant port."

"This will ruin her if she turns you down."

"She won't."

"Then do not risk it! Court her here."

Thomas looked at her sideways, his jaw set.

"I have made up my mind, Aunt. She is coming with me now."

Edith's stomach dropped. How would this look? She knew her nephew's habits, and, if he had his way with Jocelyn before their nuptials, he would throw Jocelyn aside—leave her ruined and abandoned, having to fend for herself. Edith knew he would.

A portrait of a young girl hung on the wall behind Thomas. Edith stared at the sad expression on the girl's face.

My Jocelyn.

Her husband Gearoid had named their daughter Jocelyn Eadu Donnell. He adored her. But when Jocelyn, a beautiful young lass, came to them to announce she was in love with an Irishman, Geariod locked her away from the world. No child of his would breed with the locals. But the girl was resourceful. She escaped and went to her lad. It took weeks, but Gearoid found her and brought her back to the house. Edith watched the maids scrub the grime from her daughter's body, but no matter how hard they scrubbed, she would still be ruined.

"You should have drowned yourself and saved us the heartache," Edith had pronounced calmly.

Jocelyn had stared at her defiantly.

"Next time I will," she said.

Days later, Edith watched Jocelyn flee her home and run to the ocean's shore. For months they looked for her, but to no avail. The lad denied hiding Jocelyn and soon found another lover.

The daughter who stole her husband's heart was gone, and Edith feared she had sent the girl to her grave.

A tear slowly came to rest on her quivering cheek. Hastily, she wiped it away and composed herself before Thomas saw.

"My dear Aunt, do you have affections for this girl?"

The words stung.

"I have a heart!" she retorted.

"Of course you do." He turned to the portrait. "She was named Jocelyn, if I recall correctly. My mother talked dearly of her. She had hoped for an arrangement between us, you know."

"We wrote about it when you were young."

"I hope you do not think her to be the same as our Jocelyn now," Thomas mused.

"Of course not. I am not a fool," she hissed back. "I still hope she will return to me even to this day."

"Do not delude yourself with such daydreams. Your daughter is gone, and the woman in your home is not your family. Take the money, Aunt. You need it more than a pretend daughter."

Edith looked up, eyes reddened with pain, speechless.

"Do not cry, old woman. I do not have the time."

Thomas tossed the book on the desk.

"I would not dream of it," Edith said, rallying.

She straightened her dress and looked haughtily up at Thomas, every bit a lady of station.

Thomas moved in. "I am being generous with my offer, but if you decide to deny me what I want, I promise you, I will strip you of your home and allowance, and you will be forced to the streets."

Edith's eyes widened, and she could only nod at his malevolence.

"I'm glad we came to an understanding." Thomas straightened his vest, looking once more at the portrait. "I would never have married her. You should be glad of your changeling," he sniffed.

He strode past Edith.

"I have a wife to pursue," he flung behind him as he left the room.

Edith knocked on the door of Jocelyn's room before she entered, surprised to see the girl standing at the window with her eyes closed. The cold air made Edith shiver.

"What are you doing? That draft will kill us both," Edith exclaimed, rushing to the window and pulling it closed.

"Did Thomas talk to you?" Jocelyn asked.

"He did."

"Did he tell you he is going to help me?"

"Yes, and I thought you would need help packing."

Edith walked over to the closet, pulled out several dresses, and laid them on the bed.

Guilt crept up in the old woman. Was she selling her soul along with this girl's life—all for a chance at celebrity?

"You could come," Jocelyn's soft voice pulled Edith from her musings.

Edith stopped fidgeting with a dress and looked at Jocelyn.

"I fear I cannot. This is my home, and I will not abandon it. When you find where you belong, you will feel the same," Edith said. She stood, walked to the door, and turned, sadness lingering in her eyes. "I am going to call for Helen. She can help you with the rest of your things."

Jocelyn nodded, letting the old woman go.

William and a young servant boy carried Jocelyn's trunk. Thomas pointed to the carriage outside but did not bother to get out of the way as the two heaved the heavy trunk toward the door. He watched the staircase, waiting for Jocelyn to descend.

Edith stood behind her nephew.

Jocelyn appeared and made her way down, Helen at her heels. She smiled at Thomas, then looked to her host. The old woman's face was puffy and red, her eyes worn and sorrowful.

Edith had fed her and kept her, and Jocelyn was grateful. When Edith opened her arms, Jocelyn took hold of her and gently squeezed.

"Thank you."

"You are welcome my dear chi-ld." Edith pursed her lips and swallowed. "Oh, I will miss you. Do hurry back and tell us of your adventures. A letter here and there will also be most welcome."

She knew the old woman was holding back. The high pitch of her voice gave it away.

"I will try." Jocelyn released herself from Edith's embrace and saw her lightly shaking. "What is it, Mrs. Donnell?"

Tears bled from the old woman's eyes, but her gaze traveled to Thomas.

"I pray you will be happy."

He stepped forward. "We must be off, otherwise the departure will be delayed," he said impatiently.

Jocelyn turned to Helen, whose face was filled with remorse.

"Do you have to go?" she wept, hugging Jocelyn.

Her heart went out to Helen, but Jocelyn would return one day. She would make sure of it.

"This is the only way," Jocelyn whispered into Helen's ear.

"The only way for what?" Helen asked.

Jocelyn beamed. "For me to go home. To know my own name."

Thomas coughed, interrupting the two. He extended his arm to Jocelyn. Not understanding this gesture, she instead walked around him toward the door.

Edith winced at the breach in etiquette.

"Weeks of training," Edith whispered mournfully.

Helen held tight to Jocelyn's hand, following her closely.

"I will miss you, Milady," she said, sniffing.

Helen squeezed and let go, stopping at the threshold.

"I will come back," Jocelyn assured her.

Thomas placed his hand on Jocelyn's back and guided her out the door. She swiveled around to see Edith and Helen in the great stone doorway, the tall windows of the upper floors, the smoke drifting from the chimneys.

Should I stay?

Come back to me, the ocean pleaded again.

It was settled. She could not stay if she wished to. The voice beckoned her, and she would find it.

Chapter Ten ☙

A carriage rolled to a stop in front of Aidan as he inspected the last crate to board the ship. The sky was blue and clear, a perfect day to set sail. He knew it was Thomas's transport and went over to greet him. Black velvet curtains blocked his view into the carriage. The horses snorted at Aidan as he approached the small door, manned by the footman. The man bowed his head and swung the door open. Thomas stepped out, wearing a purple coat and a matching hat with a large purple feather tucked into the bill.

The hat was gaudy even for Thomas.

Good God man, are you serious? Aidan barely refrained from rolling his eyes.

"The ship is stocked and ready to set sail," Aidan announced.

"I'm glad. The sooner we start this voyage, the sooner we are back in England."

A footman reached a hand inside of the coach. The carriage shifted with the weight of someone standing. A golden shoe, embroidered with delicate pink and blue flowers, stepped down onto the footrest. The footman leaned back, holding onto Jocelyn's hand as she emerged from the compartment. Aidan's heart raced as she stood before him, radiant in the gold dress that hugged her tightly.

A breeze danced between them, whirling her potent perfume.

"What are you doing here?" he demanded.

She smiled at him. "I am going with you."

"Excuse me?"

She could not board his ship. His crew would be in an uproar. Aidan turned to Thomas.

"Thomas has offered his help and passage aboard your ship," Jocelyn continued.

Aidan stood incredulous as the footman pulled trunks from the back of the carriage and placed them on the ground.

"Has he?" Aidan fumed, anger rising in his cheeks. Thomas knew the crew's superstitions. "I would like to have a word with you, sir."

Thomas simpered and nodded for him to talk.

"Alone," Aidan ordered, walking away from the carriage, his eyes shifting away from Jocelyn's.

Jocelyn watched Aidan turn his back to her. He was furious. But why?

"My dear, this will not be long," Thomas assured her before turning to a crewmember. "You there," he said to a sailor, who brushed his dirty hands on his shirt. "Be a good man and grab the luggage."

The sailor cursed under his breath, stomping toward Jocelyn and the carriage.

"Miss," the man said, nodding his head and weatherworn hat at her.

She smiled at the tired soul. His dirty white beard hung down, resting on his chest. He reached for her trunk with scarred, sun-spotted hands.

"Bloody 'ell," he said, dropping the box. "George! Come'n give me a 'and, will ya?"

"I can help you, sir."

"There's no need, miss. Me 'n George can 'andle these trunks."

A boy no older than fifteen rushed to help the man with the luggage.

Jocelyn fiddled with her necklace. Her fingers brushed against her chest. It was lacking something important, but Jocelyn couldn't remember what it was. She dropped the necklace against her skin. It was ridiculous for her to stand alone and wait. If Aidan were angry, she wanted to know why. Picking up the hem of her dress, she walked as close to the men as she dared, eavesdropping.

"What do you mean she is coming with us to India? Bloody hell, Thomas, the men will be in near revolt if she steps onto the boat!" Aidan argued in low tones.

"She will also be traveling to London," Thomas said casually, picking dirt from his fingernails.

"If she needs to get to London, send her on a passenger vessel! Not a working merchant ship!"

"She is to travel with us. I would offer to venture to London before India, but that would mean a delay in cargo, and I will not have the money wasted. Also, she cannot be unescorted in London. She is a lady."

"Then she should stay here," Aidan barked.

"I do not understand why it is such an ordeal," Thomas dismissed. "It is not as if the ship will sink with one more body aboard."

"These men have beliefs, superstitions," Aidan warned. "If Miss Jocelyn travels with us, they'll believe the ship cursed to shipwreck—or worse."

"Do you believe in these superstitions?" Thomas charged.

"Of course not. But they do, whole-heartedly."

"Let them. But Miss Jocelyn will be on my ship, and I do not care if I have your permission or theirs."

Jocelyn leaned forward, disturbing the dust-covered rocks under her shoe.

Thomas and Aidan both turned to face Jocelyn.

She watched Aidan's face for a glimpse of hope that he still wanted her, but his expression was cold and his eyes angry. She swallowed hard. Aidan dropped his stare to the ground.

"If it is too much trouble, I can..."

"Don't be ridiculous. Everything is fine," Thomas said, taking her arm. "Isn't it, Mr. Boyd?"

Aidan didn't like Jocelyn linking arms with Thomas, let alone losing control over his ship, but he had no choice.

Damn it!

With a nod, he walked past her and Thomas, shouting, "Day is wasting. Come on and move your legs! This ship will depart within the hour!"

Jocelyn watched men run to the ship. A few sailors stayed on the dock, attending the ship's moorings.

"Miss Jocelyn?" Thomas asked, drawing her closer. "Shall we begin our voyage?"

"Are you sure I should be going?" Jocelyn asked, pulling her arm free.

"Yes."

"Aidan seemed cross with the idea."

Thomas shook his head, chuckling.

"It does not matter what Mr. Boyd thinks. That is my ship. If I say you sail, you sail."

He guided her toward the waiting vessel.

Aidan tried not to make eye contact with Jocelyn as she

walked the boarding plank to the deck of his ship, rough waves rocking the hull. Instead he watched his men, waiting for the first to try to run her off. One by one the shipmates turned their attention from their chores to Jocelyn. A sun-browned sailor with an overgrown beard stepped forward.

"Miss, yer goodbyes are better said on land," he snorted.

Jocelyn stared at the sailor then around at his fellow mates, bewildered by the large crew. Aidan clenched his jaw as Thomas strutted up behind her, possessively taking her arm once more.

"Chap, she is a part of this voyage. She is our guest."

The astonished men looked at each other. Aidan approached the group quickly as the seaman leaned in and whispered into Thomas's ear.

"Death comes ta any ship that carries a woman, no matter 'ow beautiful she be."

Thomas reared back his head and laughed uproariously. "That is absurd!"

Jocelyn could see fear in the men's eyes.

"There is nothing funny about this," Jocelyn declared. *How dare he laugh!*

Thomas spun and faced her.

"On the contrary, my dear. It is idiotic."

"No, it is not." Jocelyn pointed to the sailor in front of her. "He is afraid. They all are."

The men roared at such a suggestion. Aidan's sharp whistle quieted them.

"We have a lady in our presence, men. Behave," he commanded.

Although the men lowered their voices, Jocelyn could still hear them whisper to each other of the dangers if she stayed.

Is it true? Can I bring down this magnificent ship? How?

"I will not go."

Jocelyn picked up her skirt and turned to leave. She quivered, knowing she was walking away from her only opportunity to find answers about her past. Swallowing disappointment, she tightened her fists and walked toward the boarding plank.

A large wave slammed the side of the ship, scattering Aidan, Thomas, and the crew across the deck.

Jocelyn locked her knees and stood her ground on the rocking vessel. The ship pulled away from the dock, moving out to the sea. The plank plunged into the water as the straining ropes docking the large vessel to land unraveled with the force. The men clutched the rails. The old sailor with the long white beard, panting against the ship's mast, gazed at Jocelyn. He rose and slowly walked to her.

The old sailor took her hand. He stared for a moment before dropping his hand from hers. He lifted his grungy jacket to his nose, avoiding her intoxicating scent.

"You shouldn't leave the ship, miss."

Jocelyn's fists loosened.

A few of the sailors stepped forward, bewildered.

"Nicholas?"

"Men!" he yelled to them. "We don't want 'er to leave us. We will not make it from this port if she does." He turned to her. "Breathe more calmly, Milady."

Jocelyn noticed the ship's rocking mimicked her quickened breathing. She took a slow, deep breath, looking into the clouded but focused eyes of the grizzled seaman before her.

The sea let go of the ship, allowing it to rest calmly again in the harbor.

"You do not need this man's permission to board my ship," Thomas said, moving to her side.

Aidan stood with his crew, as amazed as they were by the outburst of the ocean and Nicholas's statement. Of all of the men, Nicholas was the last, he thought, to allow her onboard.

Mr. Marklee approached them.

"Master Corwin, where would you like the lady's belongings?"

"In the captain's quarters," Thomas said to his steward, glaring at Aidan.

Aidan's eyebrows lifted. He opened his mouth but closed it when his eyes met Jocelyn's. He exhaled in defeat, turned, and walked away.

Aidan's anger washed over Jocelyn. Where was the man who had kissed her?

"Is there another place?" Jocelyn asked, but the steward was gone, along with her belongings.

"None suitable for a lady," Thomas said authoritatively.

He took her arm and walked her to the front of the ship. She saw Aidan curse under his breath when he tripped over his own shoes. The day before she longed to watch him, and when he kissed her, she had given away a small piece of herself. But now, the moments she had shared with him began to fade. The ocean was beneath her, waiting for her.

Mli, I can feel you, the ocean whispered, gently bringing the ship forward.

Shivers crept up her spine. She was getting closer.

Chapter Eleven ෯

The boat swayed in rhythm with the dancing waves. Jocelyn watched the water through the large porthole, framing the disappearing land. They had been sailing for a good four to five hours, but she could still hear the men running above to secure the sails. She tried to venture to the deck but was stopped by Mr. Marklee. He told her to wait until the ship was settled before coming up. She grew more anxious by the minute to breathe the salty air but didn't want to upset anyone. A wave splashed against the large window. She watched the water drip down the glass. She picked up the hem of her dress and sprinted from the room.

Passing two sailors who were making their way down into the galley, she ran onto the upper deck. The dull planks were soaked with water from the breaking waves. Jocelyn walked to the ship's rail, craving the open sea. The blue sky merged with the blue of the waters, giving the illusion that the ocean completely surrounded the ship. The call had never been stronger than it was at that moment; its song rang in her ears. The cool breeze dared her to stand on the rail and jump. She fought the desire as she observed the hull slice through the blue waters. She reached her fingers over the rail, wishing the vessel were only a few feet tall so she could caress the clear waves.

Aidan's voice was dull compared to the ocean's song. Jocelyn didn't notice it until he rested his arms on the rail next to her.

"I hope my quarters suit you. I imagine it's not up to your standards, but, on the open sea, you survive with what you have," Aidan said, surveying the waters.

Not knowing how to respond, Jocelyn stared at her hands on the wooden rail, the only thing between her and the ocean.

"Thomas tells me you'll be accompanying us to India and London."

Aidan watched her nod. He didn't like the cold silence between them, but this was not Edith's manor. It was his home, the one place he was comfortable and in control — but with her presence, everything was out of alignment. Even the movement of the ocean seemed spontaneous instead of rhythmic. He pushed himself, ready to supervise the crew, but Jocelyn grabbed his palm. Her cold fingers stung.

"You're freezing! You shouldn't be up here in this cold breeze," he insisted.

"I know you don't want me here, but I need to be. You won't understand, and I don't know how to explain it, but this is my only way home."

She squeezed his hand.

Aidan looked down at their intertwined fingers. He felt a tingle warming his skin, despite the coolness of her grip.

"You do not know where your home is."

She shrugged. "I know it's out there," she said, nodding in the direction they were heading.

"Out there is a big place," he said, gesturing toward the horizon.

Jocelyn laughed. Aidan indulged himself in a smile then remembered his place on the ship, his men around him. He was not alone with her; eyes were everywhere. The tingling lingered as he walked to the bow of the ship, leaving her to face the welcoming sea.

Night fell quietly. The men still scurried around the ship, securing every rope in its place. Aidan avoided dinner with Thomas and Jocelyn and ate with the rest of his crew, under the stars. He knew Thomas would not think it was out of the ordinary, for throughout their entire journey to Ireland he ate with the sailors, leaving Thomas alone with his thoughts. But he feared Jocelyn would not understand that he was not avoiding her, but the man who employed him.

Finished with his meal, Aidan stood from the wooden bench that was lined with sailors. His trousers rubbed against his thighs as his legs stretched to their full length. The rough fabric caught against the fresh burn, demanding Aidan take care of his wound. He grabbed a lit brass oil lantern and a bottle of gin and left the mess hall to find privacy to examine his injury.

He ducked into an empty room. Barrels of gunpowder filled the small space. The sulfur stung Aidan's nose as he put the bottle of gin on top of a black powder container and pulled down his trousers to look at the burn. The swelling had gone down since the day before, but it was still crimson red. Aidan pulled the lantern close to his leg, careful not to touch the hot metal to his skin. The circle with three waves was clear against his pale leg. Aidan bent closer. Faint burns of the gears branded his skin, but none of the marks appeared infected.

The ship oscillated as Aidan put the lantern down, lifted the gin, and pulled the cork. Balancing against a barrel, he poured the alcohol on the damaged skin to protect it from any infection. The burn stung, but it was clean. Aidan pulled up his pants and re-corked the bottle.

He pulled the trinket from his pocket and held it in front of the lantern's dancing flame. The copper gears and wired coral silhouetted against the light. Aidan pushed his pinky finger into the small opening to touch the small machines. It was cold.

"How did you burn me?" Aidan asked.

Linking his fingernail with a gear, Aidan rotated the clock one click. A small spark stung his finger, forcing him to tug his finger away from the trinket. Aidan grinned as he peeled off a splinter from a barrel. He slid the small piece of wood in between the gears and turned. The medallion lit up as it burned his fingers. Aidan released the medallion, dropping it to the ground. The trinket hit the wood planks of the ship and rolled toward the barrels of gunpowder.

"No, no, no," Aidan said as he jumped toward the hot trinket, grabbing the object before it could burn the wooden container. Bouncing it between hands and blowing on it, Aidan cooled his treasure. He peered down at the trinket. A small wheel jutted out of the protective coral.

"Damn it."

Positioning the trinket in front of the flame again, Aidan assessed the damage. The small wheel protruded, dislodged from the gearbox in the center of the coral. Aidan pulled out the wheel and put it on the lid of the barrel.

He examined the floor for any other parts that could have fallen off, but he only found small specks of dirt. Aidan rubbed his mouth in frustration as he reexamined the design. He slid the small wheel back into the coral, hoping it would fall into place and fix itself, but the small copper piece dropped onto the barrel. There was no way he could fix it. He pulled a handkerchief from his pocket and wrapped the trinket and the small wheel before slipping it into his pocket. He had to find someone who could repair it.

Aidan found an empty cot next to Nicholas. The old man snored, leaving Aidan doubtful that he'd find any sleep. He searched his pocket and pulled out the trinket, fiddling with the broken gear. He didn't notice when the snoring stopped.

"Threefold," Nicholas grumbled.

Aidan jumped, dropping the trinket onto his chest. He looked at Nicholas, who stared at the coral.

"What?"

Nicholas pointed at Aidan's chest where the trinket lay.

"'Tis a threefold."

Aidan shook his head.

"What is a threefold?"

Nicholas sat up and stretched out his hand. Aidan hesitated, not wanting to hand him the coral but too curious not to. The old man slowly turned it over in his hands, caressing it with his fingertips as if to devour whatever power it might hold.

"A symbol. Did you find it?" Nicholas waved the trinket at Aidan.

Aidan shook his head.

"'Ow did you get it?"

"I bought it. What does it mean?"

Nicholas ran his fingers around the curves as he spoke.

"Other world, mortal world, celestial world."

"I don't understand."

"'Tis not from these parts."

"I figured such."

"Good."

Nicholas handed the trinket back to him and began to roll over to his side.

"Nicholas, I still don't understand. What does 'other world, mortal world, celestial world' have to do with this?"

"Everything!" Nicholas exclaimed.

"Old man, I do not do well with riddles."

"I know, but you did not find it, therefore you 'ave no idea who it belongs to. And if you did, by the luck of the sea, you'd 'ave to believe in the superstitions of an old man."

As quickly as Nicholas stopped talking, he began to snore.

Stupid old sea-dog.

Aidan put the coral and its lost gear back into his pocket. He should have given it to Jocelyn on the beach, but instead he kissed her, and she had passed out. When he had left, he told himself she would be better off without him. Settle down with a fine bloke. He never expected her to be on his ship sailing across the world.

He imagined her curled in his bed, his blankets touching her bare skin.

Chapter Twelve ⚇

Jocelyn tossed and turned on the flat mattress as the ship gently rocked everyone else to sleep. Earlier she'd examined Aidan's room without disturbing anything—his mother's old books that had begun to tear at the binding along with a glass jar filled to the rim with shells and rocks from the sea, each one as unique as the other. The atmosphere of the room was comforting to her. She breathed it into her memory, knowing she would have to give it up once she was home.

Sleep allured her, but it stayed just out of reach for what seemed like hours. Finally, it took over.

A woman's face emerged through the fog of Jocelyn's dream world. She was beautiful even though panic widened her blue eyes as she screamed. Jocelyn floated, unable to move.

"Swim, Mli!" the woman screamed.

A monster of a man, dressed in brass chest plates, gripped the woman's waist and pulled her into him. He wrapped his arms around her chest, securing her arms under his huge biceps.

Two long scars, embedded over both eyes down to his chin, crinkled as the man smiled at Jocelyn.

His hand danced to his side, pulling out a long dagger. He gripped the copper handle, his knuckles turning white from the pressure of his grip. The woman struggled to free herself as the blade transformed from sliver to burning red, steam rising from the sharp edge.

"You can't do this," the woman pleaded, peering into his face.

The man's grin grew as he savored the moment of torment. Jocelyn kicked to unfreeze herself, but she still couldn't move.

"But, my lady, I can."

The woman's terror-filled eyes landed on Jocelyn.

"Swim!" the lady screamed.

In one swift movement, the man slid the blade into the woman's stomach, cauterizing the open skin, and slid it up, gutting her.

The woman bellowed in pain.

The man pushed the woman forward, releasing her arms. The woman's hands pushed the wound back together, holding onto the last bit of life left in her. She looked up at Jocelyn, fear washing over her beautiful face.

"Don't watch, my little one."

Without warning, the blade slit the woman's neck.

"No!" Jocelyn screamed.

The woman's eyes fogged as her life faded from her body. The man focused on Jocelyn.

"You're next," the man echoed through the fog.

Jocelyn woke bellowing in pain. Sweat dripped from her brow as tears streamed from her eyes. She could feel her heart pounding to be set free. Clutching her chest, she tried to calm it but couldn't. Through the fierce beat in her ears, she heard men rushing past her door to the deck.

A wave crashed into the side of the ship, knocking Jocelyn

out of bed and a wooden chair to the floor.

"Where the bloody 'ell did it come from?" a sailor shouted outside of the door.

Jocelyn steadied herself with the fallen chair and grabbed her long robe from the edge of the rocking bed. Covering herself, she rushed to peek out the door. Men shoved each other up the stairs toward the moonlight flooding the deck. Jocelyn followed the last sailor to the surface, her heart beating faster with every step. Her breath came rapidly, matching the rhythm of the pounding waves.

Water splashed her as huge waves punched the side of the vessel. Each drop that trailed down her skin tingled, leaving her wanting more. She hurried toward the rail to meet the roaring sea.

"There's not a cloud in the heavens. Where is the storm?" a bewildered sailor called to his mates.

Jocelyn, hanging over the rail, reached out, aching to touch the ocean's raging fury.

Nicholas grabbed her first. "Miss!"

She looked into the brown eyes of the old man. He held on tight.

"Calm yourself, miss."

"Why do you stop me?" Jocelyn finally breathed out.

"Yer walking too close to the edge, and that be dangerous fer all of us."

Nicholas let go of her. She stumbled back as Thomas rushed up the stairwell and ran to her.

"Jocelyn—what are you doing?" he yelled over the pounding sea.

She stared at him, unable to answer.

Thomas turned his glare on Nicholas. "And you, old man. Do not ever touch her again. Do you hear me?"

"Of course, sir," Nicholas responded, looking down at his feet.

Jocelyn watched Nicholas lower his eyes as his fellow sailors scrambled to secure loose sails, broken equipment. With every long second, her pulse slowed, and her heart sank, her longing for the wild sea dulling with each passing moment.

"You are right. It was silly of me to come up here. I believe I am in the way. Good night, sir."

She turned and walked to Thomas.

Nicholas had seen men as large as bears weep after such a show of the ocean's temper, but he could tell the girl was sad she couldn't be part of it.

"If only you knew," he whispered under his breath.

He watched Thomas take her arm and promptly escort her to her quarters.

"Look! God has favored us ta travel onward," a sailor yelled.

Nicholas looked out at the ocean. It lay flat, a few shimmers of moonlight smiling on the gentle waves.

Thomas, sickened at the idea of the crew seeing Jocelyn in her nightclothes, roughly pulled her to the captain's chambers.

"You're hurting me," Jocelyn accused, trying to pull her arm free.

Without stopping, he unlatched the wooden door and stomped inside, tossing her in front of him and slamming the door.

"What the hell were you thinking, you stupid girl?" He brushed his hair from his face. "Look at yourself." He pointed to the robe that covered her nightdress. "No respectable lady would dare tramp around in her undergarments in public. How dare you?"

"Why should it matter to you what I wear?" she yelled back.

Thomas stepped forward, and Jocelyn stepped back, bumping into Aidan's small desk.

"Everything you do affects me now."

"How so? You are nothing more than my escort. You have no claim over me."

He slammed his fist onto the desk.

"I am so much more!"

She flinched at the *thud*. A knock on the door distracted Thomas.

"Who the hell is it!" he snarled, swinging the door open to reveal Aidan.

"Thomas! What are you doing in here?"

"It is my ship—I can be wherever I please. Now, what is it?" Thomas barked.

Jocelyn didn't budge from the desk, her eyes imploring Aidan for help.

"I came to make sure Miss Jocelyn was not affected by the storm."

"She is fine."

He looked past Thomas at Jocelyn. "Are you?"

Both men watched her nod without taking her eyes off Aidan.

"You've done your duty. You may leave," Thomas ordered.

She shook her head at Aidan, her cheeks pale with fear. Thomas began to close the door, but Aidan stopped it with his hand.

He saw Jocelyn hold her breath with the movement of the

closing door. He had to get her out of the room and away from Thomas.

"I need every person on deck to make sure everyone's accounted for."

She nodded to him and tried to walk out of the room, but Thomas blocked her escape.

"You have seen us, and you know we are here. We do not need to be a part of your head count!" Thomas exclaimed.

"I do see you, but my first mate has not, and he does the counting around here."

"Then tell him we are fine."

Thomas squeezed the door.

"I would, but I have to go to the lower decks to inspect the ship. Gregory would assume you fell overboard, and you can imagine the delay that would cause."

"Get dressed," Thomas said curtly to Jocelyn.

At that moment Aidan noticed Jocelyn wore only a thin robe over her nightdress. The fabric clung to her body, showing every curve. He turned his head and spoke to Thomas.

"You could tell Gregory Miss Jocelyn is in her chambers: therefore, she would not have to be so inconvenienced."

Thomas grumbled but agreed.

"We will finish this conversation later," Thomas called over his shoulder as he slammed the door.

Jocelyn inhaled the salty air as she rushed to the door and locked it. She leaned against it. The cold metal clasp of the lock felt good against her back. Her hands trembled against her legs. She slid down to the floor and waited, in fear, for Thomas to return.

Chapter Thirteen ෯

Jocelyn woke to a loud *thump* against the door. She sprang from the floor and rushed to the other side of the room, not knowing if Thomas had a key to her cabin or not. Sunlight beamed through the window that overlooked the everlasting sea. Dust motes hung in the still air. Under the crack of the cabin door, she watched the dark shadows of heavy footsteps pass to and fro.

She knew breakfast was going to be served soon, and she would have to face Thomas. Her stomach turned, and she wished Helen were there to guide her through the day. If only she could stay hidden in this room. Still, the idea of being so close to the ocean yet trapped inside scared her more than his rage. Opening the chest filled to the brim with her clothes, she searched for her least favorite dress.

She found the bright purple velvet material and pulled it out along with Aidan's coat. She put the dress down on the bed and held up the brown coat. Helen must have packed it. She folded the coat over the back of Aidan's desk chair and picked up her dress. The heavy fabric draped to the floor as she looked it over.

Isabel had made this dress for church. It covered every

inch of Jocelyn's body—other than her hands and face—and hung more loosely than the other dresses. She put it on and looked at herself in the mirror. The material covered her completely, but she still felt exposed.

She tightly braided her hair back, twisted it into a bun, and pinned it in place. Her hands still shook as she turned and walked out of the captain's quarters toward the galley.

Waking before the duty change, Aidan strolled the deck of the ship, looking it over for any major damage, but his mind was elsewhere. He knew taking a woman on his ship would be dangerous for her. Not knowing how to react to the ocean's uncontrollable rage could harm anyone, but with Jocelyn, the ocean seemed to be an old friend and nothing to fear. But the man she was with was another story. If Thomas dared lay a finger on her, his death notice would be signed and followed through by Aidan. But he could only protect her as long as she was on the ship, and he would have to be a gracious host to both her and Thomas. He quickly picked up his pace, making his way down the stairwell to prepare himself for breakfast.

Wearing his cleanest, whitest shirt, Aidan paced the dining room, waiting for his company to arrive. He twirled a strand of his hair with his index finger. A soft cough behind him announced his first guest. He spun on his heels to face Jocelyn. The purple dress and her hidden hair did not suit her.

What are you wearing?

Then he remembered the tone Thomas had used with her, and he understood why she would shield herself so. He looked up from the dress to her eyes.

"You look well."

Jocelyn looked down at her dress.

"You like this?"

He shook his head no.

"Me either," she said, looking into his eyes. "I am glad you are here."

"I am too," Aidan said.

He started to walk toward her but stopped when Thomas came up behind her.

Jocelyn jumped when Thomas rested his hand on her back.

"Sorry I'm late, but I had business to tend to. I see Aidan will be joining us this morning."

"I am—and for dinner also. I have Gregory manning my post for the time being."

"Are your men sick of dining with you?" Thomas asked.

Aidan smirked. "I believe they are. Now they can gossip all they like behind our backs."

Thomas's lips curled. "I suppose they can. Sit."

Aidan took a seat as Thomas guided Jocelyn to the table.

"I must say, Jocelyn, that color suits you well. It brings out your eyes in such a manner," Thomas remarked.

Aidan smiled at Jocelyn and the bright purple fabric. Her eyes were as beautiful as the moment he first looked into them, but the dress only brought out the despair they failed to hide.

A skinny man in a stained apron bustled into the room.

"Captain," he said.

"Yes, Henry?" Aidan asked.

"You be eating dinner here now?"

"Yes."

"Very good," Henry said, staring at Aidan.

Aidan ran his fingers through his hair, readying himself for

Henry's grumbling.

"What is the matter?" he asked.

"The men be complaining about me cooking. And I be up ta my neck in potatoes, you see..."

"What are you getting at, Henry?" Aidan asked.

"Only, that yer breakfast will be late."

"It is always late," Thomas added, folding a napkin and placing it on his lap. "You, Henry, are lucky you were not left in Bantry since there was not enough time to hire another cook. If you wish to stay employed, you will make it your sole life's work to feed me and my guests on time."

Thomas lifted a cool gaze to Henry.

"I only be late one other time." Henry shifted a hopeful glance to Aidan.

Aidan opened his month to defend his cook.

"What if you had extra help?" Jocelyn spoke up.

Aidan and Thomas both looked at her.

"I would 'ave more time. Yes, more help would do," Henry chirped.

"I'm sorry, Henry, but I have no one to spare," Aidan said.

"I could help," Jocelyn offered.

Aidan shook his head.

"You will do no such thing," Thomas ordered. "When this man took this job he knew the requirements."

"What do you need help with, Henry?" she asked.

"The gentleman be right, miss. Ye don't belong in the galley."

Henry looked at his feet.

"I will make that decision. Now, what needs to be done?"

Aidan was surprised at her boldness and turned to see if Thomas's blistering temper was ready to explode.

"No, you will not!" Thomas demanded.

"How will you stop me?" Elegantly, she shifted in her seat to face both Aidan and Thomas. "I do not believe it is good manners to lock your guest in her room, nor any of the other threats you are thinking. And Henry," Jocelyn said, turning to the nervous cook, "I will be in the galley every morning before breakfast, with or without your permission, and if you do not use my help, then I will bore you with the endless lectures on etiquette I learned from Thomas's aunt."

Henry's eyes locked onto Aidan's, who was doing his best to hold back laughter.

"I would listen to the lady," Aidan said.

"Thank ye, Milady."

Henry gave a bow to her, which she returned. He then turned and rushed toward the kitchen.

Aidan began to pour clean water into small wine glasses.

"That was foolish of you," Thomas said calmly, taking a glass.

"Why not help him? I have nothing else to do," Jocelyn said.

"Have you ever worked in a kitchen?" Aidan asked, handing her a glass.

She shook her head. Aidan could see Jocelyn trying to peel potatoes with a force of determination and pride for her work. He knew there was no way to dissuade her from the hard and messy job.

Her hands are too delicate. She won't last a day.

Would it hurt to let her try to make up her own mind to quit? It would save everyone the frustration of convincing her otherwise. He glanced at Thomas. He sat stiffly, his back arched inches away from his chair, quietly drinking his water and staring at Jocelyn.

"Aidan?" Jocelyn asked softly.

"Yes?" Aidan answered, watching her childlike expression.

"Have you seen every aspect of the ocean?"

He shook his head. "The blue is too big for one man, especially my age, to have seen all of its glory."

"Why would you want to?" Thomas blurted.

"Why would he not?" she quickly replied.

"There's nothing but water in every direction. You, my dear, have only been on the sea for a day," he said knowingly. "The excitement will end, and the boredom of the same scenery will set in." Thomas turned to Aidan. "I bet in a week's time she will beg for land."

"I will take that bet," Aidan said, admiring the way Jocelyn bit her tongue.

"You believe me to be wrong?" Thomas asked.

"I am not bored with the sea and still marvel at its simplest form. Why would she be any different?"

"Because she doesn't belong here!" Thomas countered. "But if you wish to lose your money, then I will not turn you down."

"What is a bet?" Jocelyn asked, scratching her scalp under the tight bun.

"What a silly question," Thomas laughed.

She bit her lip and looked down at the table. Sensing her humiliation, Aidan graciously answered.

"He will give me money if I win, or I will give him money if I lose."

She took in the information then glared at the two men.

"How can you fathom to give money away on my actions! If even I do not know my own future, how would you?"

"That is the fun of it," Thomas said.

"I will not be a game for the both of you to play!"

"My dear, you already are," Thomas said smugly.

The next morning, the sky was half-lit when Jocelyn strode into the galley. Henry sat, slumped over a bucket on a small three-legged stool with sacks of potatoes surrounding him. He quickly slid a slender knife under the brown, wrinkled skin of the potato in his hand. Just as quickly, he dropped the detached peel into the quarter-full bucket.

Henry raised his head, wiping the front of his apron against his forehead, and noticed Jocelyn.

"I wasn't expecting ye this early, miss," he said, setting the knife down on the rim of the bucket.

"Do you wish for me to come back later?"

He shook his head as he stood and arched his sore back.

"Are ye sure ye want to be doing this?" he asked, tossing the naked potato into a sack with others like it. "I don't mean no rudeness to yer offer, but I don't 'ave the time ta waste iffen yer just trying ta hide from our employer. There be just too much work ta be done, you see."

"I wish to help you. I thought my intentions were clear yesterday morning," she answered. She sat down on the stool and picked up the knife and a potato. "Now, how do you do this?"

His pale lips curved into a smile when he saw the determined look on her face.

"Just cut and slide, thinly. There be no waste on me watch."

Jocelyn slowly peeled the first potato while Henry watched. She focused on the blade cutting into the rough texture. Leaning closer, her vision magnified, revealing the knobby edges of the multi-brown layer unraveling from the potato's body. The room disappeared, leaving only her, the knife, and the potato.

As she began to drop the peeled potato into the sack, Henry grabbed it and looked it over. It was as if the potato had been grown without skin.

"Very good, but quicker."

She nodded, picking up the next one. She turned the root in her hand, feeling every curve. Jocelyn rolled the blade through her fingers as muscle memory took over. The knife was not just metal, but an extended limb. In four quick movements, the potato was stripped of its coat.

Wide-eyed, Henry gestured for her to hand it over. The second was as perfect as the first.

"Amazing. Ye can stay."

Satisfied, Jocelyn grabbed another potato and slid the knife under its skin. She knew one thing about herself—she could handle a blade.

Aidan made it his priority to be near the galley. He would nonchalantly walk past and peer inside. Each time he observed Henry and Jocelyn enjoying an amusing conversation, though he thought it impossible with Henry's constant jabbering about the other sailors.

The sun drifted over the sky, quickly turning morning into evening. Aidan made his way to the galley once more to find Jocelyn covered in flour. She clapped her hands and pointed.

"I fried pork!" she blurted. "Come and see."

She moved out of the way to show crackling, spitting pork

sizzling in a pan.

He breathed in the meal to come. Pepper and dried rosemary, mingled with the simmering pig, set his stomach growling. It had been a long while since the meat had not been burnt and dry. Today, he noticed Henry took pride in being a cook.

"You have outdone yourself," he said to Henry.

"And it is on time," Jocelyn added, leaning over the dish.

"Speaking of time, you should clean up before dinner," Aidan said, pointing to her splattered dress.

She looked down at the mess.

"I quite like it," she said, brushing away brownish flour from the dirtied fabric.

The powder also lay sprinkled on her hair and cheeks, darkening her pale complexion. Breaded though she was, Aidan stood transfixed as her eyes beamed out to him through her dusty coating.

"Is it becoming?" she asked.

"Excuse me?" Aidan managed.

"Is it becoming?" Jocelyn smiled at him. "The dress."

She swept her loose hair from her eyes, inadvertently spreading more flour on her face.

"Here."

Aidan gently brushed her cheeks with his fingers, wiping away the flour. He stopped, but his hand lingered. He glanced to her lips and back to her eyes. A crackle of frying oil brought him back to the kitchen.

"There, " he said, dropping his hand. "Water will help you more than I can."

Jocelyn closed her eyes tight and turned her head from him. His words had stung her, and he didn't know why.

"Henry, thank you for all of your help. I will be back at the same time tomorrow."

She bowed and rushed out of the room.

"Poor thing," Henry said, wiping his hands on his apron.

"What do you mean?"

"She don't know where ta belong."

"What did you give her to do?" Aidan asked.

"Everything! She be the hardest 'elper I ever 'ad. Surprising fer a lady."

"There's no way of getting her out of here, is there?" he asked.

"I 'ope not."

Henry turned back to his kitchen as Aidan left, chuckling to himself.

Refreshed, Jocelyn opened the door and walked into the dining room. She had rid herself of the kitchen's grime and was now attired in a form-fitting white dress. She didn't want to hide tonight. Thomas and Aidan stood when she entered, and Aidan pulled out her chair.

Her nose twitched from the smell of alcohol. She spotted a brandy stain on Thomas's shirt collar and watched as his unsteady hand sloshed more onto the table.

Henry arrived soon after with their dinner. Each white plate boasted a generous portion of fried pork lying atop a mound of smooth mashed potatoes.

Jocelyn held in her excitement, waiting for the men to take the first bite. Aidan cut into the tender meat and placed it eagerly into his mouth.

"Delightful. Can I expect dinner to be this great every

night, Henry?" he asked with a wide smile.

"We'll see," Henry answered with a hint of pride.

Thomas slowly took a bite. He leaned back into his chair and nodded to Henry.

Henry's lips twitched, hiding a smile. He turned and rushed out to serve the other sailors.

"At least it was on time," Thomas said, taking another bite.

Jocelyn's heart raced as she watched the men eat, waiting for one of them to ask how her day was. She shifted in her chair, looking down at the plate and then up, nearly bursting to explain the myriad of tasks it took to make such a masterpiece.

"Henry spoke highly of your help," Aidan said, taking up his wine glass.

"I am so glad to assist him. It was delightful to be of use," she replied.

"Use," Thomas snickered before he took a drink of brandy.

Jocelyn ignored the comment, deciding not to wait for further prompting to talk of her labors.

"I peeled potatoes and rolled biscuits—and Henry let me fry the pork," she boasted.

"You did a fine job," Aidan complimented.

Thomas pushed the half-eaten plate away from him.

"You are of a different class and should not take a fancy to such work."

"What class am I?" Jocelyn asked, her excitement quickly vanishing. "I don't remember who or where I am from, so how would you know of my standing in your world?"

"It is what I say it is!" Thomas said. He gulped down the remains of his drink and looked at Aidan. "Well, Captain, do you believe that Miss Jocelyn belongs in a kitchen?"

Aidan turned and examined her before he shook his head. Jocelyn rolled her eyes.

"See. Mr. Boyd agrees with me..." Thomas slurred.

"I don't know where she belongs, but I imagine it would be her choice," Aidan interrupted Thomas.

"For God's sake, look at her hands. No woman of working class would have her hands," Thomas blurted.

Jocelyn looked down at her smooth palms. An image of Helen's callused hands came to mind. She quickly folded them under her napkin.

"I agree she is more delicate than most of the working class, but..."

"Good God man, more delicate! That is an understatement."

Thomas stood and walked over to Jocelyn. He quickly grabbed her arm and pulled her from the chair.

"What are you doing?" Aidan and Jocelyn blurted simultaneously.

Aidan tipped his chair over as he jumped out of his seat.

"Look at her figure. Her hair."

Thomas lifted a strand of her soft hair and rubbed it between his fingers. Jocelyn pushed away from him and backed toward Aidan.

"Mr. Corwin, I believe you have had one too many drinks tonight," Aidan cautioned, inching toward her.

"Of course I have," Thomas thundered, taking his seat. "But that does not diminish my point. She is not like any woman you or I have ever seen. And I will not let such a beauty go to the gutters of the world because she likes to peel potatoes." He turned and glared at Jocelyn. "What if you don't find your home? What if you have no one? What will you do? How will you survive? Not everyone is as nice as I am."

"You might want to head to your chambers, Mr. Corwin," Aidan said.

"I will when I'm damn ready," Thomas exclaimed, keeping his eyes locked onto Jocelyn. "You don't have an answer, do you?"

"I can survive," she whispered.

"Like you would have if my aunt had not found you and clothed you?"

"That is enough!" Aidan demanded. "Why be so cruel? She has done nothing wrong."

Thomas swiftly faced Aidan. "This life is harsh. The sooner she learns it, the quicker she can begin to understand her place in the world." He leered at Jocelyn "These notions you portray —this divine freedom from my society—do not exist. You are nothing more than a woman with no family or wealth. You cannot survive without a man looking after you. You belong nowhere other than a man's home. Which home you choose will determine the rest of your life!"

Thomas hiccupped, sliding down in his chair.

The room rang with condemnation. An overwhelming sadness rushed over Jocelyn as she bit her lip.

Aidan wanted to rush to her and tell her the world didn't work this way, but he could not lie to her. Thomas was right. Unless she found her home, she would have to make a decision someday to marry or take on a less respectable career if she wanted to stay alive. Only in her own home would she be safe from the Thomases of the world. He silently prayed they were heading in the right direction.

Chapter Fourteen ൭

The days slowly turned into weeks. Jocelyn continued to help Henry but decided not to talk about it to either Thomas or Aidan. She began to feel alone. Even the comfort of the sea could not rescue her from her worries. Thomas's words had struck her heart. What if she never found her way home?

Remember, remember!

But no new memories rose in her. The burdens of reality weighed her down. Every evening, she watched the sun fade into the water, wishing it would take her with it.

Aidan tried to comfort her with tales of his travels. Soon, many of his men chimed in with their own stories of the high seas. For a while, Jocelyn fantasized about being a part of their adventures in different lands, privy to the mysteries they had stowed away.

Aidan saw the wonderment on her face slowly fade to worry day after day. He hated to see the transition in her, but nothing could stop it. The damage was done.

At night, he would find a quiet place and try to pin the gear into place in the small coral trinket, telling himself that if he could fix it, he could give it to her, and she would emerge from her depression. But every night the gear would only roll out of the coral onto the table. He could not fix it or her.

The winds began to change as they drew closer to India. On deck, he could feel a storm approaching. He rushed to find Gregory, who was asleep on his cot. Aidan swung the netting aside, waking his first mate.

"I need you wide-eyed and ready," he said. "We are coming upon a storm."

Gregory nodded, blinking away the sleep. Aidan left in search of Jocelyn.

He found her stooped over, peeling potatoes, lost deep in her thoughts.

"Miss Jocelyn, I believe it best that you make your way to your chambers. A storm is coming."

Aidan saw the spark in her eyes—the same as the first time he had met her knee deep in the ocean.

"You need to go now."

He had a feeling she was hiding other plans.

"I will."

He left her and rushed to the upper deck.

Jocelyn's senses began to awaken. She could smell the rain in the distance. She nodded and put the potato down, wiping her hands on her apron. She waited until his heavy footfalls faded before she made her way up.

The ship rocked as small drops of rain pelted the deck. Jocelyn breathed in the mist of the clouds above. The ocean screamed at her. It had been quiet for too long, and now it wanted her. She kept her balance as the boat swayed with the angry movement of the rough sea. She ran to the closest rail and stared out at the darkness. Small sparks of light flashed in the sky, and thunder followed shortly after. She could feel the damage that was coming their way, and she welcomed it.

Nicholas rushed on deck with his tools and lantern in hand

and saw Jocelyn reaching out to embrace their doom. The hard wind blew her hair and dress back. He knew the ocean was going to take her and the ship with it. He dropped his tools and ran to her.

"You'll be the death of us," he yelled, but she didn't move.

He grabbed her shoulders and turned her to him, holding up the lantern. Jocelyn's eyes appeared to be black as the ocean until lightning struck in the distance. Then her eyes sparked too. Nicholas fumbled with the light, startled by what he saw. Jocelyn grabbed it from his hands.

"I know what you are! Yer one of 'em. All of my life I've talked of you, but 'ere you are. I 'ad my suspicions from the moment you walked on, but yer real."

"What are you talking about?"

Jocelyn handed the lantern back as a large wave rammed into the side of the ship, sending her and Nicholas against the rail.

"There be no time for that." He pointed to the men running around. "You are their only 'ope." His finger stopped at Aidan. "We and the captain will die tonight iffen you don't stop this."

Jocelyn watched Aidan as the rain beat down harder. He looked worried, which scared her. He had not feared the ocean until now, and she could see he knew the storm would soon get too rough to handle.

"What can I do? I can't control this!" She looked back at Nicholas.

"Only yer kind and God can control this," he said grimly.

"I don't understand."

"Why do you think you are 'ere? They want you back."

He pointed out to the open water.

"Who?"

Jocelyn wiped her hair from her face, the dark clouds

swirling around her.

"The keepers of the sea!"

"You're not making any sense," she shouted.

Sailors darted and slipped over the wet planks, rushing to get the sails down.

"Wot do you hear?"

"I hear you."

"No! Wot is the ocean doing to you? Wot is it saying?"

Come to me! the ocean screamed.

"It is screaming. Can you hear it?" *Am I not alone?*

"No. Tell it to stop. Keep us safe."

He ran to his tools and picked them up before he joined the crew.

Turning to the black waters, the smell of death invaded her, and she began to long for the ship to sink. Nicholas knew what she was, and, if he died, so would his knowledge. Confused but angry, she yelled back at the screaming ocean.

"No more!" she demanded. "Not yet! I need more time!"

The ocean cried back as another wave drove against the side of the careening vessel.

Jocelyn grabbed the rail. The ocean began to sing to her, a melody of impossible notes. She looked around the ship, but her body cried for her to go to the water.

It could be over right now.

Her eyes then locked onto Aidan's desperate face. She could feel his pain of losing her. Gripping the ship's helm with his right hand, he reached for her with the other, begging her to come to him. She in turn reached for him, but the ocean's shriek tore her away. With his pain still in her heart, she began to sing the melody back to the ocean. The lurching ocean slowed its deathly roiling.

Aidan couldn't make out what Jocelyn was doing, but he

had to get to her. He yelled at Gregory to take over the wheel and ran toward her, but a wave spilled onto the deck, knocking him down. He rose to his knees, spitting out saltwater. The water did not strike Jocelyn. She stood in defiance of the raging waters.

Jocelyn felt the power of control pulse through her veins. The ocean submitted to her will, the water heaving less and less as the ship began to steady itself. The rain continued to pour down, but the sea took no notice of it.

Who am I?

Aidan regained his footing when she stopped singing. She walked to him, her head held high, the glow of nobility around her. He wanted to thank her but didn't know what for.

"I told you to go to your chambers," he said. "You could have been killed."

"I would never have been hurt."

Chapter Fifteen ෯

Waking with a headache, Jocelyn sat up in bed and rubbed her temples, remembering the dark hours with vivid flashbacks. Nicholas's words echoed strongest.

Yer one of 'em.

Forgetting the pounding in her head, she briskly dressed and left her room.

She strode past the galley, her mind set on reaching the upper deck and finding Nicholas so he could tell her everything. He knew what she was. Her heart beat faster as she stepped onto the stairs. A raspy voice broke her advance.

"It's early for you to be up," Thomas said, hoisting a hot mug to his lips.

Jocelyn turned, irked. "No earlier than you."

"I could not sleep anymore," he said, tapping his temple. "A lot on my mind."

"I will leave you to it then."

She turned back to the stairwell.

"My thoughts are of you," he insisted. "Even during that dreadful storm, my mind could only think of you."

Jocelyn rolled her eyes, the same way she had seen the servants do privately in response to Edith's niggling orders.

She kept her back to him.

"You should search for more worthy entertainment then. Hopefully in India you can find such a thing."

She took another step toward the stairs.

"You mock me in such a delicate tone, my lady. But, you see, you owe me a debt. I was hoping to just wipe it away without this conversation, but your stubbornness has left me no other option."

Jocelyn turned. *What?*

"I see you are a little confused." Thomas swallowed his tea. "Do you know what a debt is?"

She shook her head.

"It means you owe me."

"I owe you nothing."

"How about this journey?"

"You invited me!"

"In a way, you could have thought of it as an open invitation, but everything comes with a price, my dear."

"I've heard enough." Jocelyn headed for the stairs, then turned. "I am sick of your endless search for power over me — power that you will never have."

She climbed toward the open sky.

"I bought you! I own you."

She stopped, her eyes level with the deck.

"No one owns me."

"I wager differently. I paid a rather high amount. Why else would you be here?"

Jocelyn marched down the steps to face Thomas, her anger boiling.

"You are a sick man!"

"It does not change the facts."

"I am a person..."

"You are a woman, and I am a very wealthy man. If you deny me, I will have to find a way to make up for my lost investment, and you will owe me every penny I've spent."

"Who do you think you are to demand such things?"

She could hardly breathe. Her eyes burned with saltwater. Thomas stepped close.

"You have until England. I am a gentleman, and you will be my wife. I will not demand anything until then."

"You cannot make me!"

A single tear escaped, tracing her horrified face. She felt something break within her. She wiped the drop away; it felt unnatural and forbidden, as if such grief would bring consequences.

"You will be surprised at what I can do," he said gravely.

Thomas turned to leave, then stopped and thrust his mug toward her.

"Be a dear and put this away," he said.

Jocelyn, dumbstruck, took the mug. As he left, she pulled her arm back to throw the cup at the back of his head, but someone stopped her.

"Kill 'im when no one is watchin,'" Henry whispered, holding onto her arm.

Jocelyn tugged her arm free and raced up the stairs.

Jocelyn ran across the deck to the bow of the boat. She ached for the ocean. She wanted it to surround her and hold her in a tight embrace. She stumbled once but caught herself before she fell. Lifting her dress higher, she continued to run, knowing something was changing within her. Last night she was what she should be—powerful—but now the power was gone, and she was sinking in this world, losing parts of herself over the journey. Something foreign was invading her, something, she knew, that would kill her if she stayed.

She readied herself for the long dive, but two strong arms locked around her waist and pulled her. Jocelyn tried to push away, but the grip was ironclad.

"Stop it," Aidan demanded, turning her to face him.

"I don't belong here. Let me go."

She shoved her arms into his chest and pushed, but he only held her tighter.

He could see she had been crying.

"What happened?"

She looked up at him. His voice stirred something in her; not as strong as the ocean, but strong all the same. She stopped pushing and just let him hold her.

"Thomas told me that I belong to him. He bought me."

"No one can buy you."

Jocelyn could see a flicker of anger in his eyes as he tried to stay calm. She felt a flutter in her heart. He was her ocean here. He could protect her. She felt safe. She leaned into him, placing her head on his chest.

Surprised, Aidan could only think of holding onto her and never letting go. He breathed in her scent, sliding a hand down her back.

Jocelyn felt the electricity in his fingers. She looked into his eyes. Nothing else mattered but him.

Could he be my future?

She stood on her toes and gently kissed him. A surge of emotions rose in her, and she pulled away from him, her mind racing.

He looked down at her, seeing nothing else. One kiss was not enough. He pulled her back into his arms and passionately kissed her, his body shielding her from his world.

Neither of them noticed the flickering light in Aidan's pocket.

Chapter Sixteen ෯

Jocelyn ran her hands up his chest to his neck, tracing her fingers over the stubble from neglected shaving. She threaded her fingers in his dark hair, drawing him closer to her. The gentle ocean caressed the ship, moving it forward.

Aidan moved away, breathing heavily. He grabbed her hand.

"Come," he whispered, ushering her below deck.

Jocelyn followed as Aidan made his way through the hallway toward her room. The blueprint of the large ship was etched in his mind, allowing him to hide them in doorways when other sailors marched the corridor. Finally, he slid open her door and guided her in behind him.

The sunlight seeped through the windows, dusting the room in golden light. Aidan let go of Jocelyn's hand and shut the door behind her. She moved to the middle of the room, fully aware of the absence of bystanders. She turned to face Aidan.

His back pressed against the door, he forced himself not to reach for her.

"I need to go," Aidan said.

Jocelyn took one step toward him then stopped.

"Then go."

Aidan shoved away from the door, his long stride closing the gap between their bodies. Jocelyn's arms wrapped around his neck. She pressed her body against his. Their hunger for each other grew with every kiss. He touched her face, drifting away from her.

"I must go," he said, gasping. Her blue eyes glittered with the morning light.

"I don't want you to."

She stood on her tiptoes to kiss his chin, lowering her lips to his neck.

Aidan moaned as Jocelyn's lips brushed his collarbone, her fingers tugging back his shirt. He grabbed her shoulders, pushing her away from him.

"You don't know what you are doing to me."

"I have an idea."

Jocelyn's smile increased his vexation.

"I shouldn't be alone with you, and we shouldn't kiss in front of anyone. It could ruin you."

"Ruin me? This isn't ruining me."

The irritation in her voice cut through the thick air.

"You do not understand, Jocelyn. You are not supposed to be alone with a man without a chaperon."

Jocelyn swiped away Aidan's hands and paced the room.

"I am not a child. I don't need anyone making decisions for me."

"I am not trying to make you angry. I am trying to protect you."

Aidan stepped toward her.

Jocelyn froze, staring at the man she wanted, but the anger growing inside of her prevented her from going to him.

"Protect me from myself or from your world? I can't tell

the difference anymore."

"I should go."

Aidan unlatched the door.

"Why did you bring me here if you were just going to
leave? Why didn't you walk away on deck?"

"It was the only place I could be near you without others
watching. I am a fool. I am sorry," Aidan confessed.

The anger in Jocelyn shot to the ceiling, leaving her.

"You are a fool." Jocelyn walked to him, sliding her hand
over his shoulder to the door, and slid it shut. "And here we
are. What a mess we are in," Jocelyn said.

Her eyes flicked with gold as the ocean pushed against the
ship, rocking it.

Unable to stop himself, Aidan leaned in and softly kissed
her lips.

"How we will ever figure this out is beyond me," he said.

Jocelyn peered up at him, studying his dark eyes, the tip of
his nose, his moving mouth. She bit the corner of her bottom
lip, ravenous for more. She exhaled.

Aidan stepped back into the door as a fury of sweet
fragrance of broom and honeysuckle flooded his senses,
overtaking him. Forgetting etiquette, his mind focused on
Jocelyn's face. She glittered—she was so beautiful. He inhaled
more of her; the perfume soaked into his skin.

A large wave hit the side of the boat, splashing onto the
windows.

He grabbed the back of her head, covering her mouth with
his. She kissed him back, demanding more of him. He lifted
her into his arms and carried her to the bed, their mouths
never unlocking. Laying her down, he covered her body with
his.

She wiggled from his weight, positioning herself to get

comfortable under him. Her heart raced as his hands drifted down her back, lifting her to him. He kissed her earlobe. A wave of desire shuddered through her; she arched her back.

Her body jolted, remembering the same passion from someone else. Someone else kissing her neck. Jocelyn closed her eyes, trying to block the man's face, trying to focus on Aidan, but the memory broke through her barrier. The man's black eyes sparkled with his smile as he reached out his hand for her.

Jocelyn opened her eyes to Aidan nuzzling her neck. She turned her head away from him in search of the overwhelming desire for him, but it was lost. She was left only with the image of the stranger's penetrating eyes.

Aidan lifted off her. She gazed up at him. The sweet, gentle Aidan was gone. In his place was a man consumed with one thought. Her. If she asked him to jump overboard, he would.

He lowered himself to kiss her, but Jocelyn brought her hand up, blocking him.

"Wait," Jocelyn whispered.

Aidan took her arm, kissing her wrist.

"Why?" Aidan asked with another sweet kiss.

"Maybe you're right—you should leave."

Jocelyn's heart screamed *no* as the words left her lips. She wanted him to stay with her. To cover her with more kisses. To hold her. But this man from her past lingered in the quiet spaces of her mind, begging her to stop.

Aidan stared down at her, lips frozen on her arm. She was right, but he didn't want to leave her. He wanted to stay in her arms forever.

"I want to stay."

Jocelyn stretched up and lightly pressed her lips to his.

"I know," she said, shifting him off of her.

Aidan lay, looking up at the ceiling, unable to move.

"I feel like I am sinking when I am around you," Aidan whispered.

Jocelyn sat up. "Why?"

"Because my world is not the same with you in it, and I am losing control of not only it, but myself."

Aidan rolled to his side, gazing at her.

Worry washed over Jocelyn. She wanted Aidan to want her. To love her. But her heart was torn, trying to remember what she had lost.

"Do you want me to leave?" she asked, trying to hide her fear of his answer.

Aidan sat up, facing her.

"No." He cupped her face in his hands. "I want to sink deeper."

Jocelyn smiled as he kissed her.

"I will leave, but I will dream of you."

Aidan stood and walked toward the door.

"Aidan?"

He turned and stared at the beautiful creature sitting on his bed.

"I know."

Aidan opened the door and stepped out.

Jocelyn stood on her wobbly legs, arguing with herself whether to run after him or not. She went to the door and locked herself in. She knew if she went after him it would lead to him sharing her bed. The ocean seesawed the ship, shaking the loose items to the ground.

Jocelyn walked to the window, opened it, and stared at the raging sea reflecting the rays from the sun above. The white tips of the waves crashed down, beckoning for her to step out and leap into its embrace. Jocelyn steadied her heavy breathing, ignoring the call of the ocean. She touched her lips, still tasting him. The ocean was going to have to fight harder if it wanted her back, for part of her heart had become Aidan's.

Aidan peeled off his coat, dropped it to the ground, and slid onto his cot. His lips still tingled from Jocelyn's kiss. He closed his eyes, picturing her face. His heart pounded within him. The snoring of the sleeping men, who worked the night shift, bounced off the wooden room, echoing back as the ship rocked with the ocean.

Aidan knew that nothing would be the same. He could not give her up even if it meant his livelihood. His world was hers now. This would be his last voyage.

They could live in a cottage near the ocean. He could fish. He would make a world for them. He turned over, facing the wall. The coral pressed into his leg. He sat up, releasing the pressure of the solid object. Searching in his pocket, he pulled out the trinket. He dug deeper, looking for the small gear, but he only fished out lint.

He stood, frantically turning his clothes inside out.

"Damn it," he whispered.

He sat on the cot. His feet dragged on the floor as his bed swung. He rubbed the trinket in his hand.

It was still beautiful; he could still give it to her as a present when the time was right. No one would notice the missing gear, except him. He held the medallion up, looking through it. But it was not whole, and the idea of giving Jocelyn anything broken turned his stomach.

He grabbed his jacket and shoved the medallion into the

pocket. Folding the tough fabric around the trinket, he placed it on the cot and laid his head on it.

He closed his eyes and dreamt of how to give her everything she deserved.

Chapter Seventeen ⚬

Aidan spent every spare minute with Jocelyn during the weeks following that morning. He waited outside the galley for her to finish assisting Henry. When she stepped into the passage, he would pull her to him. He tried to keep their meetings discreet, but their heated embraces blurred all else around them. At dinner, he would graze his hand against hers under the table. He did not care of his crew's suspicions, but he prayed Thomas would stay naive to the situation until they finally docked in London. There, Jocelyn and he could display their love openly with no worries of Thomas.

One crisp morning, Aidan tapped his toe against the galley wall, waiting for her.

He could hear Jocelyn's voice through the open door.

"Are you sure you don't need any more help for the day?" she asked.

"Get out of 'ere, girl," Henry laughed.

Jocelyn skipped through the doorway into Aidan's arms. She kissed the tip of his chin before pulling him forward.

"Come with me," she said.

They ran through the passageway hand-in-hand to a dim corner of the ship.

"Tell me again," Jocelyn begged.

"About what?"

Aidan kissed the top of her head.

"Your mother and father."

Aidan ran his fingers through her hair, sweet perfume radiating from each strand.

"You're intoxicating."

"Aidan, tell me about them."

He shifted uncomfortably.

"They were poorer than church mice. Why do you want to hear this again?"

"I like the way you talk of them."

"Well," he exhaled. "They were poor, yet they loved everything they had, including me." Memories of his mother's arms opened wide, waiting for him, flashed before him. "She would wrap her arms around me and whisper, 'My Aidan, you are my gift.'" He stopped.

Jocelyn watched as Aidan grew silent and looked out to sea through a small porthole.

"I've never told anyone that before. When they first put me on the ship, I was angry. I thought I hated them, but they were trying to give me a trade. And they did. I haven't seen them since I was eight."

Jocelyn pulled away from him.

"Why haven't you found them?"

"I'm afraid of what I will find. Their love was unlike any I have seen. The way my father smiled at her from across the kitchen, and how she blushed when he kissed her. It is odd what I remember."

"I don't remember my parents. I don't even know if they loved each other," Jocelyn said, intertwining her fingers with his.

"What do you remember?" he asked, taken aback.

"About love?"

Aidan laughed. He cupped her face in his hands.

"Sure."

"No one can own or demand it. It is either there, or it's not. Your heart is the one that chooses."

"My heart?"

"Yes." She placed her hand over his heart. "Your heart."

The strong beat pulsated through her hand to her own soul. Jocelyn looked into his eyes.

"How does one's heart know such things?" Aidan teased.

Jocelyn stood on her tiptoes, eye-level with Aidan. Aidan's laughter stopped as they stared at each other.

"Your heart burns when they are not near. The fire inside consumes you until your lips find theirs."

"And if your heart doesn't find them?" Aidan asked.

"It would stop beating. Leaving you with a dead heart."

Aidan pulled Jocelyn to him, kissing her deeply.

Jocelyn wrapped her arms around his neck, burying herself deeper into him. His skin smelled of the salty air and oak.

Aidan let her breathe for a moment before kissing her again. Jocelyn closed her eyes, letting everything go, even the ocean.

Mli, where are you? The voice of the ocean called out.

Jocelyn's eyes shot open as a memory rushed into her conscious mind.

A man with dark blue eyes held his forehead against hers.

My heart will stop beating if you don't come back to me, Mli. It will die without you.

Jocelyn looked over the man's face. He was flawless. She grazed her lips over his.

I will come back to you. I am yours.

Aidan's fingers sliding up her back brought her back to the cabin of the ship. He was still kissing her.

Jocelyn stepped back, breaking the embrace.

"Is everything all right?" Aidan asked, searching her eyes.

Jocelyn could paint every detail of the man's face if she could paint, but she locked the memory away. Aidan was her future. She was happy here with him. But something burned in her heart. Part of her didn't belong here with him. The part that longed to dive head first into the never-ending ocean.

"Nothing." She ran her fingers down his jaw line. "I thought I remembered something."

"That is a good thing," Aidan smiled.

Down the nearby corridor, a crewmember slammed a door and began making his way toward them. Aidan kissed Jocelyn's hand before letting go.

"You first."

He gestured for her to walk in front of him.

Jocelyn moved forward, giving distance between them. Hiding their love from the world. She walked to the interior of the ship as the sailor rushed past them, taking no notice.

Aidan watched the man disappear up the stairs to the main deck.

"Have you ever loved anyone?" Jocelyn asked, turning back to him.

"I'm sorry—what did you say?"

"Have you ever been in love?" she asked again.

He watched her mouth form the word love.

"Able hands on deck!" Gregory yelled from above, echoed by a few crewmembers.

Aidan kissed Jocelyn's lips and then her hands.

"I have to go. It is the changing of hands and my presence

is needed."

Jocelyn watched Aidan rush toward the deck before making her way to the galley. The sway of the ocean moved in harmony with the smooth-running vessel.

"Did you give 'im yer heart?"

She jumped at the sound of the quiet, raspy voice.

"Nicholas?"

"Miss."

He bowed his head.

"What are you doing down here?" Jocelyn asked, hearing Henry humming in the kitchen.

"Do you love 'im?" Nicholas asked.

Jocelyn looked up at the tall man, but he would not meet her eyes.

"Whom do you speak of?" she asked coyly.

"You know of whom. I've witnessed yer small affections. Most of the crew have, but we be loyal to the captain. But yer Thomas…"

Her blush faded. "He is not my Thomas."

"He be not as foolish as you believe," he said in a stern voice.

"You offend me with such questions."

Nicholas brushed the air away from his nose.

"I be worried fer me captain. Stop trying ta hypnotize me!"

"For God's sake, what are you talking about?"

"That smell."

She sniffed, the smell of salty bacon wafting in the air. *Crazy merdia.*

"I have never loved before, how would I know if I do now?" she asked.

"You would know. I've watched you an' the captain, and you do not understand the sorcery you 'ave 'im under."

Nicholas swallowed. "You will kill 'im."

"I will not."

The words tasted like a lie.

"But you will die first."

Jocelyn looked at Nicholas's sorrowful face.

"Will you be the one killing me?" she asked, knowing the answer.

Nicholas took a step back, shaking his head.

"I would never, Milady. Never a woman and most definitely not you."

"Then how do you know if I will die or your captain?" she whispered as she saw Henry's shadow approach the doorway.

"Tales of yer kind tell me so."

My kind.

She wanted to demand him to speak of all he knew, but what of Aidan?

"I know I am not like you, but I am beginning to like this way of life. I fear you will tell me what I am, and it will all change. I don't want this to disappear," she replied.

"You've already begun ta change, Milady. You can feel it in yer heart, and I can see it in yer eyes."

"Is it a bad thing to feel this way?" she asked, her voice trembling with the emotions that coursed through her.

"Miss Jocelyn, is that ye?" Henry asked, poking his head into the hallway. He glanced at Nicholas. "Good day."

"Good day," Nicholas grumbled.

Henry nodded, assessing the situation. Nicholas was crazy, but usually right about things. He wasn't dangerous to anyone unless you stole his lucky boots, and Jocelyn was no thief. Picking up on the note he had left off, he began humming again as he shuffled back into the galley.

"You belong out there." Nicholas pointed to a porthole

overlooking the blue water. "You've been out of it fer too long, and I fear you do not know the worse is yet ta come."

"Then tell me."

The words slipped from her mouth. She would have welcomed this revelation months ago, but now she was afraid.

"You are a creature of the sea. A mermaid."

Jocelyn laughed, running the word through her mind.

"Aren't we all creatures of the sea? Especially the ones on this ship?"

"No, you come from the sea and belong there as a fish does. Land is not yer home and never will be. Yer kind governs the oceans with powers not of my world, and you don't belong here. You will die iffen you don't go back. That is the way of things."

Nicholas looked down at his well-worn boots.

Tears welled in her eyes and spilled onto her suddenly hot cheeks. He was right. She had never belonged anywhere, but she felt she belonged here.

"Why can't I remember?"

"I was told of a mermaid years ago who was tricked onto land, but the memory of the ocean faded as she became more human. Then, she died. Lost from her world."

"Why?" Jocelyn asked.

"They say she withered from this earth and demanded the ocean ta take her, but her lifeless body was returned by the rolling waves."

Jocelyn clenched her jaw, wiping away a loose tear.

"How did she become human?"

"Her medallion was taken."

"What medallion?"

"You have one. All of yer kind do. It be a gift the sea gives you ta return. An ornament of sorts, they say hers be made of

He looked her in the eyes for the first time.

Edith's coral trinket.

"It was never hers," she whispered.

"Wot?"

"Is that how you go back?"

"With the medallion?" Nicholas looked confused.

"Yes. Will I become a mermaid again if I have it?"

He nodded. "I believe so."

"I know where it is."

"I'm glad. The sooner you go back, the better."

After examining his maps and compasses, Aidan went in search of Jocelyn. He found her sweeping the floors of the galley. He leaned against the doorway and watched her extend her arms while she danced with the broom. She was all he needed in this life. He planned to approach Jocelyn with a proposal after they reached London. The trinket, hidden in his pocket, would be her engagement gift.

When she saw him, she pulled the broom close and inhaled deeply. Aidan saw the subtle change in her. He could feel she was carrying a burden. He walked to her, but she shied away as if in search of something.

"Is everything all right?" he asked, standing near the cutting table.

She nodded, moving uncertainly to a stack of metal dishes used for the sailors. She slowly began to put them away in the small cabinets, the clanging of tin breaking the quiet.

He watched her delicate movements for a few seconds

before crossing the kitchen and taking her by the shoulders.

"What is it?" he asked.

Jocelyn leaned into him.

"I am so lost," she said into his chest.

"No, you're not. There is a reason why you don't remember your home. Maybe it is time you make a new one," he said, closing his eyes.

"I cannot," Jocelyn said, her eyes swelling with tears.

Panic stirred in Aidan's heart at the thought of her leaving.

"Of course you can."

"You don't understand." Jocelyn looked into his eyes. "I barely do myself. There are forces stronger than you or I involved in this. We cannot control or change what should happen."

"I don't understand. You are not telling me everything I should know."

"It is better you do not know, but I must return to Mrs. Donnell's. She has something of mine I cannot part from."

He could not turn the ship around if he wanted to—the currents and food supply would not allow it. But why the sudden change of heart?

"You said you were trapped there. Why would you want to go back?" he asked.

"She took something from me, and I must have it back."

Aidan saw the sorrow on Jocelyn's face as she avoided his stare.

"I cannot turn this ship off course without jeopardizing my men. You will have to wait until we get to London before we can venture back to Ireland."

"That will take months!"

"Whatever it is, you have lived without it this long," Aidan said, pragmatic yet gentle. "Time does not seem to be an enemy in your situation."

Footsteps echoed through the hallway. Aidan backed away from her as two sailors walked past the door.

"I will help you, but I cannot right now," Aidan said, taking her hand once the sailors were gone.

"I understand."

He saw a look of dread wash over her face. He would do anything to make her happy and to keep her with him. His hand dipped into his pocket, taking hold of the trinket. Slowly, he lifted it from his pocket, thinking of how to ask her to be his wife.

Jocelyn turned as Thomas walked into the room.

"How can you endure the smell?" Thomas asked, covering his nose.

Aidan's heart sank as he slipped the trinket back into his pocket.

"Mr. Corwin," he said, turning to face Thomas.

"Captain. Miss Jocelyn." Thomas nodded to her. Jocelyn bowed before she returned to putting the dishes away.

"May I have a word with you, Captain?" Thomas asked.

"About?" Aidan asked, worried about leaving Jocelyn alone with her thoughts.

"I believe I would like to venture to China after India, and thought I would have a word with you about it—in a more cheerful environment, if you please."

He turned toward the dining hall.

Jocelyn, eavesdropping from across the room, felt an eddy of fear in her belly as Aidan looked back at Thomas, confused.

"We do not have anything to trade in China," he answered.

Thomas looked at Aidan coolly.

"Oh, but we do," he said, turning once more and making his way to the dining hall.

Chapter Eighteen ໒ྀ

"Opium!" Aidan repeated.

"Yes," Thomas said, leaning back in his chair. "There will be a little difficulty obtaining it, but I believe I have worked out most of the problems."

Aidan shook his head. "There are more than a few—not to mention the Chinese government—who expressly forbid merchants to bring opium into port."

"This is true. But if we can have the delivery ready in two months and can be in port during the early morning, the government will never know."

Thomas turned and poured himself a glass of brandy.

"You are putting all of our lives at risk! Besides, there's no way we can make it in that timeframe." He stopped, thoughts clicking as he watched Thomas sip his brandy. "At what port in India do you plan to make land?"

Thomas turned and grinned at Aidan. "Smart man. Calcutta. You are a good captain. I know you can manage the time constraints."

"That's on the other side of India," Aidan protested. "We have not set up buyers there for this voyage! And no ship can travel at the speed you demand to get us there." He rested his hands on the table, shaking his head. "You are going to risk this entire voyage to venture into new trade. Why not plan for a later date?"

"And allow other companies to seize this opportunity? I will not do that." Thomas took a seat at the head of the table. "I have plans of my own and wish to travel back to England as soon as possible, but I will not halt this trade and neither will you."

Aidan clenched his teeth, holding back rage. "I am captain, and it is my responsibility to guide this ship and its crew to safety. I see no good in this greed."

"I don't care what you see. If you will not captain this ship, then you will step down, and Gregory will be promoted," Thomas said calmly.

"What?" Aidan exploded. "I pilot this ship—not Gregory or any other man!"

He slammed his fist down on the table.

"You need to remind that temper of yours who owns this ship, and if it must come down to Gregory, you'll have no one to blame but yourself."

Aidan stared holes into Thomas and thought of his still-green first mate, directing the ship to its doom.

Thomas smiled. "I can see you have made up your mind. Set course for Calcutta. We have two months."

Jocelyn kept watch on the corridor as she finished her chores in the galley.

"You're making me 'ead spin. I'll finish here. You just get out of me kitchen and do what ye need to do," Henry said, taking a stack of dishes from her.

"No. There is too much work."

Jocelyn sighed and went to the counter to cut the potatoes. As she did, Aidan walked past the doorway without slowing down.

"Captain must be in a hurry today," Henry said, rubbing his hands on his stained apron.

"That was the captain?" she asked, dropping the potato and knife and removing her apron.

"I'll be seeing ye at dinner," Henry laughed, taking her place with the potatoes.

"Thank you, Henry," Jocelyn flung behind her as she ran out of the galley.

She hurried to the deck in search of Aidan. The ocean calmly moved the ship forward. Jocelyn could hear it humming from the blue depths, but she pushed it away. She needed to know what Thomas was talking about when he said China—and if they were going there, where was it? She spotted Aidan standing near his first mate, who manned the ship's wheel.

She picked up her dress and glided up the stairs, keeping her eyes on Aidan. Gregory checked the compass as Aidan gave him new coordinates to Calcutta.

"And we are to be there in 45 days? How will we manage such speeds?" Gregory asked, easing the wheel to the left.

"I do not know, but our employer has high hopes we will make our new deadline."

Aidan looked up when Jocelyn stepped on deck.

Impatient to speak to him, she quickly but elegantly slipped between the two men.

Aidan bowed his head. "Miss Jocelyn, what brings you on deck?"

"I wish to know where we are heading," she said simply, noticing Gregory shift nervously. "Are you all right?" she asked.

Gregory swallowed and turned to Aidan.

"May I take my leave, Captain?"

Aidan nodded as he tried to mask a smile. Gregory bowed to Jocelyn without looking at her, clumsily making his way to the lower deck.

"Is he ill?" she asked, watching Gregory scurry away.

"No. I believe you make him nervous."

"Why? We have been on the same ship for almost two months now."

"He is a true sailor and is rarely around a real lady," Aidan said. "Let alone one as beautiful as you."

"You exaggerate."

"Do I?"

"No more of this nonsense. I need to know where we are going," Jocelyn demanded.

"We are still on course to India, but we have a new port to visit after."

"China?"

He nodded and looked down at the compass.

"Canton, China, to be exact."

She looked out at the open sea. A gust of cool wind blew her hair from her face. She was traveling farther away from the only thing that would release her memories.

Parkena. "Where is China?"

Aidan looked up from the compass and pointed northeast. She followed his finger and squinted out at the horizon.

"Thomas wants us there in two months. But even with the wind and the good weather we've had, no one has traveled to China in four months."

"There is nothing you can do to travel faster?"

"No, not unless the currents and wind magically pick up speed—there is no way humanly possible to do so."

"Currents?"

"The pull of the water," Aidan answered as he checked the compass and turned the wheel.

"If it increases in speed, will we make it?" Jocelyn asked. *Ouniome. Home.*

"Yes, but we have no control over the ocean," he said absent-mindedly.

Jocelyn smiled, biting her bottom lip.

"You're right. You have no control over it."

Dinner was quiet. Aidan avoided most of Thomas's attempts at conversation, and Jocelyn was lost in her thoughts. A soft knock on the wood door lifted everyone's attention.

"Come in," Thomas demanded.

Gregory poked his head in.

"Captain, you are needed on deck."

Aidan nodded to his first mate then looked at Jocelyn. She smiled, knowing he was searching to see if she would be all right alone with Thomas. Giving a reassuring nod, she watched Aidan leave the room with Gregory.

"Finally. Alone," Thomas announced.

Jocelyn focused on the bowl of potato and leek soup in silence as Thomas shifted in his chair.

"You have heard of the changes?" Thomas asked.

Jocelyn nodded, stirring the soup.

"Do not worry about the extra time; soon we will be in

England."

Jocelyn tried to tune him out, but his deep voice boomed in her ears.

"I will introduce you into society with a ball. No expense spared, of course."

"Do you enjoy all of that?" she asked, watching the soup drip from her spoon.

Thomas looked at Jocelyn's suddenly tired face.

"Of course—and soon you will enjoy it as well."

"I don't think I would."

Jocelyn fumbled with her spoon, knowing his piercing eyes were leaving their mark on her.

"Of course you will," he said.

"I appreciate what you're doing for me, but when I find my home, I will stay," she announced.

"I understand you want to know where you are from, but as a woman you need to think about your future and where you stand. Truly, Jocelyn, what do you think you will find that I cannot offer you better?"

"I don't think you understand, Thomas. You have nothing I want. It is getting late, and I wish to retire."

Jocelyn stood before he could respond and walked toward her chambers.

Thomas threw his napkin down on the table and stood.

"You, my lady, have no means to turn me down. Do you understand? I own you. You are bought and paid for!"

She continued to the door.

"Goodnight, Thomas."

Once out of the dining room and away from Thomas, Jocelyn ran to her room. She bolted the door, pulling the handle to see if it would budge. She sat near the porthole and waited patiently for the late hours of the night.

The bright stars were sparkling through the windows of her room as she silently crept to the upper deck with a small lantern to light her way. A few sailors sat on barrels, on watch but more asleep than not. Jocelyn tiptoed barefoot between the shadows to the head of the ship.

She pressed herself to the head rail and looked down at the ocean, her view blocked by the figurehead. A young woman's face, carved of wood, stared up at her, pointing the way of the ship. Jocelyn squinted to see the figure's fin. She was examining the half-woman, half-fish when a quick movement in the water caught her attention. She lifted the lantern over the rail and peered at the dark sea. A pair of eyes reflected the light and stared at her. Mesmerized, she leaned closer. A head lifted from the water.

Jocelyn dropped the lantern into the ocean, gasping. The small flame threw light on a man's face as it disappeared into the water. Jocelyn's heart raced as she rushed around the rail, looking for the being that had vanished in the cold water. The melody from the ocean began to rise when a loud splash rang on the other side of the ship.

Jocelyn stopped and pulled herself on the rail to look down. Nothing but the black ocean looked back. She pushed her body further, balancing on her stomach, only the tip of her toes still touching the ship.

Is that you? the voice asked.

"Who are you?" Jocelyn asked, waiting for the voice to answer.

Nothing. She leaned further still against the damp rail, but a screech stopped her.

A few of the sailors roused themselves and rushed to the opposite side of the ship, looking for the source of the noise.

The sudden movement of the men broke Jocelyn away from her search for the unknown creature. She began to whisper to the ocean.

"You need to move quicker. We head to Calcutta and then to Canton. Quicken your pace so I may join you sooner."

She closed her eyes, picturing the waters moving faster and faster with the wind rushing around the ship, propelling it forward. Jocelyn opened her eyes, waiting for a jolt of acknowledgment, but nothing happened. A yawning sailor approached her.

"It be early fer you, miss, ta be out here," he said as she turned toward him.

"I know," she said. *This was a waste.*

She exhaled and followed the familiar path to her cabin.

"You can stay, miss. I meant no orders fer you ta leave," the sailor said, watching her.

"I have gotten enough fresh air, and I am tired," she whispered back. "I am not needed out here."

Chapter Nineteen ෧

Jocelyn slept in later than usual, and when she woke, her eyes burned from the bright sunlight engulfing the room. She slumped out of bed and ambled to a small mirror above a washbowl. She stared at her image. Dark circles ringed her eyes. She tried to rub them away, but to no avail. She looked back at the bed with its welcoming white blanket. In a haze, she dragged herself to it, devoid of energy.

What is the purpose? I will never make it to my ouniome.

"All men on deck!" a sailor yelled behind her door.

Jocelyn froze in front of the warm bed, listening to men running past her cabin. She turned to her window and scanned the horizon for storm clouds, but blue skies filled the view.

The tempest must be in front of us.

She ran to the closet and pulled out her cleanest dress and Aidan's coat, accidentally dropping it to the ground. Jocelyn picked it up and held it to her nose. His scent still lingered on the heavy fabric. She knew she should give it back but was afraid to. It could be the only thing she would have to remember him when her journey ended.

She buried the coat in the closet as a loud knock sounded on the door.

"Miss?" came Henry's voice through the wood.

Jocelyn rushed to the door and cracked it open. Henry, catching his breath, pointed up to the deck.

"'Tis a miracle — 'urry, miss."

"What is?" she asked, opening the door to follow Henry. A brisk breeze reminded her of her thin attire.

"'Urry, miss! No one knows 'ow long it'll last!" he yelled, rushing back to the upper deck.

"What?" Jocelyn yelled back, but Henry didn't reply.

Slamming the door, she pulled her nightgown over her head and dropped it to the ground. She stepped into her dress and laced the back as she ran out the door toward the deck.

Jocelyn emerged to see a deck full of crewmembers leaning over the side of the ship. An insistent wind pressed her dress to her legs and blew her long hair back. She spotted Henry with a large smile talking to one of his mates, pointing east toward India.

Jocelyn trudged into the wind. The invisible force hugged her with cold arms. Goosebumps prickled her skin from the excitement in the air.

She stopped at the waist of the ship and squeezed between two burly sailors. She gazed down into the ocean. White water splashed up from the fast-moving current.

A *thud* sounded behind her. Swiftly, she turned to find a shoe not far from her.

"You'll be one shoe short iffen you don't learn ta properly tie them," Nicholas yelled up to the sky, rushing to pick up the battered boot.

Jocelyn cast her eyes upon a young boy, who had helped her with her luggage in Ireland, with his legs wrapped around the main yard of one of the three masts. The boy secured the main topsail to the yard before he leaned over to holler back at

Nicholas.

"They may not be as lucky as yers, but I 'aven't lost one yet!"

Nicholas laughed, placing the shoe on top of a nearby barrel.

"Why are they removing the sails?" Jocelyn asked, her eyes glued to the boy scurrying fearlessly across the yard.

"The wind be against us. It only slows us down," Nicholas answered, leaning on the barrel. "I take it this gift from God 'ad a little help?" he asked, pushing his hair back from the salty wind.

Jocelyn smiled. "I believe so."

Nicholas spit into the water. "Be careful, lass. There may be many half-witted men on this ship, but with such displays even the simpleminded will begin ta question their luck."

"You talk in riddles."

"Wot do you think they will do ta you iffen they knew wot you be?" Nicholas pointed to the excited crew.

What would they do? She studied the men.

"The fearful will put you back into the ocean, even if you look human."

"I have not harmed them. Why would you say such things?"

"You, no, but yer kind has. Death is known to follow the ship with a mermaid attached to it."

"Then why did you let me on?" Jocelyn demanded.

"It seems safer ta me ta 'ave you on this ship then not. And I fear the lives of this crew relies on yer well-being."

"What are you saying?"

"If you die, we all die," Nicholas said, staring at the boy climbing down the main shrouds.

The lad jumped to the deck. She gazed across at the other

men, cheering their inexplicably fast progress.

"Should I make it stop?" she asked.

Nicholas tracked the swift currents below before shaking his head.

"You 'ave them fooled fer now. Just be mindful of wot you are and who yer with. People do funny things with the unknown."

He grabbed the shoe from the barrel-top and tossed it to the boy, but the wind caught it first. Nicholas laughed, watching the lad chase it across the deck.

"Can you make it go faster?" he asked with a wink.

The current sped the ship toward India day after day. Aidan marveled at their extraordinary luck. He navigated his ship by the currents of the seasons, but never had he found one that kept such speed nor lasted so long. It was as if the ocean knew his destination and was determined to get him there.

Thomas gloated at the timing of such friendly waters, which made Aidan almost wish for the currents to slow so they would miss their illicit cargo. But the pace only picked up. He figured if this current kept its speed, they would be in China with a few days to spare. The idea of helping Thomas gain a footing in the opium trade sickened him, but as he played with the trinket in his pocket, he was glad they would soon be on their way back to England where he would, hopefully, gain Jocelyn's hand.

He weighed the dangers of stealing Jocelyn away from Thomas, calculating how to sneak her off the ship once it was docked on English soil. Thomas's reputation of his temperament was well-known throughout his employees, especially Aidan. Christopher confided in Aidan about his son's behavior in brothels and pubs, where Christopher paid large sums to wipe away Thomas's sins.

A man who enjoyed the sorrow of other's torments had no hope of growing into anything good. Without knowing the elder Corwin was in the beginning stages of consumption, Aidan was asked to fetch Thomas from a bawdy house in Bristol.

Knocking on the large door as cat calls from harlots echoed down the dark alley, Aidan kept his face covered with the brim of his hat, protecting his identity from the drunk man linked to a prostitute, stumbling on the cobblestone.

The door swung open to a skinny woman with few teeth smiling up at him. Her dress hung from her shoulders, showing her collarbone and sagging breasts. Gaudy jewelry lined her fingers and neck. She must have been the Madame of the house.

"Wot you be looking for, son?" The woman hissed like a snake luring its prey.

"I am in search of Master Corwin."

"He's not here. But there are other pretties who might entertain you."

Aidan took a step back, distancing himself from the mistress of the house as the overpowering stench of brandy and lack of hygiene escaped from her mouth.

"I was told he was here."

"He was, but he's gone now," the Madame said.

"Do you know where he's gone?"

"Home, I assume. He lost a large amount of money to Sir Markus at poker. He was in no mood for a companion."

"Thank you for your help."

Aidan bowed and turned to leave.

The mistress grabbed his arm before he could escape the dread of lost souls.

"He owes this house a large sum for his entertainment."

Aidan shrugged the woman off.

"I will let his household know."

"Make sure you do, now." The woman smiled up at Aidan, dropping her grip. "Are you sure we can't entertain you for a spell?"

Aidan shook his head no before tramping through the mud and grime of the city. He turned the corner, exchanging one dark alley for another. A man stood at the corner, whispering to a lady-of-the-night's ear of sweet things he would give her if she would give her services for half price. She laughed in his face and pushed past him. The man slumped forward, trudging passed Aidan.

Shadows climbed the narrow alleyway, darkening the street with secrets. Aidan quickened his step, running right into Thomas. Blood covered Thomas's knuckles and his white shirt.

"Bloody hell man, watch where you're walking," Thomas slurred.

"Master Corwin!" Aidan said, gaining his footing.

"Do I know you?"

"I am an employee of your father's."

Thomas pointed. "That's right. You are the amazzzing cabin boy. Did the old man tell you the grand news yet?"

"I am here to fetch you and bring you home. Barron Corwin insists we are quick."

"An errand boy now. Already de-promoting you before your promotion. What does the old man want?" Thomas fiddled with the sleeves of his shirt, drops of blood staining the fabric.

"He didn't say. Are you hurt, sir?" Aidan asked.

"Don't worry. It's not my blood. Take me home, good lad. Let's go see the old geezer."

Aidan ground his teeth as Thomas twirled in the streets, dancing to the music in his head. Someone was hurt badly by the amount of blood on Thomas's body, and the man beamed with triumph.

The next day Aidan read in the papers of Sir Markus's body being found in the river near the brothel.

If Aidan and Jocelyn were to live happily ever after, Thomas could never find them, and Jocelyn could never return to Edith's manor. But that would come later. Right now the current pushed the ship forward toward his future.

"Thank you," he breathed to the unknown force.

Every night Jocelyn would lie by the open window in her room and talk to the shifting sea. The first night under the gray clouds she only spoke of the current and India. The next night, after hours of listening to the ocean sing to her, drifting asleep on the rough wood sill of the window, breathing in the damp air, Jocelyn's eyes fluttered open to an echo calling her.

Where are you? the masculine voice asked, bleeding in with the haunting melody of the ocean.

At first Jocelyn barely heard it as her eyes blinked away the sleep fogging her consciousness. But when she did not answer, the voice grew stronger. Bolder.

She jumped to her feet, believing someone was in her room. The shadows on the wall swayed with the slow rocking of the ship as if in a dance with a drunk partner. Jocelyn fumbled to light a lantern, burning her finger. Her skin glistened white as an instant blister bubbled up. She pressed the wounded finger into her mouth. The cool saliva on her tongue stung the damaged skin for an instant before the dull throb took its place. She held up the oil lantern as her eyes explored the room for the voice's owner—her finger still attached to her mouth. The flame flittered wildly as if mimicking her racing heart. The room was empty except for Jocelyn and the dancing shadows.

Feeling childish, she grabbed the pillow she had been sitting on and made her way to the bed.

A worried voice intruded on the silence of the room.

"Where are you?"

The voice was different this time. It echoed through the window into the room instead of inside her head.

Dropping her pillow, Jocelyn ran to the window and looked down the long drop to the dark waters. If someone were down there, she could not see him. She pushed herself farther out the wooden frame, trying to hear the voice again. The feeling of eyes watching her made her pull back into the safety of her room.

"Wait!" the voice yelled.

Slowly, she peered out again.

"It is you." Relief washed through the voice. "Are you hurt? Did they hurt you?"

Jocelyn shook her head no, not remembering ever being hurt by anyone.

"Are...are you the ocean?" Jocelyn stammered after a few moments.

"You don't know who I am?" The voice cracked.

"No, who are you?"

"I am part of the ocean, as are you."

The voice was gentle and strong. One she knew her whole life.

"I know you."

She settled herself in front of the window.

"You do, Mli? Say my name. I need to hear it," the voice begged.

"I know you, but I don't know your name."

The water splashed below. Jocelyn searched for the maker of the sound, but only saw the ripples that were left behind, fading into the moving ocean.

"Why do you call me Mli?" she asked when the voice wouldn't reply.

The voice was quiet. Jocelyn peered down at the ocean.

"Tell me who I am, please," Jocelyn begged.

"I can't."

"Why not?"

"I can't help you unless I am with you. Wait for me."

"I can't," Jocelyn answered.

"I have found you, and I'm going to bring you home."

"Who are you?" Jocelyn held tight to the frame, pushing her body out of the window, searching.

"Your friend," the voice echoed.

"Who am I?"

Black eyes peered up at her as they reflected the moonlight.

Confused by her own calmness, she folded her arms on the window's edge and used them as a pillow, looking down at the eyes.

"You are my Mli."

Jocelyn's heart raced at the word "my."

"You're tired. Sleep."

"Will you go?" she asked, hoping he would not.

"I will stay."

Heat rose in her cheeks—and the hope she soon would know herself at long last. Closing her eyes, she listened to the voice hum with the rocking of the ocean.

Chapter Twenty ⚕

Jocelyn woke once more to the sun streaming into her room. She stretched her stiff arms, yawning. When she finally stood, wobbling on sleepy legs, the memory of the voice seemed to be a dream. Rubbing her tired eyes, she replayed the encounter in her mind. The strength of the voice comforted her, helped her feel not so alone, out of place.

She fixed her hair in the mirror before peering out the window at the moving water. Narrowing her eyes against the brilliant sun, she looked for any sign of life that might be lingering below. Tears welled in her eyes, making everything blurry.

Turning back to the room, she whispered, "It couldn't have been real."

I am as real as I was last night, the voice boomed in her head.

Jocelyn's breath stuck in her throat as she stumbled back to the window. The bright glare of the sun on the water blinded her. Quickly she closed her eyes.

"Where are you?"

No one replied. She leaned out now, trying in vain to pinpoint the location of the voice over the rhythmic lapping of the sea against the ship's hull. A knock on the door made her gasp, and she hit her elbow on the edge of the window frame. She tried to rub away the pain as she stepped to the door.

"Who is it?" she asked.

"Aidan."

Aidan never came to her room anymore unless there was a problem onboard. Jocelyn leapt to the door, swinging it open. He stood with his hands behind his back.

Aidan couldn't help but notice she was out of breath.

"I did not mean to disturb you, but I was worried."

Jocelyn put her arm on the door and rested her body against it.

"Why are you worried?"

"You never came to the galley for breakfast."

"What time is it?" she asked, turning to the window, the white light pouring through.

"Noon," Aidan said, looking at the dress she was still wearing from yesterday.

His eyes followed it up to her exposed arm on the door. A line of fresh blood trickled down. Without thinking, he grabbed her, surprised by a rather large cut on her elbow. She pulled back.

"What are you doing?"

"What happened?" he asked, leading her into the cabin and leaving the door open.

She turned her head to look at the gash. "I bumped it."

"Where?"

He helped her sit down on a bachelor's chair as he advanced to the washbowl and filled it with water. He opened a cabinet that held a porcelain bowl and pulled out a wooden box.

"The window."

Jocelyn examined the wound, fascinated by the way the

blood clustered together and slid down her arm. It smelled bitter and spicy.

Aidan set the washbowl on the floor and dunked a hand towel inside. Tucked under his arm was the wooden box. He knelt beside her, set the box down, and opened it. Jocelyn saw a red velvet-covered interior with small, labeled medicine bottles lined in rows, tied to the top of the box. The bottom was filled with neat rows of cotton fabric. He pulled out the wet towel from the bowl and gently covered her open wound.

"*Parkena!* That hurts," Jocelyn yelled.

"I am sorry, but we have to clean it. Is the window broken?" he asked, removing the towel.

Jocelyn shook her head. The cut stung, but this quickly gave way to a stronger sensation: Aidan's large, gentle hands moving up her arm, sending warm vibrations through her body.

Aidan cleaned the towel before wiping the remaining blood from her arm.

"How did you cut it then?"

"I hit it."

He grabbed a bandage from the box, wrapped her arm, and tied the dressing.

Jocelyn admired the white fabric that protected her wound. The rough texture of the bandage rubbed against her skin when she bent her elbow, but if she could get used to Thomas and life aboard a working ship, she could get used to that.

Aidan stood and walked to the open window. He ran his fingers along the edges of the sill, but they were rounded. He leaned out the window just as a loud splash rose from the waters below. Aidan spied the waves for a good minute, but nothing came to the surface. He turned his attention back to the window itself. The protruding wood that hung from the ship was cracking from many seasons out at sea.

"Were your arms outside the window?" he asked, reminding himself to have the outside of the ship re-sanded and sealed before the next journey.

Jocelyn only nodded, afraid if she told him the reason she was looking out the window, he would think her mad.

"Try to avoid putting your arms out there. The wood is rotten and jagged." He looked up at the high sun before he pulled himself back in. "Lunch should be ready soon. You might want to change before you come. Also, could you check in with Henry? He's acting like an old maid with all of his worrying."

"About me?"

"You seem to have more than just me under your spell." Aidan kissed her forehead, then headed to the cabin door. "I need to make my rounds. I'll see you in the dining hall."

Jocelyn bit her lip. *Stay with me,* she pleaded silently.

As he left, a low *thud* sounded against the outside of the ship.

Finally dressed for the day, Jocelyn crept to the galley and peeked inside. Henry was still at work. The aged man bent over the stove, lighting dry wood. Stacks of peeled potatoes spilled over the counters. Jocelyn tiptoed into the small room.

"How ye be?" Henry asked without turning his head from the struggling flame.

"I am fine," Jocelyn answered, resting her back against the wall.

"Are ye sick?" A worried tone edged his voice.

She smiled at his kindness. "I am well."

Henry turned and looked at her.

"Yer paler than normal."

He grabbed a mug from the cabinet and poured warm coffee. Jocelyn watched the steam rise lazily from the cup as he held it out to her.

"Drink," he ordered.

She took the hot mug and held it to her nose.

"Wot are ye doing?" Henry asked, observing her.

"I like the smell of coffee more than the taste," she responded, inhaling the bold scent.

"Smelling it'll do ye no good. Drink, lass."

She sipped the dark liquid, the rich flavor covering her tongue, then warming her throat.

"Is the ocean keeping ye awake?"

He slid a large pot onto the burner and dropped the potatoes into it. Water splashed over the side.

Surprised by the question, Jocelyn stalled, taking another sip of coffee.

"With the current going the way it is, a lot of the crew ain't sleeping."

"Do they hear anything?" she blurted out.

"'Ear what?"

He looked over his shoulder at her.

"Voices or something similar?" Jocelyn raised her eyebrows, anxious for Henry to answer.

"Well, some say the ocean talks to 'em. When ye are on the water for so long, a few of the crew just can't 'andle it."

"Handle what? The ocean?"

"Everything. The endless blue. The loneness. Everything that comes with being out ta sea. After a while, they begin ta see and 'ear things that ain't there. Superstitions don't 'elp, but they can't be stopped."

The aroma of dried pepper and salt blended with hot potatoes slowly became the only thing Jocelyn could focus on.

"What happens to the crewmembers who hear the voices?" Her voice wavered.

"Some leave at the dock. Some go to the sea."

"Into the sea?" Her stomach churned.

"The voices tell them to." Henry waved her to the gangway. "You go and eat. Captain was saying we'll be in India in a few short days."

"So soon?"

She placed the nearly full mug on the counter. If coffee was for anybody, it certainly wasn't for her.

"The current is doing the work. A true miracle if I say so myself. Now go. They be waitin' for ye."

Jocelyn walked into the dining hall, expecting Aidan and Thomas to be waiting for her, but instead the two men were hunched over a large, round cloth. The thick, painted material covered most of the table. Aidan ran his hand across the dried blue paint that occupied most of the space. Green and brown overlapped to form a mass surrounded by the blue body with waves painted in. She stretched her neck as she walked forward, trying to follow his finger.

"By my calculations, we should be here." Aidan's finger stopped inches away from the brown mass on the canvas. "As you can see, we have maybe three days until we dock in Calcutta."

"I told you time would not be an issue." Thomas gazed at Jocelyn as she leaned down to observe the painting. "You look better than I expected."

"What were you expecting?" she asked, gently guiding her fingertips over the smooth blue of the map. *Beautiful.*

"When you missed breakfast, we thought you might be ill."

Thomas sat down as Aidan watched her hand glide along the same path his hand had taken.

"I am fine. I was tired and didn't realize the time." Jocelyn looked up at Aidan. "What is this?"

Aidan couldn't help but smile. "A map. See, India is here."

He circled part of the green and brown mass. 'India' was spelled out across it, with smaller lettering for the ports and cities.

"It is wonderful." Her eyes danced with delight.

"It is an old map," Thomas said.

Aidan frowned at Thomas's comment. This map was no more than a year old. He began to fold it, minding the delicate edges.

"Henry said we were close."

Jocelyn took a seat alongside the men, staring at the map even as Aidan finished folding it.

"Closer than I could have imagined. For some reason God has favored us," Aidan said, placing the map into a satchel.

"As He should," Thomas declared, playing with the ruffled sleeves of his shirt.

The smell of boiled potatoes filled the room. Soon, Henry arrived, carrying their meals.

"In a few days, my dear, we will have a real meal," Thomas said as Henry placed a plate in front of him.

"This is not a real meal?" she asked, smiling up at the cook who gently handed her a plate of potatoes and roasted chicken.

"Thank you, Henry."

He nodded as he made his way to Aidan.

"Good God, no! This is barely edible. I speak of a meal that will reach your soul with its spices," Thomas said, cutting the meat.

"The meal you speak of sounds rather dangerous. I wouldn't want anything to invade me. I like the simplicity of these meals," Jocelyn said, her stomach growling in agreement.

"I must concur with Thomas on this one," Aidan spoke up, taking his plate.

Jocelyn blinked at her captain. Nothing Thomas said was agreeable.

"I have never had such a meal as I have had in India. I'm surprised Henry hasn't mentioned his delight with the food yet," Aidan said.

Henry stopped before he reached the doorway.

"'Tis a private matter, a man and 'is food, Captain. She will see fer 'erself."

Henry bowed his head before he exited the room. Jocelyn faced Aidan.

"Do we bring the food on board?" she asked.

A rush of excitement filled her. If Henry felt so passionately about the food, how could she refuse?

"No. We will be dining out, and in three days, no less," Thomas answered. "Mr. Boyd will be our guide. Won't you?"

"Of course," Aidan answered. He had visited Calcutta on many accounts and knew the territory well.

She beamed. She would not be alone with Thomas — Aidan would make sure of that. India waited for their arrival with promises of exotic foods and, she hoped, a faster way back to Edith's.

Chapter Twenty-One ⚛

India came sooner than Aidan expected. The current had somehow picked up even more speed. Two weeks faster than any other voyage. He marveled at the landmass growing in the distance.

Thank you.

Seagulls hovered over the ship, begging the young sailors for the stale biscuits hidden in their pockets. With fresh provisions miles away, a few relinquished the hard bread. Nonetheless, the gulls bravely landed in the bow, webbed feet hopping to and fro, fighting over crumbs.

Aidan appeared on deck as the sailors sat by, entertained by the winged scavengers.

"Get those birds off my ship," Aidan ordered.

Hastily, the boys ran at the birds, arms wide open. All took to the air except one. The gull waddled, squawking at the sailor, nipping at his hands as he swatted at it. With a final protesting *caw*, the gull half-flew, half-hopped to the other end of the ship. Aidan watched the defiant bird and shook his head.

Bold thing.

Jocelyn emerged from the belly of the ship. The ornery gull hopped toward her.

She beamed at the creature like an old friend.

"What are you doing here?" she asked.

The bird turned his head, eyeing her, the same way the gull had done at Edith's. The humid air stuck to her skin.

"You are far from home."

The bird shook its feathers.

"Go home," Jocelyn laughed, shooing her feathered friend to the sky. She blocked the sun from her view, watching it take flight. It soared toward the blurry greens and browns of the earth on the horizon.

"Is that India?" she asked as Aidan walked to her.

"Yes," he said.

She focused her eyes to get a clearer picture. The world around her drifted from her view as the forthcoming destination magnified.

She pointed, unable to make out the bobbing specks brushing the edge of the new world.

"What are the brown dots in the water?"

Aidan looked for the dots, but only saw the coast. He extended his brass telescope and raised it to his eye. Boats sailed along the rim of the terrain toward the ports, miles away.

He moved the telescope away from his eye and the ships disappeared.

"How did you see those?" he asked, handing her the telescope.

She hoisted the spyglass, watching the brown specks turn into large ships. She quickly moved the telescope away from her eye and blinked. The large ships turned back into dots. She laughed as she repeated the trick over and over.

"This is amazing!"

"Yes, it is," Aidan said, eyeing her keenly. "Those ships are miles away. How could you see them without the telescope?"

She lowered the looking glass and stared out over the water.

"I just do," she said, looking up at him with an innocent smile.

She longed to share her secret, but Nicholas's warning loomed in her memory. Without saying a word, Jocelyn handed back the telescope.

Aidan could feel her pull away from him as she slipped the cold brass of the telescope into his hand.

"You don't have to answer my question," he said quickly, wishing otherwise. "But if you did, I think I could understand, whatever your answer may be."

She shook her head.

Heedless of who might be watching, Aidan reached for her, but she stepped back.

"I told Henry I would help him," she said, turning toward the galley.

"He can wait."

He wanted to hold her close and make her safe—even against his own inquiries—but something told him to let her go. She stole past him without a sound.

Throughout the rest of the day, the crew made their guesses as to when the ship would dock in Calcutta, but nothing was certain until Gregory declared it to be noon tomorrow. Jocelyn tried to sleep, but the excitement of arriving in India, then eventually China—and, more importantly, her journey back to Edith's for her coral medallion—kept her mind racing. After an hour of staring at the ceiling, she finally lit the lantern, grabbed her pillow, and trundled to the open window. She plopped the pillow on the sill and laid down her head, thrilled by the warm night air and the light from the full moon dancing on the bejeweled water.

The moonlight revealed everything. She turned down the lantern until the flame disappeared.

"Is anyone there?" she asked, repeating the same question she had bashfully asked the night before. She waited but received the same response—nothing. "I do not know who or what you are, but I feel more alone not having you here. Why is that?"

The ocean's cry quickly answered her. It had been some time since she'd had the urge to surround herself with water, but now she could feel her heart begging her to surrender to the bottomless blue eternity. An anguished tear escaped her eye and fell into the ocean. That single tear was all she could give for now. The idea of sinking into the deep waters frightened her.

Chapter Twenty-Two ꙮ

The ship docked while Jocelyn and Henry cleaned the galley. Henry made it very clear lunch would not be served onboard. Once the ship was attached to India, he would be off in search of supplies, including ale and local foodstuffs.

A young boy ran into the kitchen. Jocelyn recognized him as the lad from the sails. She looked down at his feet. He still had both shoes.

"Wot is it, George?" Henry asked the bright-faced youth.

"I'm ta collect the missus' clothes," George answered with a shy smile.

"You'll wot?" Henry demanded.

George's smile melted away. "Fer washin.'"

"It better be." Henry glared at the lad.

"Sir Corwin's man told me to," George said in his defense, standing taller.

Jocelyn looked down at her grease-stained dress. Nearly her entire wardrobe was stained in one way or another, and each dress had an odor of its own.

"I'm ta collect it afore the burden is unloaded," James added.

"What is 'the burden'?" she asked.

"The cargo." Henry turned back to the few remaining dishes. "Milady will 'ave 'er laundry waiting fer ye by 'er door."

"'Ow long'll that be?" George asked, tapping his finger on his thigh.

Henry spun, clutching a dripping plate, to face the boy.

"As long as it takes 'er."

George nodded and raced out of the galley.

Jocelyn untied her apron, looking around the unusually clean kitchen.

"You shouldn't be so harsh on the young boy."

"I wasn't harsh. Ye should go take care of yer clothes before the young lad comes knocking on yer door."

Jocelyn pulled dresses and undergarments from the closet, and, after giving them a cursory whiff, threw them into a pile on the floor. She halted at the purple dress, which she had worn only once during the voyage. She placed the violet garment to her nose. A hint of soap still lingered on the material. Holding up the dress, she examined it. It was still ugly, no denying it.

The small wood-lined cabin was warmer than it had ever been, and the idea of being hugged by the thick fabric made her face scrunch in disgust. She dropped the dress onto the bed.

She sniffed the last four dresses in the closet and tossed them into the mounting pile before returning to the hideous purple frock. She pulled off her soiled galley-dress, but the fabric stuck to her sweaty limbs. She tugged at the dress, peeling it from her skin. Standing in a corset and chemise,

Jocelyn fanned her face.

What a change from Edith's.

The dampness in the air covered her. Exhaling, she pulled the purple dress over her. Dots of sweat spread across her brow as she peered into the small mirror, and her shoulders drooped from the weight of the fabric.

One day. I only have to wear it for today.

The dress was smothering.

Gathering up the laundry, she put her things in three sacks. She panted as she dragged the sacks out of the cabin. The job done, she pushed the door shut and sat on the edge of the bed, taking deep breaths.

It wasn't long before she heard a knock on the door. Expecting it to be George, she opened it to find Thomas standing there. She sucked in air, surprised to see him so close to her bedroom. She closed the door to a crack, peering out at him.

"I see you are ready."

Thomas examined the purple fabric curling around the door.

She searched outside the threshold for the sacks of clothes, but none were there.

"But you may rethink your attire. It is far too humid for you to be dressed in such a manner."

"I agree, but all my other clothes need laundering. I will manage with what I have," she said, shifting in the sticky fabric, drops of sweat trickling down her leg.

"No, you will not."

"As I said, Thomas, I have no other."

"You will. India has the finest silks, and I have already arranged for you to be fitted for a new wardrobe."

Jocelyn shook her head.

"You will not last an hour out in this weather. It is a gift to you," Thomas added.

"A gift." Jocelyn laughed aloud as she repeated the word. Thomas smiled. "Yes."

"The same as the voyage here or my stay with your aunt? Your gifts, sir, have strings attached. Now, if you'll excuse me, I would like to get by."

She opened the door to walk out, but Thomas stood his ground.

"What I said earlier was out of line, and I wish I could retract it, but I cannot," Thomas said.

"No, you cannot," she agreed.

Thomas did not rise to her taunt. Instead, his voice softened as he fiddled with his fingers.

"I do not wish for you to think of me as the monster I have portrayed myself to be," he said with apparent humility. "I have grown up in a world where I have received most, if not all, of my wishes. And when denied, I acted like a spoiled child. I apologize for that. I wish to start over, and a new wardrobe is my peace offering."

Speechless, she looked Thomas over. He stood taller, shifting his hands behind his back and lifting his chin high. Everything about him was exceedingly superior: his pressed suit, shined boots, clean-shaven face. Meanwhile, a tickling drop of sweat ran down her calf. She scratched it with the back of her foot, but another replaced it. Jocelyn knew the dress had to go. Thomas's declaration came with many unstated obligations, but she had to get to Edith, and he was the one with the ship.

Why not take the clothes too?

"I will owe you nothing," she said flatly.

"Nothing."

Chapter Twenty-Three ⚛

Aidan folded a dirty shirt and placed it at the bottom of a long canvas bag. He picked up his breeches by the ends and swung them out, brushing off any loose grime. The hand-sewn pockets unfolded, dispersing the treasures in them. The glint of copper from the little light in the cabin drew Aidan's attention to the soaring gear. He dropped the breeches on the cot, keeping his eyes on the gear, hoping not to lose it again.

The copper pattered against the wooden planks, rolling away from Aidan. He jumped toward the lost piece as it slid between two wooden boards.

"Bloody hell!" Aidan yelled, shoving his fingers into the tiny space.

They compressed against the walls of the floor, not allowing him to free the gear. Sitting on the ground, Aidan searched his pockets for something to grab the gear. He found his knife.

He slid the blade into the crack, moving the gear forward, rolling it up the side of a board. The knife's sharp edge carved into the plank with ease. The ribbed edge of the gear poked over the side of the board, almost free of its hiding place. Aidan pushed his index finger against the gear, holding it against the blade. Lifting his knife out of the hole, he rolled the gear onto his palm.

He stood, ran to his coat, pulled out the coral medallion, and slid the gear into it. He had to get it fixed before losing another piece of the delicate gift. He put the trinket into his breast pocket and grabbed his clothes, shoving them into the bag. Throwing the heavy baggage over his shoulder, Aidan strode out of the cabin.

Aidan paid the dues at the port then escorted the cargo, searching for merchants to buy his unclaimed goods. With a delay of other merchant ships, the trades came easily and quickly.

After collecting payment and dropping off his dirty clothes to be laundered, he proceeded to Taylor's Emporium, where the finest Indian creations were sold to the wealthy. He had been instructed to meet Thomas and Jocelyn there.

Aidan found the building with little trouble and entered the crowded, stuffy room. Tables filled with china plates, silks, tapestries, and rows of other exquisite merchandise lined the large room, along with white linen tents stocked with lightweight, colorful clothes for the pampered to purchase.

On the morrow, he would barter with the silk, tea, and spice traders for the cargo bound for England. The negotiating and managing of the trades made the day long. In the midst of it all, he would have to make time to go with Thomas to get opium, which he had never done before. But at the present, he had to search out Jocelyn and Thomas.

This will be an awkward evening.

He wished he could grab a quick bite and then make his way back to the ship to rest. He didn't want to leave Jocelyn alone with Thomas, but his eyes were begging for sleep.

Only a few hours and then rest, he promised himself.

He scoped the open room before poking his head into every tent, searching for Thomas and Jocelyn. In the fourth tent, he found a slender man leaning over a table stacked with watches and clocks. Aidan's feet moved forward, in search of Jocelyn, but his eyes focused on the man's small fingers working on a timepiece. The man slid in a brass gear and screwed it into place with ease. He looked at Aidan, lifting his magnified glasses onto his head.

"Take a moment to explore, sir. You never know what you will find," the man said.

Aidan stopped. He scanned the table and the watches.

"Did you build all of these?" Aidan asked.

"Most. Some I've bought. Others I've found, but every one is a great buy, sir."

Aidan picked up a pocket watch and opened the back. The inner workings appeared to be the same as the trinket.

"Do you ever fix anything other than watches?"

"Like what, sir?"

"Jewelry?" Aidan asked, reaching into his pocket.

The man sighed, pointing.

"There is a fine jewelry maker at the end of the building."

"I don't think he can help me." Aidan held out the coral trinket. "Please take a look. I will pay you."

The man smiled at the word *pay.*

"Let me take a look then."

The man's knobby fingers tightened over the design, lifting it away from Aidan. He flung down his glasses as he peered into the mechanics of the coral shell. He stared at Aidan, his mouth open.

"What is this, sir?"

"I do not know, but it's broken. Can you fix it?"

"I don't know how to fix this. I don't even know what it is."

Aidan grabbed the trinket and shook it over the watchmaker's hand. The small gear dropped onto the man's palm.

"Can you reattach that?"

The man held up the gear. He pulled the trinket away from Aidan, turning it over, leaning closer.

"Three shillings."

The man looked up, waiting for Aidan to protest.

"Fine. How long?" Aidan asked, resting against the table.

"Not long. Not long at all."

The watchmaker grabbed his tools and sat down. He moved the watch he had been working on out of the way and replaced it with the medallion. The copper workings in the cream coral popped in color against the crisp white cloth it lay on. The man guided the tiny gear into the trinket with tweezers, placing the missing piece between larger gears, locking the teeth of the gears together.

Searching through a wooden box, he pulled out three miniature screws, each one slightly different than the other. He grabbed the first with the tweezers and positioned it. The screw was too big. The man pulled it out, dropping it back into the box. Lifting the smallest of the three, he screwed it tight.

"There," he said, lifting it to show Aidan. "Good as new."

Aidan reached into his pocketbook, pulled out three shillings, and handed them to the watchmaker.

"Thank you," Aidan said.

The man passed the trinket back to Aidan.

"Do you know what it does?"

"It is jewelry. It doesn't do anything."

"You've been misled, sir. This is mechanics, not fine art. It has a purpose once it's turned on."

Aidan smirked. "How do you turn it on?"

"I have no idea. I didn't make it. Have a nice day, sir. Try to stay cool."

The man turned back to his workstation.

Aidan bowed his head before leaving. He opened his breast pocket to hide the trinket. He could finally present it to Jocelyn. Searching the large room, Aidan spotted Thomas and two other older Englishmen, sitting and waiting in front of hanging sheets of bright red curtains.

Aidan walked through the auditorium to the booth, brushing against the new clothes—mostly women's attire hanging on racks. He took a seat next to Thomas. The two Englishmen bowed their heads to him before returning to their conversation.

Thomas kept his gaze on the red drapery.

"Are you done for the day?" he asked Aidan.

Aidan nodded. "We need to talk about tomorrow."

"What about it?"

"I need to know the details of the trade," Aidan said as a heavy-set woman appeared from behind the red curtain in a beaded, white silk dress and a large silk hat. Her gray-tinged, blonde hair did not match her youthful expression.

She twirled for one of the Englishmen, who clapped for her without stopping his conversation. The woman cheerfully smiled, prancing to a large mirror to survey herself.

"I know the details," Thomas said.

"I know you do, but are you negotiating or am I?" Aidan asked, putting his head down and rubbing his eyes.

"We will see tomorrow."

"I need to know now. Sir Corwin, I do not feel comfortable..."

Thomas rose from his seat. Aidan raised his head to see Jocelyn emerge from behind the curtain in a blue silk dress embroidered with flowers and small beads draped from the bodice. He couldn't help that his jaw slightly dropped at the sight of her. Aidan quickly stood.

"Are they both with you?" the heavy-set woman asked.

"Yes. This is Mr. Corwin and Mr. Boyd," Jocelyn said, smoothing her hands down the beautiful fabric.

The woman extended her hand, but Thomas only nodded as he corrected Jocelyn.

"Baron Corwin."

The woman let out a little giggle. Aidan stepped forward, took the woman's hand, and kissed it.

"And are you a Baron also?" the woman flirted.

He smiled and shook his head.

"Just a captain."

"Mr. Howard!" the woman yelled over her shoulder.

The gentleman who had clapped for her got up and hustled to her side.

"Yes, dear?"

"This is my husband, Mr. Howard," the woman announced to the group.

The man bowed as the woman introduced Thomas, Aidan, and then Jocelyn. He stopped and gazed at Jocelyn's face before he bowed to her.

"And I am Mrs. Howard, but everyone calls me Anne," the woman said. "Your Jocelyn and I became acquainted in the dressing room."

"You should let the young woman finish her shopping, my dear," said Mr. Howard.

"I will, but I was wondering if you would like to join us for supper. Your Jocelyn said this was her first visit to Calcutta, and the idea of fresh eyes excites me," Anne said, taking Jocelyn's hand. "My dear, you're freezing."

Aidan could not handle a prolonged evening of dining filled with etiquette and spoke up before Thomas could.

"I am sorry, but we have arrangements already."

"Oh," said a disappointed Mrs. Howard.

"Maybe next time," Mr. Howard added.

"Maybe," Thomas mocked before turning to Jocelyn. "You look ravishing."

"How about tomorrow?" Jocelyn asked, watching Anne. The woman talked a lot, but happiness radiated from her. She liked her.

"Yes, why not tomorrow? We can dine at the club." Anne shrugged hopefully.

"We have business to attend to tomorrow," Thomas said, taking in a deep breath.

"What business?" Jocelyn asked.

"We have a trade to attend to."

"Is Jocelyn needed?" Anne asked, still holding onto Jocelyn's hand.

"No..." Thomas began.

"Then it is settled," Anne interrupted. "The men will go about their business, and we will spend the day together."

Aidan smiled at the way Anne had manipulated the situation to her benefit, but he could see Thomas was about to lose his temper.

"That would be grand," Jocelyn answered with a friendly smile.

"Then it is settled," Thomas said.

Hiding a smile, Aidan watched Thomas bite his tongue. Mr. Howard extended his arm for his wife and escorted her back to the dressing room. Aidan turned, ready to defend Jocelyn for speaking up. Instead, Thomas was as civil as a magistrate.

"You must get one in every color," he said, inspecting Jocelyn's dress.

Something is wrong, Aidan thought to himself.

Thomas gave the address of the clubhouse and Jocelyn's room number to the Indian saleswoman, who carefully folded and boxed the last dress. Speaking to a young boy in Hindi, she placed the last bundle next to a large stack of packages and hatboxes. The child nodded and wrote down in English, *Room 14. Miss Jocelyn. To be delivered tonight*, before he tied the parcel with twine.

Jocelyn walked to stand next to Thomas, who was signing the bill, and Aidan, who impatiently tapped his finger on the counter. She wore a short-sleeve, pink cotton dress that hung loosely from the waist down. She inhaled the freshly dyed and cleaned material on her shoulders.

Much better.

She turned her attention to the young boy as he spoke rapidly to the saleswoman. She listened and watched as he spoke. At first it was muddled, but soon she recognized words, and quickly the conversation became clear to her.

The saleswoman replied in Hindi to the servant boy.

"The purple dress in the dressing room—just get rid of it. But don't let the lady see. The rich man wants it gone."

The woman smiled at Jocelyn as she spoke. Jocelyn quickly turned to Thomas.

"Where will we find a translator?" Thomas asked Aidan.

"In the market. We will need one for tomorrow, unless your seller speaks English," Aidan said. He noticed Jocelyn's irked expression. "What is the matter?" he asked.

Thomas smiled at her.

"Yes—my dear, why are you frowning?"

"Why would you tell them to dispose of my clothes? I know the dress is hideous, but you have no right," Jocelyn accused.

"What?" Thomas asked, looking at the saleswoman, then back to Jocelyn.

Jocelyn pointed to the stunned saleswoman.

"She said you wanted it gone."

Aidan shook his head. The whole time they were waiting for the dresses to be boxed and paid for, the woman had only said, "Thank you" in very badly pronounced English. The rest of her conversation had been in Hindi, which neither Thomas nor he understood.

"When did she say this?" Thomas asked, astonished.

"Just now!"

Jocelyn turned to the woman and began speaking Hindi to her.

The men quickly looked at each other, then back at her. The saleswoman, with wide eyes, nodded and pointed to Thomas. Jocelyn turned and glared.

"She has no need to lie to me."

Thomas ran his hands through his hair.

"How did you do that?"

"Don't change the subject! Why would you tell her to throw my dress away? Someone spent a long time making it for me. Not you."

Jocelyn placed her hands on her hips, waiting for an answer.

"Answer the lady," said Aidan, hoping for an explanation of Jocelyn's sudden multilingual prowess.

"The dress is outdated and unfashionable. You have no more use for it. You can't hold on to everything," Thomas protested. "Now, how did you speak to that woman?"

She shrugged. "The same way I speak to you, Aidan, or any other person." From the corner of her eye, she saw the large stack of new clothes. "What did you do with the rest of my wardrobe?" she quickly asked, her hands clenching into fists.

"You have no use for those things." Thomas cracked his neck nonchalantly before turning back to Aidan. "Well, I guess we found a translator."

Jocelyn trembled with anger, remembering Isabel's small, worn hands sewing the trim of the dresses, and the way Helen had adored them. She closed her eyes to block her tears.

"This was never a gift, but another trick."

Thomas smirked. "Don't be so dramatic. It doesn't suit you."

Without thinking, Aidan turned on Thomas.

"Why do you insist on tormenting her?" he asked defiantly.

"Tormenting? This woman has finer attire than the queen herself, and you have the audacity to accuse me of impropriety?" Thomas laughed richly and glared at Aidan. Leaning toward his captain, he whispered, "Do not think I am blind to the way you look at her. You are walking a very thin line."

Aidan ground his teeth and glanced at Jocelyn. Every strand of him wanted to quit Thomas's employ, demand his pay, and stay in India—but he could not do so without losing her. Whatever was at Edith's was too valuable to her, and it was far too dangerous to be poor in Calcutta. He had to get her to England at all costs before he ended his association with the baron.

Thomas faced Jocelyn.

"May we eat now?" he asked sarcastically.

"I am not eating with you!" Jocelyn said hotly. She then said to the saleswoman, "Please box the purple dress and send it with the others."

"What will you do then—eat dirt?" Thomas asked.

"If I have to," she said.

Aidan approached Jocelyn protectively.

"We must all eat, and it is far too dangerous for you to be wandering the streets of Calcutta alone in search of food," he cautioned. "If you don't mind, it would save me a good deal of grief if you would..."—he swallowed hard—"eat with Thomas and me."

Jocelyn lifted her eyebrows, knowing Aidan would like nothing less than to keep Thomas's company for the evening.

"If it will save you trouble, then fine," she said, pushing past Thomas.

"Good lad," Thomas said with derision, walking after her.

As he watched her confident gait—pink cotton ruffling in the coming evening breeze, the lights of Calcutta before her— Aidan could feel Jocelyn slipping away from him as the waves do the shore.

Chapter Twenty-Four ෨

In another town, the placid white paint and tan-tiled roof adorning the outside of Horse Head Tavern might have signaled a like interior, with reasonable drinkers and drink. Not in Calcutta. The place was so crowded with drunken bodies Jocelyn could not even see the ground. She followed Aidan as he pushed his way through the mass of singing sailors to an open area of tables and chairs. He gestured for her to sit. Shouts and songs and swearing ricocheted around the small room, ringing in Jocelyn's ears. Aidan said something to Thomas, but she was deaf to it. Thomas sat on her right and Aidan on her left. Still standing, Jocelyn finally sat down, bewildered by the fevered cacophony around her.

"What do they serve?" she asked.

"I'm sorry, I didn't hear you. What did you say?" Aidan asked.

She leaned over the table.

"What is there to eat?" she yelled.

As she did, the bawdy bar song carrying on behind them shifted to a dulcet melody of love. Aidan peered at her, trying to piece together the fragments he heard. Jocelyn flattened her lips and stared at the stained, round table.

At least I can hear myself.

"Curry and pilau rice is my favorite," Aidan said finally. "They also have fish and other game."

She could feel his eyes on her. She peered at him, cheeks flushed. Despite the chaos, he seemed right at home, relaxed. He smiled at her warmly. For a moment, as she looked back, the beehive of a room seemed less crowded.

Thomas looked around, wincing and waving his hand under his nose.

"What is this place, and what is that God-awful smell?"

Jocelyn sniffed the air. Fresh fish and burning wood mingled with the musk of sailors, merchants, con men, and more. It reminded her of the ship.

"What smell?" Aidan asked, looking over his shoulder.

Most of the men stood, holding large, metal mugs slathered with foam. Thomas shook his head, glaring at Aidan.

"This is not at all what I would call a suitable dining environment."

"It is good to keep an eye on your crew even when we're not on the ship, especially in foreign lands. Your father advised me of such," Aidan said, looking Thomas in the eye.

"I imagine my father's words, as wise as they are, were meant for you, not me."

"On the few voyages when your father accompanied me to India, he always chose to dine with his sailors."

Thomas pursed his lips.

"I am not my father," he said. "Tomorrow we will be dining at the club the Howards mentioned, preferably without that dreadful woman's company."

Thomas forcefully folded his napkin on his lap.

Jocelyn's back stiffened with the remark.

"She was very nice to you in the brief moment you met

her," she said.

"Nice, yes. But she is unbelievably common. Imagine the conversation we would have to endure."

Thomas raised his hands to the heavens as if soliciting divine assistance.

Jocelyn drew her eyebrows together and set her jaw.

Anne is a fine, kind lady—how dare you, you impotent junicom! She swallowed her anger. *I have to get back to Edith's.*

"She was very nice and did not seem common to me, but sincere," Aidan remarked.

"Thank you," she said sweetly. "Perfectly said."

A waiter dressed in all white stopped at the table.

"What can I get you?" he asked in perfect English.

"Red wine. Deer curry with pilau rice, and the lady will have the same," Thomas said imperiously, avoiding eye contact.

"And you, sir?" he asked Aidan.

"An ale and the rest the same," Aidan replied pleasantly.

The waiter nodded to Aidan before withdrawing to the kitchen. A gentleman in a long, brown coat and a black top hat moved past the waiter to an empty table behind Thomas.

Thomas saw him first.

"What the bloody hell is on that man's head?"

Jocelyn and Aidan turned their attention to the stranger.

Jocelyn observed the gent take off his coat, then fold it and place it on the back of the chair, displaying a blue silk jacket with a white cravat. The stranger's face was hidden from her view, but his stature was perfect. Black trousers hugged his long legs and disappeared into knee-length black boots. He seemed to be Aidan's height, but slimmer in build. Jocelyn noticed other sailors pointing to the gentleman and whispering. The man sat with his back to her, flinging the tail of his blue jacket away from the seat of the chair.

"I hope everything is running smoothly," Thomas said as the waiter brought over their drinks, then scooted directly to the well-dressed patron.

She looked down at her wine, playing with the rim of the glass, then up at the stranger again. Sweet honeysuckle perfume kissed her nose. She shook it away, but the smell was familiar and called to her.

"As smoothly as it can. I just hope tomorrow will do the same," Aidan answered.

Jocelyn tuned out the conversation at her table and zeroed in on the waiter and the mysterious customer.

"What can I get you?" the waiter asked.

"Water," the man said in a tranquil voice.

She froze with her finger on the glass.

"Anything else?" the waiter asked with some irritation.

"What would you recommend?"

All the sound in the room seemed too quiet as she only heard the gent's voice.

"Curry is the main dish and one of the local favorites," the waiter said briskly.

"Then I will try that."

The man shifted and lifted his chin to the server, his profile now visible to Jocelyn.

Staring, she leaned forward and knocked over her wine. It spilled everywhere as the glass landed on her lap, then rolled and crashed into pieces on the wooden floor. Immediately attended to by Thomas, Aidan, and the waiter, she tried to push them out of her view. It was Aidan's warm touch that finally brought her gaze back to her table.

"Jocelyn, are you all right?" Aidan asked, taking her elbow and guiding her to her feet.

"I'm fine."

"Watch out for the glass."

She looked down at the red wine seeping into the cracks of the floor and the puddle of wine on her new dress, now clinging to her lap. She pulled the fabric away from her skin.

A long heavy coat draped over her shoulders.

"I hope this will help," a soothing voice said. A soothing voice she knew well.

Jocelyn spun around as the coat slipped off her shoulders. The stranger deftly caught it and, putting his arms around her, gently wrapped her in the coat and buttoned the top black button.

She looked directly into his aqua-green eyes and held his gaze. She smiled, watching the colors shift to turquoise, then blue.

"I know you," she whispered.

She had seen him before in her dreams.

"Do you?" the man asked, returning the smile.

Aidan stepped forward to interrupt, but Thomas was quicker.

"Thank you for your service. I will make sure your coat is returned to you. Jocelyn, you should button the rest to cover yourself," Thomas said.

Wine dripped from the hem of her dress. The man turned to Thomas, still smiling.

"You must be Mr. Corwin—or should I call you Baron?" the man asked.

"I am, and Mr. Corwin is fine. Do I know you, sir?" Thomas asked.

"I am called Benlar," the man answered.

Aidan couldn't help himself.

"What kind of name is Benlar?" he asked, sizing him up.

"*My* name. I see your table is not fit for dining. Won't you join me at mine?"

Benlar led them to his table as the waiter rushed to the kitchen for rags and a broom.

"That would be lovely," Jocelyn answered for the group.

Aidan grunted but followed anyway. Benlar graciously pulled out Jocelyn's chair before seating himself across from her.

"So, Benlar. You never answered my question. How do you know who I am?" Thomas asked, taking a seat between Jocelyn and the gentleman.

Aidan stared at Jocelyn, who appeared to be mesmerized by the stranger.

I cannot lose her.

"I have been looking for you. I have a business proposal I would like to discuss with you and your captain," Benlar said before nodding to Aidan. "Mr. Boyd."

Aidan, surprised by the man's knowledge about his name and profession, could only nod in response.

Who are you?

"What kind of business proposal?" Thomas asked as a young Indian girl brought a tray of food, water, and wine.

She quietly set down the plates and drinks. Both Jocelyn and Benlar thanked her in Hindi. The girl beamed at the gesture and backed away from the table, bowing.

The arrival of the yellow curry and grilled vegetables halted all conversation. Jocelyn bent to her bowl and inhaled the sweet, spicy scent. She looked at Aidan and smiled broadly.

He smiled in return, relieved to have her attention once more. He poured the curry over his rice, and Jocelyn did the same.

"This smells divine," she said as the golden curry engulfed the rice.

"Taste it," he urged.

Jocelyn took a small bite. The sweet curry rolled on her tongue before giving way to a piquant tang that nearly brought tears to her eyes. She blinked, smiling, her senses awash with discovery.

Aidan savored her reaction as if he himself were tasting the food for the first time.

"You see? Nothing like it," Aidan said.

She nodded and took another bite, a low whimper escaping her lips.

Benlar and Thomas followed the same ritual of covering the rice before they ate their food. Aidan noticed Benlar's eyes darkening with each bite.

Like Jocelyn's.

"Your business proposal?" Thomas asked, pausing to take a drink of his wine.

"I need to travel to England, and I hear your ship will be voyaging back soon," Benlar said plainly.

Aidan ground his teeth at the idea of another passenger on his ship—especially this one.

"We don't have the accommodations to take on any passengers. Maybe the next ship," Thomas answered.

"I will pay you."

Benlar handed Thomas a small black leather purse, tied at the opening. Thomas shook it. The heavy coins clinked inside. He opened it, looked inside, closed it, and turned back to Benlar.

"You can have that now," the stranger said. "I will give you the same amount once I am in England."

Thomas nodded. "It is a generous offer."

Aidan shook his head and stole a glance at Jocelyn, who held her napkin to her face to hide a smile.

This will change everything.

Chapter Twenty-Five ☙

After dinner, Aidan, Thomas, and Benlar walked Jocelyn to the local inn. She had noticed Thomas and Aidan glaring at Benlar, but the man focused only on her. The clerk at the front desk smiled at Thomas.

"The packages are in her room, sir," the clerk told Thomas before turning his attention to Benlar. "It's good to see you again, Mr. Benlar. Your suite is ready as you requested."

"Good man," Benlar answered, grabbing the key held out by the clerk.

Thomas dug in his coat pocket, pulling out three keys with room numbers etched into the metal. He handed one to Aidan then reluctantly passed one to Jocelyn as well.

The four walked up the stairs to the second floor in search of their sleeping quarters. Jocelyn's room was first in the long hallway. Even as she stood in the doorway and the small group broke to go to their own rooms, Benlar stood a moment longer than the other men, studying her face. Heat rose to her cheeks, but still she faced him. She knew him.

When he finally left and went into his room only a few doors away, she could still feel his presence. It surprised her to see Aidan leaning against his doorway down the hall, watching. She smiled and waved before retiring to the stylish room.

Dark brown wallpaper with large white flowers covered the walls. Jocelyn ran her hands across it, touching the petals. A wooden four-poster bed with a feather mattress filled the middle of the large room. It was covered with pink silk sheets, and a flowered comforter lay at the foot of the bed. Netting, hung from the ceiling, draped over the sides. A washstand with a blue, flowered pitcher and washbowl stood in the corner, a round mirror above them. An oil lantern glowed near the washbowl. She inhaled the clean fragrance of the room and walked to the washstand.

Staring at herself in the mirror, Benlar's brown coat engulfed her. She pushed her nose into the brown leather. It smelled of salt and sand. She closed her eyes and thought of the beach at Edith's manor, the crash of the waves meeting the soft sand. She opened her eyes and saw Aidan catching her on their first meeting, then kissing her.

Jocelyn took off the coat and placed it on the footboard. She looked at the dried wine stain on her pink dress, then at the large stack of white boxes.

She walked to the stack and opened one box after another until she found one filled with new nightdresses Thomas must have picked out. She shook her head. Everything was new. The only reminder of Edith's home was the hideous purple dress hidden in a white box among the new garments.

Jocelyn undressed and pulled the nightgown over her head. She folded her soiled dress, placed it in the washbowl, and covered it with clean water, watching the clear liquid go pink from the stain. Exhausted, she padded to the bed, dropped onto the feather mattress, and fell fast asleep.

The haze tasted of honey. Jocelyn spun around as she floated alone in the dark abyss to face the scarred man. Small amounts of blood misted around them as the woman's dead body floated away. The light shimmered off the polished pearls around her neck that were stained red.

The man's eyes were black and focused.

"You are next," he said, lifting the burning blade.

Jocelyn kicked away, but the man grabbed her arm, pulling her to him. He pressed the flat surface of the knife to her forearm.

Jocelyn bellowed as her skin boiled from the blade's touch.

"This is all because of you," he said.

The man yanked the knife up from Jocelyn's arm, her burnt skin peeling away with the blade. The pain paralyzed Jocelyn's body as she struggled to breathe. The man raised the blade above Jocelyn, ready to strike.

"You will be the last."

She heard his voice cracked with sorrow, not because of killing her, but because the killing would stop. The physical pain from her arm fell short as the heartbreak of losing loved ones engulfed her. The safe world that was hers had been taken by this man called Fiar. The pain dissolved into anger, leaving a metallic aftertaste on her tongue as the surrounding waters stilled and grew quiet, waiting on Jocelyn to grow into its keeper.

Fiar brought down the knife, aimed for her heart. Reflexes took over, and Jocelyn raised her hands to block the deadly blow. But the waters took it as a command and parted, separating her from her killer and knocking the knife from his hand. It struck the sand deep below.

Fiar's expression of shock matched Jocelyn's, but he didn't waste time dwelling on what had just happened. He advanced again, this time faster and more determined to have the job done.

Fluttering backward, Jocelyn tried to flee, but Fiar was fast. He grabbed her waist, pulling her to him. His fingers slid to her throat and squeezed.

Jocelyn pushed her hands into his chest and screamed. A rush of water whirlpooled around them, shoving them upward.

The man's arms flailed, letting Jocelyn go. Kicking with everything she had left, Jocelyn darted through the water, praying the sea would keep him from her, but his evil had touched her skin. She knew he would haunt her until he was dead. Diving deep, Jocelyn knew the only way to survive would be to kill him first. She swam for the knife. In the distance, she could see Fiar diving toward her.

The storming waters raged as her heart pounded in her chest. The knife was within reach, but so was Fiar. Plunging her hand into the sand, she gripped the knife and snapped her tail to the middle of the storming water.

She spun to glare at the man struggling to swim through the current wrapping around her. Raising the knife over her head, Jocelyn aimed.

"You will never see the light of day again, Fiar," she yelled, releasing the blade from her fingers.

The water stopped moving long enough for the knife to somersaulted into Fiar's left eye.

The man screamed, fighting the swirling water to move his hands to his head.

Jocelyn watched the man struggle. Everything in her wanted him dead. She balled her fists, afraid to move forward to finish what she had started, but the hatred for him consumed her. He must be punished for everything he had done. Jocelyn shook with rage. The water fed off her, spinning faster, making it hard to see Fiar bellow in agony. Jocelyn stretched the contracted muscles in her hands as vengeance became her life force. The water listened to what she wanted and shot into the heavens, taking Fiar with it.

Alone with the woman's floating carcass, Jocelyn panicked. The ocean should not be controllable. It was its own. But it had responded to her. The gentle current that caressed her skin ran deeper into her veins. She was the ocean.

Reaching for the person who had protected her, Jocelyn grabbed the woman's cold hand and pulled the body to her. She brushed her fingers against the woman's face, struggling to breathe.

"Don't leave me," she pleaded, but the woman's soul was gone, leaving behind an empty corpse.

A soft knock forced Jocelyn awake. She was in her bedroom. Tears soaked the pillow. She sat up and rubbed her eyes, trying to see in the dark—not sure if she dreamt the sound or if someone was outside her door. Raising her left arm, she ran her fingers over the scar, now knowing where it came from. Someone tapped against the door again.

"Who is it?" Jocelyn mumbled as her stomach turned with fear. The shadows on the walls stared down on her. They had a mind of their own, dancing with the wind and the moonlight. They were her guardians, ready to attack.

Jocelyn clenched her jaw, swallowing the terror. The dream was real, and Fiar's threat was still alive. This was one memory she wished would have stayed buried with the waves of the ocean.

Open the door, the voice from the ocean implored.

Jocelyn gasped when she realized the man she was seeking might be standing outside of her bedroom. She jumped to her feet and ran toward the entrance to her chambers. Her past was waiting behind that door. She cracked it open and stared up at Benlar. He was fully dressed in his top hat and overcoat. Leaning against the doorframe, he smiled down at her.

"We need to talk." His voice was that of the ocean's.

Jocelyn caught her breath as she studied his eyes—they lingered in the back of her mind, tormenting her to remember all of him.

She opened the door, and he walked in. He closed it behind him as she stood near the frame.

He reached out and touched her face, making her flinch. Benlar quickly withdrew his hand.

"Sorry," he whispered.

He moved to the bed and sat. Jocelyn knew somewhere in her past she would have crawled onto his lap and kissed him, but not now. He was a stranger with a face that haunted her and a voice that called to her. He had all the answers she needed; all she had to do was get him to tell her.

"Who are you and why are you here?" she asked.

Pain washed over his perfect face.

"I'm Benlar. Your friend. I'm here to take you home."

"And where is that?" Jocelyn's fingers twitched with the excitement of finding out where she belonged.

"In the ocean."

"How can that be?"

"Your English is better."

Benlar played with a loose string on the quilt.

Jocelyn stared at him. "How many languages do I speak?"

Benlar lifted his hat off his head. Jocelyn fought the urge to run her hands through the ash blond hair that fell over his ears.

"About two hundred."

Her heart thumped in her chest. "That's impossible."

"Not for us. Humans have to learn how to speak. We just need to hear the words. Meanings, pronunciations are passed down to us."

Jocelyn's legs quivered. She sat down on the ground.

"Where did you go?" Benlar asked, staring down at her.

She wrapped her gown against her legs.

"I don't know. I woke up on the shore."

Benlar slid off the edge of the bed and stood across from Jocelyn.

"You promised you would come back to me."

"I don't remember you." Her voice cracked as the sorrow of losing the memory of being loved filled her. Her gaze drifted to his lips, wondering how many time she had kissed him. "Were we lovers?" Jocelyn asked, lifting her stare to his eyes. Her cheeks blushed from asking such a personal question.

He nodded. Benlar kneeled and wrapped her in his arms.

"Why don't I remember?" she whispered.

"I don't know. But I'm going to take you home and protect you."

"Protect me from what?"

Benlar rubbed her back. His body heat warmed her.

"From everything."

Jocelyn melted into Benlar. She inhaled him, smelling the ocean on his skin. He was her protector. Bodyguard. But the terror of the man in her dreams tormented her no matter how hard Benlar squeezed her. She feared to go where he might take her.

"We go back tonight," he said.

"How?"

"We dive in."

Jocelyn's forehead rested against a coral medallion hanging on a silver chain around his neck, pressing it into his chest. Benlar pulled away from her as the medallion began to glow. The emblem depressed into his skin, embedding itself.

"What is it doing?" Jocelyn asked, mesmerized by the working emblem becoming one with Benlar.

He lifted the chain, extracting the medallion from his skin. His face winked in pain. The white coral spiraled inward like a shell cut in half, glowing. The rotating copper gears shined against the white light. Jocelyn peered up at Benlar's eyes. They were black.

Her heart dropped to her stomach. He was not like her. He was something different. Jocelyn shoved out of his arms.

"What are you?"

He blinked, bringing back the blue.

"Calm down, Mli. You've seen this before."

His hands rubbed her shoulders, trying to relax her. She shifted, unsure whether to stay or run.

"When the emblem is one with us, it turns on, allowing us to change."

"Change into what?"

The man with the scarred face had black eyes, just like Benlar.

"I am a merrow, same as you."

"Why were your eyes black?"

Benlar smiled. "Is that what scared you?"

"It's not natural."

"Yes, it is. We see in the dark."

Jocelyn stared into his eyes, the darkness gone.

"You can't change without that?"

She pointed to the medallion hanging on the chain around

his neck.

"No. We are born on land and then taken to the ocean once our emblems are crafted to our bloodline and destiny."

Benlar sat on the ground. She decided to trust him. Jocelyn ran her finger over the knobby edge of the coral on his chest. The surface was cold, but the gears were releasing heat, warming her skin.

"This is our way home?" she asked.

His eyes burned with desire. Her eyes mirrored his. Her body wanted him. He moved closer, decreasing the distance between them. Their lips touched. He scooped her onto his lap.

Jocelyn wrapped her arms around the neck of the man she had just met. His fingers ran up her spine, sending shivers down her—the same as Aidan's had. She jerked away from the kiss.

"What's the matter?"

"I can't do this."

Jocelyn pushed against his shoulders and stood. She paced the room.

Benlar crossed his legs.

"What if you are here to hurt me?"

Benlar's laughter reverberated from the walls.

"Is this because of that human?"

"We are all human!"

The words were familiar, but someone else had yelled them at her in her past.

Benlar jumped to his feet, the laughter gone.

"Do not throw his words at me."

"Who?"

They both stood, glaring at each other, ready to fight.

"Where's your emblem?"

"In Ireland," she replied, remembering Aidan examining it

in the game room.

"It can't be. It has to be near you. You would have never survived this long without it."

"It's not here."

Benlar shook his head. "You don't understand. You would have died without it. You are not meant to be on land for this long. You have to return."

"I don't have it."

"Someone must. We have to find it." Benlar grabbed his hat from the bed. He covered the distance between them in three long strides. "You will remember me, Mli." He kissed her forehead and went to the door.

Jocelyn turned, wanting more answers. "Who is Fiar?"

Benlar's hand dropped from the handle.

"What do you remember?"

"Him, killing a woman."

Sadness washed over Benlar's face. "Your mother."

Jocelyn's legs gave. Before she hit the ground, Benlar seized her in his arms.

"He cut her open?"

He nodded.

"Is he dead?"

"No."

"Good. I will skin him alive and leave him for the sharks to tear apart."

Benlar stared down at her. His eyebrows turned up in amazement.

"You're changing."

Blackness had invaded the blue of her eyes.

Chapter Twenty-Six ♋

Jocelyn woke early. Benlar had stayed in her room until she had fallen asleep. Now he was gone.

The sun beamed through the open window, and a warm breeze danced with the burgundy curtains, hurting her eyes. She stretched her arms, tangling her fingers in the netting around the bed, then sat up and looked out the window. Bright orange and red blossoms caught the sunlight, waving in the morning wind. She pulled her knees to her chest and watched as they almost seemed to reach for her, their rich perfume wafting into the room. She closed her eyes.

Slowly she got out of bed and grabbed a dress box from the large pile. Jocelyn pulled open the lid. Delicate cream paper covered the white satin fabric. She lifted the dress, dropping the box to the ground. Silver beads surrounded black pearls sewn into the bodice of the dress, forming everlasting flowers. String laced up the bodice, allowing it to be changed without the aide of a ladies' maid.

Jocelyn laid the dress on her mattress and slipped out of her nightgown. The white fabric cascaded around her as she pulled the dress over her head. With swift fingers, she laced the dress tight and then brushed out her hair.

Her stomach turned. The longer she was in her room, the longer Benlar had to disappear—return to where he came from without giving her answers.

Her heart begged her to sprint out of the room, down the stairs, and into his arms, but she knew if she did, her world would change. She wasn't ready to give up this world. She needed more than dreams. She needed her memories back— and she needed them now.

While pulling her hair back to wear a sunbonnet, she noticed the dress in the washbowl and pulled it out. Pink water dripped onto the hardwood floor. The once-pink dress now looked red. Jocelyn wrung as much water as she could back into the washbowl before draping the wet dress over the washstand. Her reflection in the mirror grabbed her attention as black eyes peered back at her. Jocelyn leaned closer, examining what had startled Benlar the night before. Her eyes were black without the medallion—controlled by something much more powerful. Blinking, her pupils recoiled, allowing the blue to be seen.

She needed more answers.

She made her way through the open hallway to the lobby. Green sofas crouched in the corners of the room, occupied by gentlemen smoking cigars. The overpowering aroma and smoke made Jocelyn cough. Throat burning, she held her breath and rushed toward the open, oversized doors. Once outside, she was relieved to taste the exotic aromas of India. The saltiness of the sea mingled with the herbs and flowers growing around the large, white stone inn.

"Hello."

Startled, Jocelyn turned and looked down. Benlar sat languidly on a couch, wearing a crisp linen suit.

"Good morning," he said almost musically.

Her heart skipped a beat as he stood up from his wicker lounge chair. He stepped past her and walked off the porch.

She watched him leave, not knowing if she should follow him or stay.

Benlar stopped, turned, and smiled at her. She held on to her bonnet as a swift breeze pressed into her. He laughed out loud.

"What are you laughing at?" Jocelyn demanded.

"You can make anything look appealing no matter how ridiculous it is," he said. He began walking again. "Are you coming?" Benlar asked over his shoulder.

"Where?" she asked hurriedly, picking up her dress and chasing after him. "Wait!"

"I have been," he said as she trotted to catch up with him.

He stopped to pick an orange flower. A group of massive banyan trees stretched their branches on all sides of the pair as if to shield them. He breathed in the scent of the delicate wrightia flower and tucked it in her hair under the bonnet.

"My eyes were still black this morning," Jocelyn said.

"That can't be. You don't have your medallion."

"But they were. What is happening to me?"

"I don't know, but we will find out."

Jocelyn tensed as his fingers traced her ear.

"Please don't," she said, moving away from him.

His smile faded as he looked at her.

"I will find your medallion and take you home. I promise you," he said and stepped between the plant and trees that shielded them, disappearing.

A cheery voice rang behind Jocelyn. She turned and saw Anne hurrying toward her.

"Hello."

Anne waved a handkerchief in the air. Jocelyn, trance

broken, smiled at the happy woman and walked toward her.

"Good morning."

"Oh, yes, it is a good morning. I am so glad you are a guest here. I saw the baron in the clubhouse in the west wing. Who was that man you were talking to?" Anne asked, not missing a beat.

"Benlar. He is traveling to England with us. He is a friend."

"He is quite a looker. You be careful with those types. Most of the time their affections are only skin deep. Well, shall we?"

Anne took hold of her arm and led her to an open two-horse carriage.

"Where are we going?" Jocelyn asked.

"I will show you."

The ride was refreshing. Warm air swept under Jocelyn's bonnet, and the flower from Benlar fell onto her lap. She picked up the brightly petaled blossom and put it back in her hair.

"There is no place like India, my dear," Anne mused, looking out at the beautiful landscape of white roofs, narrow streets, and waving trees.

"It is magical," Jocelyn agreed.

"That it is. But you must know with every magical place there are demons hiding in the corners," Anne warned.

She waved to a local woman who was carrying a small child on her hip.

"Demons?" Jocelyn asked, studying the woman in the road.

Her hair was matted to her head, and her clothes were beyond worn. Jocelyn smiled at the dirty toddler who clung to his mother.

"There is another world here, as there is everywhere. Now, my dear, you are more than welcome to come with me or stay in the carriage. I will understand either way," Anne said as the carriage stopped.

Jocelyn glanced over Anne's shoulder to a group of native Indians rushing toward them.

"Anne?" She pointed to the mob.

Anne turned and stood up in the carriage.

"Raahi."

A skeleton of a man walked forward from the middle of the group and extended his bony hands. She reached down, and he helped her out of the carriage.

"Anne," the man said with a large smile.

She turned toward Jocelyn and spoke Hindi very slowly.

"This is Miss Jocelyn. My dear friend."

Anne reached under the seat and pulled out a large basket covered with a cloth. The man reached out to help Jocelyn, who immediately took his hand. She climbed out onto the muddy ground.

"His name is Raahi."

Jocelyn turned toward Raahi and spoke perfect Hindi.

"It is very nice to meet you, Raahi."

Raahi's big smile grew bigger.

"You too. Now come, come. Damini is waiting for you, Anne. She has gotten much worse since last time."

Raahi pushed through the other men, his stick-thin legs leading them toward the village.

Anne and Jocelyn kept up with his fast pace.

"You are quite fluent in Hindi. Where did you study?" Anne puffed between breaths.

Jocelyn shook her head.

"I didn't."

Anne laughed, swinging the basket sideways in her hand. "You are a mystery, my dear."

To his surprise, Aidan woke late. He swiftly dressed, grabbed the coral trinket, and rushed out of his room. He fastened the collar of his shirt while hurrying down the long hallway. He stopped and looked back at Jocelyn's closed door. Taking a deep breath, he changed directions. He held up his hand to knock, but a hard cough stopped him.

"She is gone," Benlar said, leaning against his door, eyes fixed on the trinket in Aidan's hand. "Have you had that long?"

He looked from the trinket to Benlar and put the coral into his pocket.

"Long enough. Do you know where she went?"

"Out."

"Thank you."

Aidan turned and once again paced down the hallway. He shifted and saw Benlar walking beside him. Startled, he jumped, bumping his back against the wall.

"Careful."

Benlar, his hands behind his back, waited until Aidan regained his footing before he motioned him to continue down the hallway.

Aidan kept up with Benlar's pace.

"Do you know what you have?" Benlar asked.

Aidan stared at Benlar as he took in his question.

"I believe you are talking to the wrong man. Mr. Corwin should be in the lobby—you can finish your conversation with him."

He walked faster, passing Benlar. Benlar laughed. Aidan stopped and turned toward him.

"Why do you laugh?" he demanded.

"I do not wish to fight you."

"Good."

Benlar stepped closer to him.

"The jewelry you hold, the coral medallion. What would you want for it?"

Aidan shook his head.

"Nothing. It is not mine."

"I see." Benlar looked into his eyes. "You are a good man."

"How would you know?" Aidan bristled.

"I know." Benlar walked past him. "You need to give that to her sooner than planned."

"I will give it to her when I damn well please."

Aidan wanted to grab Benlar and toss him at the wall, but he stopped himself, holding tight to the trinket. Without appearing to move, Benlar was face to face with him. His eyes swirled with white and blue.

"You are nothing more than a mere man. How dare you think you could take me down?" Benlar's upper lip twitched.

"And what are you?" Aidan asked.

"So much more."

He shook his head, pushing past Benlar.

"I don't have time for this."

"That coral you have. I want it."

Aidan shook his head.

"Never. Also, find another ship. Otherwise, I will throw you overboard myself."

Chapter Twenty-Seven ✆

Jocelyn walked behind Anne as they entered a village of square wooden homes. Young children ran between the small, dilapidated houses, chasing each other. Excitement stirred in the air. She pictured the boy in the clothing shop and the young serving girl in the tavern. Both so clean, yet broken in spirit. They had hung their heads low to remain unnoticed. Here, it was different.

The children spotted Anne and ran to her, jumping excitedly and calling her name.

"Calm down, children."

Anne touched the children's heads one by one.

"Did you bring us any?" they eagerly sang.

"Not today. But next time I will."

"You promise?"

A small girl clung to Anne's leg.

"I promise, Bahula. Today, children, I am here to see Damini."

A young boy with mud splattered on his legs and face gazed at Jocelyn. She smiled at him.

"Who are you?" he asked.

All the other children turned and looked at her.

"I am Jocelyn."

"What is the matter with your eyes?" the boy asked.

"It is not polite to ask such questions, Taha," Anne said.

"Do you not see it?" Taha asked Anne.

Jocelyn looked down at the ground. Anne took her hand and pulled her forward.

"Go along, children," Anne ordered. "I have business to attend to."

"But Mrs. Anne," Taha said, trying to look into Jocelyn's eyes again.

"Taha!"

Anne looked back and smiled at the boy before he ran off with his friends.

"The boy does have a point," Anne affirmed.

Jocelyn looked up from the mucky road.

"I don't know how to explain it."

"Then don't."

She peered into Anne's face.

"You are who you are. Never be ashamed of that."

She stopped, still holding onto Anne's hand. Raahi stood in front of a cloth-covered doorway, waiting for them.

"I don't know what I am."

Anne firmly squeezed Jocelyn's hand.

"You are a kind woman, that is what you are."

Jocelyn began to shake her head.

"Gibberish."

"Excuse me?"

"My dear, look around you. These people are poorer than the dirt they stand on, but they are some of the truest people I have ever met. Most of them will die from a curable sickness before they reach my age. But none of them look at it that way. They see the moments in front of them, never missing a beat.

They dance with God in perfect harmony while we step on his feet. No respectable lady would dare to step out on this muddy ground with them, but here you are. I do not care what color your eyes are, my dear. Do not ever be ashamed of who you are."

"Anne," Raahi called, holding open the door covering.

"Coming!"

Anne picked up her dress and lightly stepped to him.

Jocelyn looked around at the bright faces of the villagers. Taha, riding a young elephant, raised his hands toward the sky, singing loudly. The other children pointed and laughed but soon chimed in.

"Are you coming?" Anne asked.

Jocelyn nodded. She rushed up the hill and entered the dirt-floored home. Raahi held open the door but did not follow Jocelyn. She stopped and inhaled the stale, bittersweet, yet welcoming air. The inside of her mouth dried as she breathed. She grabbed hold of the cracked wood supporting the hut to keep her balance.

Anne leaned over a wooden table then straightened. On the table rested a small, shrunken girl.

"Damini, I have brought a friend."

The tiny girl, who lay upon a straw pillow, lifted her head. Her face sank inward, and her yellow eyes bulged out. With all her energy, Damini smiled. She reached out for Jocelyn.

Jocelyn glided to the outstretched hand and took it into her own.

"Are you here to take me?" Damini asked.

Jocelyn looked up at Anne. Anne held back tears for the dying child.

"No. I am here to hold your hand."

Jocelyn compassionately patted the loose, brown skin.

"My mother talked of you. She said you would come..."
Damini stopped, inhaling deeply. "Please, don't leave me here."

She kept her eyes locked on Damini. The girl had a slight
glow around her that fluctuated with her uneven breaths.
Jocelyn closed her eyes, inhaling with Damini. She could feel
the energy from Damini's hand tingle in hers. She opened her
eyes to look into Damini's.

I see you.

Damini tightened her hand and nodded.

"I see you too," the girl answered.

"You see what, child?" Anne asked.

You hear me? Jocelyn said in her mind.

Damini nodded.

"Save me," she whimpered.

How?

"Take it from me. I never wanted it, but you can take it or
kill me. No more." Tears streamed from Damini's eyes. "No
more."

Jocelyn kissed the girl's forehead, praying for help. Her
lips burned on contact; she gasped, sucking in. A black mist
pushed through Damini's forehead into Jocelyn's mouth. It
tasted wonderful. Jocelyn inhaled deeper, pulling more of the
black fog into herself.

Anne rushed forward.

"Good God, girl. What are you doing? She is sick."

Jocelyn lifted her lips away from Damini but continued to
breathe in Damini's toxic energy. A small spark of light
streamed from Damini's forehead to Jocelyn, glowing through
her throat to her lungs. It stabbed into her racing heart, forcing
her to push away from the girl.

Jocelyn grabbed her chest, knocking Anne's basket from
her hand. Fresh fruit bounced on the ground and rolled toward

the door. Anne pressed herself against the wall, watching Jocelyn cough.

The urge to consume Damini was replaced by an overpowering sickness. Jocelyn's stomach was on fire and her lungs frozen. Every breath ripped through her throat. Jocelyn clutched the walls as her stomach purged a thick, black ooze.

Stepping toward the door, Anne, shaking, inched past Damini. The girl grabbed her arm.

"My father. Get my father, Anne."

Mouth wide open, Anne stared at Damini's eyes. They were clear as a mountain stream.

"Please," Damini pleaded.

Anne nodded and rushed out of the house, yelling for Raahi.

"Miss. Are you all right?"

Damini picked herself up off the table and looked down at Jocelyn, who held tight to her knees.

Jocelyn stared at an orange that rested near her foot. She closed her eyes and focused on the smell of the ripe fruit. She began to shake as her insides burned.

Damini jumped off the table and grabbed her hands, her bony fingers warming Jocelyn's.

Raahi abruptly entered the hut and started to cry when he looked down at his daughter, comforting Jocelyn. Anne, still frightened, stayed behind Raahi.

Damini saw her father and reached for him with her free hand, the other still holding tightly to Jocelyn. Anne ventured a look but stayed hidden behind Raahi.

"Damini. Hug your father," she said.

Damini stood as Anne leaned down and hesitantly took Jocelyn's hands.

"Good God, child, your hands are freezing." Anne quickly

touched Jocelyn's forehead. "But your head is burning up. Raahi, we need to get her to the city."

Still holding on to his daughter, Raahi nodded through his sobs.

"Now, Raahi!"

Raahi kissed Damini's forehead before he let her go and rushed to Jocelyn. He gently picked her up and ran out of the hut with Anne swiftly following.

White hair stroked the cheekbones of a beautifully aged woman. Her blue eyes sparkled with undying youth. Wrinkles lined the corners of her face with the wisdom of many years watching the world spin in circles. The woman held Jocelyn to her core, rubbing her back, trying to wipe away the pain that would forever be burnt into Jocelyn's soul.

Jocelyn stared at the wall of books bonded in processed seaweed—boiled down, pressed, bleached, and printed by the bookmakers of this realm.

This dream was different than the others that haunted her. The colors of the large room, brown and yellow, were clear, and the smell of salt and sand was fresh as she inhaled, tasting the dream.

What is happening? Why are they after us? Jocelyn asked.

The soft hands ran their fingers through her long, loose, brown hair.

Your grandfather is right. You are not like us. You are different— more evolved. The ocean has claimed you as its master. Do you understand, child?

Jocelyn shook her head, staring up at the old woman who

had the same eyes as she did.

You threaten the way things are down here. You are the new light that will wash over us and darken the old traditions. Traditions that many hold to keep power over all of us.

I will not revolt against all of the descendants.

I don't want you to, but we have to get you out. Away from them. As long as you are alive, they will hunt you.

The woman's voice rolled from her tongue as if for song, soothing and sweet—one meant to put children to sleep.

Nowhere is safe.

You're wrong, child. There is no time. We leave tonight.

Jocelyn bit her bottom lip, holding back a swarm of sorrow that rushed her breaking heart.

They were trying to protect me.

A worn smile lifted the old woman's face.

I know, child. That's what parents do. We die so our children can live. We leave tonight. Ready yourself for the voyage. Gentle lips pressed against Jocelyn forehead. *Bring little, my light. Where we are going, we cannot take our things.*

Jocelyn wrapped her fingers around her grandmother's wrist, holding tight to the last of her family. The steady pulse of the old woman was a reminder the world was still moving and, even though she wanted to lie down and give in to her grief, Jocelyn could not. If she broke down, she would lose the drive for destroying the descendants—the first to sink into the ocean and lift from its sands a civilization of evolved humans that ruled the sea with their knowledge of controlled metamorphosis.

She ran her fingers over her emblem protruding from her chest. Placed on her minutes after her birth on land, the medallion was the key to the underwater world, transforming her into a mermaid. The coral twisting into three waves molded with copper was her family's crest—one of the oldest.

Will we ever return? Jocelyn asked.

No, my light. We cannot.

Back at the hotel, Aidan walked into the lobby and found Thomas blowing smoke circles from his cigar into the dry air.

"I have come to speak to you about Benlar," Aidan said, taking a seat next to Thomas.

"What about him?"

Thomas pulled out a white, embroidered handkerchief from the inside of his coat.

"I wish you to reconsider taking him on board. He will be nothing but trouble, and with a woman already in our party, we do not need to stir the pot more."

"Stir the pot, you say. Well, I don't see it that way."

Thomas gently spit small tobacco flakes into his handkerchief.

Aidan shook his head, throwing his hands in the air. He looked around at the grand statues and marble tile of the club, trying to focus on anything to stop his anger from boiling over.

"You don't understand what you are about to do."

"First, you tell me how to run my trading company, and now you declare I am not to allow a paying man to accompany us," Thomas said churlishly. "If I were to listen to you, I fear I would go broke. It's too bad my father didn't spend more time teaching you how business works." Thomas snickered, raising the smoldering cigar to his mouth.

Before Aidan could respond, a tall Indian man ran into the lobby, waving his arms and yelling to a group of locals. He left as fast as he'd arrived. The group rushed outside after him. Aidan stood and walked to the large open doors.

"What the bloody hell is going on?" Thomas blustered, pushing his cigar into a glass ashtray and staring at the commotion.

"I don't know," Aidan answered, watching as the men gathered around a carriage.

The tall man bent down into the open compartment. Anne sat inside, holding something in her lap. Anne looked up and made eye contact with Aidan. Without hesitation and with instant comprehension, he rushed to the carriage.

"Out of the way!" he yelled, pushing through the small crowd.

"Oh, thank God! Mr. Boyd, it's Miss Jocelyn," Anne cried as the tall man stepped out of his way.

Aidan jumped up on the footrest and stood over Jocelyn. Anne was cradling her fragile body as a mother would a hurt child. He could only stare.

"What happened?" he asked in disbelief.

"I cannot tell you here," Anne whispered, "but we need to get her to her room quickly. We are running out of time."

He gently but firmly slid his arms under Jocelyn's limp body.

"Out of time? What do you mean out of time?"

"Soon, if not already, everyone will know what she has done, and they will all come for her."

"What happened?"

Aidan's eyes burned into Anne's.

"Get her inside, and I'll tell you everything."

Aidan swiftly carried Jocelyn through the small door of the carriage and rushed her to her room. Anne grabbed Jocelyn's bonnet before following them.

Thomas stood from his seat as Aidan hurried past him with his precious burden.

"Is that Jocelyn? What the bloody hell happened?" Thomas yelled at him.

"The weather has gotten to her. Nothing to worry about," Aidan hollered back, continuing down the hallway.

"Very good then," Thomas said, settling back down with his cigar. "But make it quick. We have a trade to make."

Chapter Twenty-Eight ֍

Aidan paced the room while Jocelyn lay motionless in her bed, her sweat drenching the covers. Anne sat in the corner, wiping her eyes. Even the sweet scent of the blooming flowers outside could not wash away the despair hovering in the still air.

"What she did was a miracle. That girl was on her deathbed, and she healed her. Never in my life have I witnessed such a thing!" Anne said in awe.

"You said we were running out of time. What did you mean by that?" Aidan asked in a calm voice, checking to see if Jocelyn was still breathing.

Her chest vibrated like a hummingbird's, moving so rapidly it was almost imperceptible.

"That girl is not the only sick child. The villagers will come to Jocelyn and demand she heal their loved ones."

He closed his eyes, envisioning a mob of desperate families carrying her away.

"How long do you think we have?"

"News travels quickly here. I saw what happened to her." Anne stood and walked over to the bed. She tenderly placed her hand on Jocelyn's head. "I don't know what she is, but you need to protect her. I do not believe she would survive another miracle."

He stopped pacing and looked into the mirror hanging over the washbowl. He stared at the reflection of the chamber.

How can I save her?

Jocelyn's body twitched, and she began to moan in pain with each spasm. The smell of the room grew thick with sweat and drying vomit. His stomach turned, but he forced himself to be strong for her.

Think! What can I do to help?

He watched Anne lift Jocelyn's head and place it on her lap. He was glad Anne was with them.

"What should I do?" Aidan asked.

"Leave..."

A loud knock on the door interrupted Anne.

"Jocelyn! Aidan! Are you in there?"

Thomas's voice thundered through the wood. Aidan rushed to the door and swung it open.

"What do you think you're doing in Miss Jocelyn's room?" Thomas barked.

"Listen to me. I will only say this once. Go to your room and pack your things. We leave on the hour, and, if you are not on the ship, I will leave you here."

"How dare you! I will have the authorities arrest you for such a threat."

Thomas pounded his fist against the plaster wall.

"By all means, do, but you will never leave India. My crew will make sure of that," Aidan calmly threatened.

Thomas's mouth dropped as Aidan shut the door in his face. He went to Jocelyn's side.

"Mrs. Howard, can you please pack Jocelyn's things?" he asked, lovingly stroking Jocelyn's feverish face.

"Of course." Without hesitation, Anne gently laid Jocelyn's head on the bed and jumped to her feet. "You will need to get your crew. Tell my man to take you wherever you need to go."

"You are very kind." He rushed toward the door, then hesitated. "Don't let anyone in here until I get back."

"I will lock the door as soon as you leave," she assured him.

Aidan, hand on the doorknob, stopped and looked at Anne, suddenly overcome by the braveness of the woman.

"You barely know her," he said softly.

"I know." Anne looked to Jocelyn, curled in the fetal position on the oversized bed. "But there is something about this girl that tells me if I don't help her, I will regret it to my dying day." She looked back to Aidan and gave him a small, quick nod. "Now go."

Jocelyn could hear feet shuffling on the hardwood floor. Using all of her strength, she peeled her eyes open. The bright sunlight blinded her. Quickly she squinted and whimpered, burying her head back into her pillow.

"Are you waking?" Anne's voice seemed slurred.

Suddenly, a sharp pain pierced Jocelyn's head and darted through her entire body, causing her to cry out in pain. Anne's cold hand pressed against her forehead. She tried to pull away from the freezing touch but could not. Her aching body shuddered with another excruciating spasm. She gripped the sheets, screaming.

"Oh, God. Dear! Can you hear me? Open your eyes!" Anne grabbed Jocelyn's shoulders.

She mustered enough strength to obey Anne's command.

Anne gasped.

"What have you done?"

Jocelyn's eyes closed as her body went limp in Anne's embrace.

The memory rushed fast into Jocelyn's mind, erasing the pain from her weakening body.

Her grandmother held tight to a round, brass lantern. The small container within held methane gas to ignite the flame trapped in the bulb. The glow gave way to the multi-colored fish that swam around them.

Jocelyn looked behind her at a golden tail that shimmered specks of blue from the light, kicking through the dark water —her tail. A knife was strapped by a leather belt to her thigh. She kicked harder, keeping pace with her grandmother, who held tight to a satchel fastened around her teal tail.

We have until dawn. Stay close, Jocelyn's grandmother ordered.

The two swam through the current of the playful sea and the large corral reef that painted the ocean floor. A hand reached through the colorful mess and grabbed Jocelyn. She released the knife, ready to strike the threat.

Where are you going? The familiar voice was soon joined by its owner, Benlar.

Jocelyn wrapped her arms around his neck, knowing this was the last time she was ever going to see him. She shook in his arms.

Mli, what's the matter?

The news of her mother's death was unknown to the

others, but her mother's dead eyes haunted Jocelyn. She
wanted to tell Benlar what had happened. The words sprang to
her mind but were stopped by her grandmother's hand
pressing her back.

We have to go, the old woman said.

Jocelyn held tighter to the only man she had ever loved.
Since childhood, he was her rock. He protected her from the
cruelties of the world with his sharp tongue—and brutal force
when necessary.

I will come with you, Benlar said with an unarguable tone.

Jocelyn shook her head, swallowing the pain of leaving her
love.

You can't come. She peered up at him. *I won't be long. Only a
few days' trip. We need to find my grandfather,* she lied.

She wrapped her fingers around his sandy blond hair and
kissed his lips with enough passion to last a lifetime.

She floated back, away from him.

Mli, I love you.

Jocelyn smiled so brightly he could not see her body
trembling with the pain of losing another loved one.

I love you too, Benlar.

Promise me you will come back soon.

I promise.

Avia grabbed her granddaughter and pulled her forward,
breaking the string that tied Jocelyn to the underworld. The
man she had loved as a child and thought would be her
eternity floated frozen in the cold abyss. She swam faster into
the unknown, knowing she would never see him again.

Chapter Twenty-Nine ෯

Aidan found his men at the tavern. He searched for Nicholas in the crowd of merry sailors. The crew would listen to the old man. Nicholas sat at a table surrounded by blokes, swapping tales of the sea. Aidan pushed through the throng and slammed his hands down on the table.

"Nicholas, we need to leave. Now! Gather the crew."

"Why the 'urry Captain?"

"It's Miss Jocelyn."

Nicholas stood, knocking his chair to the ground.

"She be all right, I pray?"

Aidan shook his head.

"They are coming for her."

"Who be coming fer 'er?"

Nicholas pulled Aidan away from the rowdy drunkards.

"She saved a girl—some sort of miracle, they say. The villagers will be coming for her, but she's so sick she can hardly move."

"I warned the stupid girl." Nicholas grabbed Aidan's shirt and pulled him close. The old man's breath reeked of stale ale. "Do they know wot she be?"

"Not now Nicholas. I don't have..." Aidan stopped. *He*

knows who she is? "Tell me Nicholas—who is she?"

With dirt-brown eyes, Nicholas stared at him.

"She be a mermaid, sir."

Aidan shook his head.

That's what I get for asking a drunken, superstitious old man—legends of the sea.

"Ready the crew," he directed Nicholas. "Find Gregory and make haste. We do not have much time."

He didn't wait for a rebuttal and left the tavern.

Anne's driver raced the carriage full speed across the dusty roads back to the inn. As the carriage slowed, Aidan jumped off and ran to his room. He threw his belongings into a small leather bag and ran to Jocelyn's quarters. He leaned into the door and banged on it.

"Mrs. Howard—it's Mr. Boyd."

The lock clicked, and Anne threw open the door.

"Thank God." Tears fell from her eyes. "She is worse, so much worse."

He looked past Anne to Jocelyn. He touched Anne's elbow and guided her out of his way.

"Tell your man to take her things to the carriage."

Anne rushed out with her head bowed, clutching her chest.

He sat on the bed next to the fragile Jocelyn. Her breathing was quick and uneven. He placed his large hand on her burning forehead and moved closer. Her once delicate, porcelain skin now appeared dry and gray against his tan hand. Drops of sweat clung to his skin from the light touch. She burned with fever. Aidan took the edge of the sheet and wiped her brow before he leaned down and whispered in her ear.

"I love you."

He took her limp hand into his and pressed it gently to his lips.

Anne's driver tiptoed into the room, picked up the trunk Anne had packed, and rushed it to the waiting carriage. Anne entered the room shortly after.

"Look at her eyes."

Still holding on to her hand, Aidan retracted an eyelid. The once indescribable blue had become a murky yellow.

"They're yellow!" he exclaimed.

He looked at Anne, desperate for an explanation.

"Damini's were the same color. She is dying."

Before Anne could say another word, he grabbed Jocelyn and lifted her to his chest. He stood, and one of her hands fell from her lap and swung with his steps.

"No doctor here will treat her," Anne whispered.

"What? Why on earth not?" Aidan asked.

"They have nothing to cure her. I tried every physician to help Damini, and everyone said the same thing. 'Let her die in peace.'"

"Dear God, what am I to do?" Aidan paced the room, thinking.

He looked down at Jocelyn's face, his love wasting away in front of him.

"Whatever you can. But it can't be done here. She will surely die if you stay. The carriage is waiting."

"Thank you."

Aidan held Jocelyn tight to his chest and hastened from the room, leaving Anne to grieve.

Thomas barked orders at the crew to stop preparing the ship for departure, but it was to no avail. Gregory spoke over Thomas, directing the crew to hurry. Ropes whipped in the breeze, and the sails swung loosely when Anne's carriage sped to a stop at the boarding ramp. Aidan yelled for the crew to grab the luggage. He ran onto the rocking ship, holding Jocelyn close.

"Is everything ready?"

"Almost, Captain," Gregory answered.

"Make it ready," Aidan ordered.

Gregory looked down at Jocelyn's motionless body.

"Is she…"

Aidan stopped Gregory before he could utter another word.

"Get this ship sailing now."

Gregory straightened and yelled at the top of his lungs, "Every man at 'is station!"

Aidan rushed forward to the belly of the ship.

"How dare you!" Thomas shrieked, stopping him.

Aidan's eyes burned with anger at his employer. Thomas looked down at Jocelyn.

"What did you do?" Thomas uttered in shocked dismay.

"India did this. I think it is best if you go to your room and stay there as much as possible," Aidan said, turning his back on Thomas.

He made his way below deck, Jocelyn's breathing still raspy and erratic as the giant chains of the rising anchor clanged against the hull.

"We are not leaving without the opium!"

Thomas followed close behind.

"We already have!" Aidan yelled over his shoulder.

Thomas ran toward the main deck as the ship pulled away from the dock.

Once in the tight corridor away from Thomas and the crew, Aidan kissed Jocelyn's forehead. His lips burned from her fever.

"You're going to be all right," he said, trying to convince himself.

A movement at the end of the gangway stopped Aidan.

"Who's there?" he asked, waiting for one of his crewmembers to speak.

"You didn't think you would get rid of me that easily, did you?" Benlar asked, stepping into view. "This ship is actually quite nice. I'll be very comfortable."

"What the bloody hell are you doing here?" Aidan demanded, pulling Jocelyn tighter to him.

"Looking around." Benlar stepped closer, staring at her. "What happened?"

"The weather."

"The weather did not do this to her!"

"And how would you know?"

Aidan tried to keep calm as a breeze whistled through the small space.

"Because I know." Benlar reached his fingers to touch her but pulled them away. "You need to get her to her room immediately."

"What are you not telling me?"

He could see the worry in the man's eyes. Benlar shook his head.

"Your ship needs a captain, and she needs rest."

Aidan wanted to argue but knew he was right. He shoved

forward.

Chapter Thirty &

The memory drove Jocelyn deep into the ocean. A storm rocked the sea. The lantern blazed bright as Jocelyn and Avia swam for the only sanctuary they had left—land.

Lightning struck the surface of the underwater world and spread out, fanning over the sea in a wave of light. Jocelyn watched the tempest forming above. Her widening pupils allowed her to see clearly through the watery depths. Thunder reverberated into the ocean and into her. Her world was breaking apart, and the heavens wept. Rain pelted the ocean, disappearing into the rolling waves.

They were close. The bottom of the ocean climbed upward toward the island where they could remove their emblems to become human once more.

I don't want to go, Jocelyn begged.

Avia swam to her granddaughter, cradling her in her arms. *I know. But we have to. We will return to the sea.*

When? Years or centuries, Grandmother?

Avia smoothed Jocelyn's long brown hair, fluttering with the current.

However long it takes.

Nothing will be the same when we return, Jocelyn said.

It hasn't been for a long time, my light. Come, we're almost to shore.

Jocelyn watched her vanishing home for the last time. The mounds of sand and coral reefs blocked her view of the village, but the luminescence from the houses brightened the ocean floor and silhouetted the danger swimming toward them.

An arrow spun through the ocean between Jocelyn and Avia.

Swim, child. Swim! Avia screamed.

Jocelyn propelled herself through the rolling sea. Thunder roared through the waters as another arrow flew past her. As she turned to glance back at who was firing the weapon, Fiar aimed the crossbow at her head. Jocelyn kicked to the right as the arrow grazed her fin and tail. Swimming faster, she ignored the burning sensation as the salt water soaked into her wound. She turned back as another merman aimed his weapon at Avia. Grabbing her grandmother's tail, she pulled her down, and the arrow missed the old woman's head.

Jocelyn stood upright on the current as the men swam toward her. The image of her mother and the death of her father fueled the anger in her blood. The ocean began to twirl as she pulled lightning through the water—inching its way deeper and deeper into the forbidden. Jocelyn's hair rose as the electricity merged with the water. Avia grabbed her granddaughter's hand.

Just swim.

But Jocelyn was done swimming. She pulled away from Avia as another lightning bolt struck the waters near the mermen. They scattered, but Fiar was determined to see Jocelyn dead. He aimed another arrow and fired.

The sharp point rotated toward Jocelyn's heart, but she did not move. She shifted her eyes to the sky to release more lightning through the water, disintegrating the arrow. Her power controlled by her hatred was at full force, ready to rip the world apart. The ocean and sky were her weapons. One by one the mermen were pierced by lighting or thrown into the sky by the current of the monstrous sea. But the one she wanted dead, Fiar, held tight to the craggy cliffs below, waiting to strike.

Avia grabbed Jocelyn's face, turning her black eyes to meet her own. The ocean raged in Jocelyn's soul as lightning struck from within her eyes.

You don't know what you are doing.

Leave me, Grandmother. Let me finish them.

Jocelyn turned to the few men, struggling to survive in the death trap.

Avia swam in front of Jocelyn, blocking the men from her view.

You will destroy everything if you continue. Stop now, child.

Jocelyn pushed Avia aside. She was in control, and no one was going to stop her from killing Fiar or anyone else who meant her harm.

Fiar lifted his bow and fired.

Spotting the arrow, Avia grabbed Jocelyn's waist and pushed her away from the deadly blow, taking the hit.

Unsure of who had grabbed her, Jocelyn's fury surrounded Avia. The ocean shoved her grandmother away, and bolts of protective lightning surrounded the old woman.

Avia shook in fear of her grandchild. The ocean calmed as Jocelyn struggled to breathe. Lost in the desire to cause pain, she had almost hurt the one she loved.

Swim, Avia said.

I'm so sorry!

The dangers of the waters disappeared as Jocelyn pleaded

for forgiveness. Neither of the women noticed Fiar swimming in the shadows.

Just swim, child. You need to leave the water now!

Before Jocelyn could move, Fiar's knife was at her neck, the burning metal boiling the water.

What a ride, girl. They will marvel at what you can do, Fiar boasted as he pulled a long tube, containing a red gas in its glass walls, from a satchel fastened to his mud-brown fin.

You can't do this, Fiar, Avia begged.

Do you wish her dead instead?

Avia froze as Fiar pushed the blade closer to Jocelyn's skin.

What do you want with me? Jocelyn asked.

It's not me who wants you, but the descendants.

And you think you can bring me to them? Jocelyn laughed.

The ocean began to spin around them, leaving Avia on the outside of the whirlpool.

Fiar pressed the tube to Jocelyn's ear as the current tore between them.

You won't remember who I am, girl.

He pulled the lever, releasing the red gas that twisted into her ear canal. But he wasn't quick enough. The current spun wide, ripping the blade from Fiar's hand. The ocean floor blistered in air pockets as the ground cracked opened. In all of her fury, Jocelyn threw the water up, shooting Fiar into the raging sky.

The sea possessed all of Jocelyn's senses. The ocean was a slave to her, and she was a slave to it. There was no balance. She knew the scale had tipped, and she could destroy everything she loved. She could never return to the ocean.

Mli?

What is happening to me?

One by one, Jocelyn's memories slipped away from her.

Avia pressed her wound.

Listen, my light. You won't remember me soon. But you will be fine. I will find you. Do you hear me? I will find you. You have to go alone.

Jocelyn looked down at the end of the arrow sticking out of Avia's side.

Grandmother?

I need to heal, but I will find you.

Avia gripped Jocelyn's emblem.

The shore is not far.

She pulled the medallion from Jocelyn's chest.

Jocelyn's eyes widened as the gills on her sides pulled inward, closing. The webbing between her fingers shifted down, hiding themselves.

Remember.

Avia pressed the medallion into Jocelyn's palm.

Don't let go, Avia begged.

Her last memory vanished from her mind as her tail pulled apart, revealing pale legs.

The ship rocked. The scent of fresh salt from the ocean filled Jocelyn's nostrils. Never before had the ocean sung to her so clearly. She tried to block its cry with the pillow, but it rang through. She opened her aching, bleary eyes and looked around her room. The sun had started to disappear, allowing shadows to paint the room. Shapes of Aidan's desk and armoire blended with the deepening darkness. She could sense someone was in her cabin but could not see him.

"Why did you do that?" a familiar voice asked.

Jocelyn looked to the only dark corner of the room. Her head pulsated with the movement.

"Who's there?" she squinted.

"Benlar."

He stepped out of the shadows and walked to the bed.

Jocelyn pulled herself up and rested against the headboard as the ocean continued to sing to her. The returning memories crippled her from standing. She had left Benlar behind in the sea, expecting never to see him again, yet here he was in her room. Her eyes swelled with tears she forbade to fall. If she fell apart now, she would never find herself again.

"Why did you do that for the girl?" Benlar asked.

"I don't know."

A surge of pain ran from her head to her toes.

"You saved her."

She blinked rapidly, trying to clear her vision.

Benlar grabbed her hand and squeezed.

"Mli."

Her eyes cleared, and she stared into Benlar's familiar and comforting eyes.

I remember everything, Jocelyn confessed.

"I could have protected you from all of that, but you left."

"I had to."

"I'll bring you to Thessa. They can help."

"I can't go to Thessa. I can't go back into the water."

Benlar sat next to her.

"I searched for you."

"And you found me. But I can't return. You don't understand, Benlar."

Jocelyn shifted, but her body refused to move, her joints frozen.

"Mli, you can't stay above."

"I have no choice."

"What you did is killing you," Benlar said.

"I still don't understand what I did."

"I don't understand it either, but your grandfather says it's written that the sea can claim one as its own. But it's a myth."

Jocelyn closed her eyes as a sudden headache exploded behind them.

"He was right, you know. His crazy lectures of half-breeds and tainted blood."

"He predicted it was because we had evolved. That our genes have changed. And the only way to stabilize a half-breed is to remove the toxins from the morphing genes. I remember."

"It's the toxins that kill them, because we're not human anymore," Jocelyn said.

The headache slowly faded.

"Her blood cells were dividing at a rapid speed, and it was creating toxins her body could not break down. Our two species are not meant to be together. I could smell death on her, lingering on her."

"We have to get you back into the water. It can heal you once you are in your true form. Then, we need to get to Thessa, where you belong," Benlar said.

"I don't belong anywhere!"

Benlar shook his head.

"You belong with me."

He reached under her and lifted her into his arms with no effort.

"What are you doing?" she asked, thinking of struggling but instead, clung tight to him.

"I'm taking you home." Benlar walked toward the door of the cabin. He stopped and looked at her. *I've missed you.*

She traced his motionless mouth but answered aloud.

"I've missed you too, but you have to leave me."

"Never, Mli."

She coughed and shivered, noticing the weak beats of her failing heart.

The cabin door swung open. Aidan stood in the doorway, dumbfounded, as Jocelyn clung to Benlar.

"Let go of her!" he said, gripping the doorframe.

"I can't do that," Benlar said.

"I said let her go!"

He charged Benlar.

Benlar swiftly stepped out of the way, and Aidan ran into the bed.

"Aidan, stop it!" Jocelyn shouted, trying to gain control of the situation. The cabin seemed to grow smaller by the second.

"What the bloody hell is going on?" Aidan begged, trying to gain his footing.

"You would never understand," Benlar stated.

"I did not know," Jocelyn said. "I'm sorry—I never wanted to hurt you."

Jocelyn watched Aidan's eyes fill with pain.

"I see," Aidan said, staring at her arms wrapped around Benlar.

"You don't understand, Aidan," Jocelyn's voice was weak.

"What is it then?" he asked, his eyes pleading for the truth.

"He will not understand," Benlar said.

Jocelyn closed her eyes.

"I am a mermaid."

Aidan stumbled backward, bumping into the washtable. He looked around the room, her belongings mixed with his, his heart breaking.

"What do you take me for, a fool?" he cried. "Just tell me the truth. I love you Jocelyn, and all you have done is run me in circles. I need an answer."

"I am telling you the truth," she said under her breath as another bolt of pain jolted through her.

She began to shake, trying to control her breathing.

"Give me the emblem."

Benlar reached out his hand to Aidan.

"No," Aidan replied. "Give her to me. Can't you see she is in pain?"

Benlar pulled her closer.

"You can't help her," Benlar said.

Aidan stared into Benlar's eyes, ready for a fight.

"She is not yours," Aidan yelled.

With one swift kick, Benlar connected with Aidan's chest and sent him sprawling on the bed. Aidan found himself on his back, trying to catch his breath while Benlar searched his pockets.

Still gasping for air, Aidan glimpsed a white coral hanging from a silver chain through Benlar's shirt.

Benlar's face lit up as he pulled the emblem from Aidan's pocket. Carefully he placed Jocelyn next to Aidan on the bed.

Through her pain, she looked at the coral. Her father's crest. Three waves enclosed in a circle. Her way home.

"You've had it this whole time?" she asked, her voice a mixture of fatigue and relief.

A single tear rolled from her yellow-tinged eyes as she turned and beheld Aidan's tortured expression.

Unable to talk, Aidan watched Benlar carefully place the trinket onto Jocelyn's chest. He pressed it down with his index finger, holding it into place. The gears shifted, turning on. It began to glow as it fused with Jocelyn's skin.

Jocelyn could feel the binding of the trinket but was again overwhelmed by the throbbing pain of impending death.

Aidan watched in desperation as Benlar ran out of the room with Jocelyn in his arms, her screams echoing down the hallway.

Chapter Thirty-One ⚆

The cool breeze refreshed Jocelyn's sweltering skin as Benlar carried her onto the upper deck. She opened her bleary eyes to the late afternoon sun kissing the rim of the blue sea, sending bright reds and oranges across the sky. She wondered if the setting sun would be the last thing she would ever see. Pain burned inside of her. She gripped Benlar's shirt, trying not to faint from the torment. If dying would stop the pain, she welcomed her grave.

The crew turned and watched the strange man running across the slippery deck, Jocelyn clinging to his breast like a pale necklace. With Nicholas's words of warning still carved in her heart, she wondered what would happen to the men once she was gone and to the people below if she returned to the sea.

"Wait," she whispered in Benlar's ear.

Focused on the bow of the ship, Benlar pressed on.

"What?"

"What will happen to them?" she asked, afraid of the answer.

"I don't know. Probably die. They all do eventually."

"I can't do this—I don't want them to die because of me!"

Jocelyn tried to wiggle out of his tight grip.

"You have to. I will not let you die."

"I will destroy it all."

Benlar held her more firmly.

"You have to let me go," Jocelyn begged the man who was her protector and lover. She understood if he left her on the ship, she would die, but if she returned below and the descendants found her, what would happen to her home and the people who lived there?

And there was Aidan.

The pull of the ocean begged her to make the leap, but Aidan's voice was stronger. Aidan cried out to his crew to stop Benlar. His voice soothed her.

She turned and saw Aidan running toward them. She hoped he would not be too late.

"I love him," Jocelyn confessed, knowing it would hurt Benlar.

Benlar stumbled to a halt and stared down at her in disbelief. His eyes raged with anger, swirling from light blue to almost pitch black.

"You love *me*."

Jocelyn cheeks burned at his words. Part of her knew he was right, but she was in love with Aidan too.

The ocean began to roar around them.

Benlar stared at her.

"You've changed," he scorned.

Suddenly Nicholas's large body charged into Benlar like a swinging tree trunk, sending them all crashing to the hard deck. Sprawled on the ground, Jocelyn cried out in pain.

Benlar lay on the wood but only for an instant. He quickly recoiled and jumped to his feet with incredible speed. Nicholas righted himself slowly.

She stared into Nicholas's fearful eyes as he watched Benlar. Benlar's shirt was ripped, exposing the spiraling coral dangling from a chain. She touched her medallion as a large wave crashed against the side of the ship. She had to control herself if she didn't want the ship to go down in the storm she was creating.

"Just let her go," Nicholas begged.

"I can't do that, old man," Benlar replied.

Jocelyn grabbed hold of a barrel on the deck and pulled herself up, her body splitting with pain. She slowly stood, steadying herself against the drum.

Nicholas's hand shook as he gripped something under his coat.

"Don't even think about it," Benlar warned Nicholas as another titanic wave pounded the ship.

Nicholas pulled a long knife from beneath his coat. In a flash, Benlar flew toward him, slapping the knife from his hands.

Benlar turned to go back to Jocelyn, but a pistol pressed into his chest. He froze.

"I will shoot you, and I will not miss," Aidan promised.

"No, you won't," Benlar said, smiling calmly.

Jocelyn, still unsteady on her feet, grabbed the rail of the swaying vessel. She watched Aidan's face to see if he had heard her confession. Every part of her begged to be in his arms. She ordered her legs to move forward, but they would not support her.

Aidan shifted his eyes from Benlar to Jocelyn.

"I don't care what you are."

Her heart leapt at his words, knowing she only had a few hours left with him.

"Well, I do," Benlar whispered.

Before Aidan could react, Benlar swatted the pistol out of his hand.

"Stop this!" Jocelyn tried to shout.

Lightning struck across the sky, illuminating the bow of the ship.

Benlar punched Aidan. Aidan grabbed Benlar's chest, grabbing hold of the warm medallion. Another blow sent him to the ground. Benlar rushed to Jocelyn.

Aidan stumbled, his ears ringing, sliding his hand over the brass handle of his pistol. Ignoring the pain, he stood, grasping the pistol. He started toward Jocelyn, but Benlar had already closed in.

Benlar grabbed Jocelyn's shoulders and pulled her close to him. Her trinket began to glow as brightly as the summer moon. He touched his own chest, trying to find his trinket to press against his bare skin.

Jocelyn turned to see the barrel of the pistol aimed at Benlar's medallion, the broken chain dangling from Aidan's hand.

"Very good," Benlar praised, still holding onto Jocelyn.

"Don't, Aidan," Jocelyn begged.

"Let her go," Aidan ordered.

Benlar turned to her.

"Don't struggle," he said.

Benlar pulled her close and kissed her lips deeply as rain spilled from the sky.

"Let her go!" Aidan yelled, cocking the gun.

In one swift movement, Benlar pushed Jocelyn overboard into the dark waves. The crew tackled him savagely.

As she fell into the sea, Jocelyn watched Aidan pull himself over the rail to jump in after her. But a dozen hands pulled him back. Too weak to struggle, she left go of the anger that controlled the storm above.

"Let me go!" Aidan screamed at his men as Jocelyn splashed into the cold water. She watched Aidan fade away. The dark waters consumed her. The heavens opened, shining down the blue light from the clear moon.

The pain in her froze with the ocean's embrace. Silence surrounded her, and she sank deeper. She tried to kick toward the disappearing surface, but her weak limbs struggled. She let go of her last breath. She felt nothing but the icy hands of the ocean.

Her heart slowed with her fall into the cold unknown. The pain that inhabited her body dissolved once the sea took her, promising never to let go. With her eyes closed, Jocelyn inhaled the seawater into her very soul, the saltiness sweet on her tongue. Her white satin dress danced with the slow movement of the underworld, brushing against her legs.

It's too late.

She opened her eyes as long strands of her hair grazed her translucent face. She ached for her lost life.

I want to go back.

She reached for the dark shadow of the ship above. To never again be near Aidan crushed her fragile heart. She pressed the medallion on her chest, her eyes drifting shut, and her heart stopped.

Specks of light glimmered off the trail of air bubbles drifting to the world above. A growing luminescence overpowered the never-ending darkness that engulfed her. Warmth filled her still heart as the forgiving ocean caressed her, whispering into her ear the silvery melody that had beckoned for weeks and weeks. She opened her eyes.

The bold light grew outward. In a flash, the overwhelming brightness shot toward Jocelyn and dived into her still body, leaving nothing but a dim glimmer that danced in front of her.

Slowly, her gaze followed the light down to her glowing medallion. She watched the brilliance from the emblem trace its way through her body, a thin, fiery thread like the tip of a hot knife sent both to burn and heal her. She lifted her hand, watching the dazzling glow beam through it. In moments, the burning light found the notches between her fingers. The pale webbing sprang a full two inches higher, joining her knuckles.

The metamorphosis had begun.

THE END

Don't miss a special preview of

Drifting

ᕮ

Book Two of the Sinking Trilogy

Chapter One ๑

Her pulse pounded through the thick waters, echoing back to her. The rising skin between her fingers held an internal flame glowing and burning through the dark sea. Jocelyn's lungs ordered her to gulp the salty ocean, demanding oxygen. She inhaled, letting the salt scratch down her throat, but the pain pushed through her ribs, tearing her flesh. She wrapped her arms around her chest and pulled her knees up, shielding herself. But she couldn't protect herself from morphing.

The flame danced down her arms, over her stomach, to her legs. She burned like a torch. Her white dress turned to ash against her scorching skin and fluttered in pieces around her. Exposed, Jocelyn hugged her legs closer, but they were not legs anymore. Her inner thighs molded together, fusing the skin that braided to her feet. Her toes pulled apart as a thin layer of skin webbed together, pulling her heel to the back of her ankle. She arched her back as the stretching tendons ached with the force. Small scales rose from her pale skin, shining like yellow diamonds against the inferno inside of her.

Cramping, Jocelyn's muscles forced her to spread her limbs from her core as the last of the transformation burned brighter. Thin, small fins growing from her elbows and her

large tail danced with the slow current of the sea. She panted
the water that rushed through her, in and out of the gills under
her breasts, tickling the tender flesh. Her lungs rejoiced. She
breathed in the water again.

The immobilizing spasm released its grip on her body,
allowing Jocelyn to have control once more. Her body
descended deeper into the ocean. The fire within her faded,
taking with it her only light. Her hope. Darkness forced its
way around her morphed body.

You are home, the ocean sang to her.

Jocelyn rubbed her hand up her thigh, pressing against
her newly acquired scales. They scratched her palm. Focusing,
her pupils stretched open, pulling away the iris and sclera until
thin rings of blue circled the windows to her soul, allowing the
elusive light from the depth of the ocean to paint her
surroundings.

Lime algae blanketed the rocks scattered across the sand.
Jocelyn's flukes hit the sea's floor. She tried to kick her tail to
swim upward, but her body was deprived of energy to spring
her forward. The rest of her body anchored onto the bed of
sand as the shadow of Aidan's ship passed over her.

Don't leave me. Please don't go.

Stretching up her webbed hand, Jocelyn reached for the
man she loved.

Her head knocked against the ocean floor as her heart
began, once again, to beat faster and faster, until the water
vibrated the rhythm back to her heavy body. Her stomach
turned as it pushed the poison from her, making her vomit.

Jocelyn remembered Damini's yellow, bulging eyes—death
waiting over the half-breed girl in Calcutta, India. The girl was
doomed from having a mermaid and human as her parents.
Once puberty started, her cells divided, fighting against each

other to become either human or merbeing, creating a poison in her system. Jocelyn had breathed the toxins out of Damini and into herself to save the girl, but it was killing her. Benlar, the merman who came to take Jocelyn home, had thrown her overboard, hoping the ocean could heal her.

Jocelyn threw up again. Her stomach contracted, squeezing out every last bit of its contents. Jocelyn bellowed in pain, pulling her tail closer to her chest as the ship drifted away on the surface of the ocean, taking with it the two men who loved her—who had kept her safe.

The ocean caressed her skin with its soft current for hours. With nothing left to spew, Jocelyn's stomach rested. She lay there, breathing in the moonlit water.

One.

She counted, moving her hands to her back and pushing up against the pressure of the water.

Two.

She raised herself to her hidden knees. Her stomach protested, making her gag. She stopped moving, waiting for her body to heal. Benlar was right; the ocean was restoring her health. She was still weak, but stronger than she had ever been on land.

Jocelyn ran her fingertips over the warm, embossed skin. She traced the three twisting waves that surrounded the triangle in the center. Her symbol was different than Benlar's. His spiraled inward like a shell cut in half. Aidan had taken it from him, imprisoning him on the ship.

Three.

Jocelyn swept the water with her opened hands, pushing up toward the surface. She kicked her tail and shot up through the water at rapid speed. She did it again, fascinated with the momentum from one movement, rushing her body toward the heavens above.

Her head shoved through the barrier of water and sky to nothing but open sea. She spun, searching for the ship, but it was gone. She was alone.

Jocelyn's lungs panted as she began to hyperventilate. She dipped her head underwater and inhaled the water, giving her relief.

"Aidan!" she screamed into the emptiness.

The air burned her eyes. She closed them as tears welled up, soothing the dryness.

Benlar! Jocelyn screamed through her mind.

I'm here.

Benlar's voice echoed in her head. Jocelyn's eyes shot open.

Mli, are you safe?

Jocelyn nodded. A small dot on the horizon on the edge of the ocean moved past the clouded night sky, exposing its location. Jocelyn focused on it. Sails. Her heart leapt.

Speak to me, Benlar demanded.

She dove under the water, swimming toward the ship.

Benlar? It was easier to communicate underwater with her mind. It was her natural language.

Are you safe? Benlar's deep voice cracked.

Jocelyn could feel his worry as if it were her own. He did not just speak words—he spoke his emotions to her from miles and miles away.

I've transformed, Jocelyn confessed.

Benlar's relief washed through Jocelyn as her body

propelled through the ocean toward him.

Go deep, Benlar ordered.

No. I'm coming to you. Don't leave me out here, Jocelyn begged.

It's not safe, Mli. I will be fine.

Doubt dropped her stomach. He was lying to her.

Don't lie to me.

So, you still feel me. Dive deep and fast.

No.

Don't trust anyone.

I'm coming back on that ship, Jocelyn pleaded.

You can't. Dive, Mli. Dive now.

Benlar's voice faded with every word.

Benlar? Benlar!

Benlar was gone. She could not feel his emotions intertwining with hers. She swam faster, closing her eyes to shield them from the piercing water. Her hands hit an attacking shark.

Chapter Two 🌀

Aidan wiggled his hands, trying to free them from the rope that kept him tied to the walls of the storage room. Blood stained the blond rope as his skin pulled away with his determination to be free.

"Will you stop that?" Benlar yelled across the room.

Aidan glared at the man who had thrown the only woman he had ever loved into the ocean to die.

"Do not speak to me." Aidan twisted his hands again, trying to gain control.

Benlar rubbed his cheek against his shoulder, wiping drying blood from his face. A deep cut extended over his forehead into his hair.

"Stop struggling. You're giving me a headache."

Aidan recoiled. "You threw her overboard!"

"Where she belongs."

"She was sick. Whatever she is, she will still die. Do you not see that?"

Benlar used his legs to push himself against the wall to stand.

"Die from what? I saved her."

Aidan did the same and stood to his feet, facing his enemy.

Both men, tied to opposite walls, leaned forward, stretching the fibers of the ropes digging into their skin.

"You killed her!" Aidan screamed.

"Then let me go, and I will save her again." Benlar lifted his chin.

Aidan leaned back against the wall and struggled to reach into his jacket pocket. On the verge of dislocating his shoulder, Aidan wrapped his fingers around Benlar's medallion. Aidan pulled out the coral trinket for Benlar to see.

"Is this what you are asking for?"

Benlar smirked as he leaned against the wooden walls of the ship.

"You know it's the only way."

"For you to escape?" Aidan dropped the trinket to the ground. It bounced then landed flat against his leather boot.

Benlar locked his eyes onto the trinket.

"You don't understand what she is. She needs me."

"She was fine until you boarded my ship."

"She will never be fine above water. This is her ocean. She has a responsibility to her kin," Benlar said.

Aidan shook the trinket from his boot. It clinked against the floor.

"Who were you to her?"

Aidan watched as Benlar slid back to the ground.

Benlar closed his eyes.

"We were lovers soon to be bound together." He opened his eyes, glaring at Aidan. "You see, Mr. Boyd, you were not the only creature in love with her."

Aidan's blood burned with hatred for Benlar. He shifted his eyes away from the merman.

"Is she dead?" Aidan asked.

"No."

"Will you protect her?"

"With my life," Benlar answered.

"You had better." Aidan shifted his boot and kicked the trinket. It stopped inches away from Benlar.

Benlar stared at the medallion.

"You'll never see her again," Benlar said, looking up at Aidan. "She will never return to you."

Aidan met his stare. "We will see."

Benlar stretched his toe toward the coral medallion. The creak of the heavy door stopped him. Both men stared as Thomas walked into the room with a pistol in each hand.

He aimed the first one slowly at Benlar's head.

"What the hell are you doing, man?" Aidan demanded.

"He killed my beloved. And you…" Thomas aimed the second pistol at Aidan. "Did too."

He pulled the trigger.

Aidan flinched, but nothing happened.

Thomas grinned. "I cannot have my captain murdered onboard. That would be bad for business. But a public hanging —that will be a sight to see."

"On what grounds?" Aidan asked, his eyes trained on the pistol still pointed at Benlar.

"Murder and mutiny, of course," Thomas answered.

"No one will believe you," Aidan snapped.

"Quite the contrary, sir. My fiancé rests at the bottom of the sea due to the quarrel between you and Mr. Benlar." Thomas took a step toward Benlar. "And you, Mr. Benlar."

He aimed the gun at his leg and fired.

The round bullet tore through Benlar's flesh, lodging against the bone. Screaming in pain, Benlar pushed down on the wound, trying to seal it. Blood seeped through his fingers, streaming onto the floor and toward the coral. Thomas picked up Benlar's only way home.

"Scream all you like, Mr. Benlar. This is not the end."

Thomas walked out, leaving Aidan to watch Benlar bleed to death.

TO BE CONTINUED...

Acknowledgements ෴

This book would not exist today without the love and support of my wonderful husband, Joshua Garner, who would talk me back into being a writer when I was talking myself out.

I would like to thank my fellow writer's group members, Kathy Boyd Fellure, Pam Dunn, and John Clewett, who have been key to making this book into reality by reading many bad drafts.

Thank you to my editor and friend, Michele Harper, who loves my characters as much as I do.

My deepest gratitude goes to my father, Steve Armstrong, who said never stop because nothing happens overnight; my three beautiful children, who would sleep long enough to allow me to create a new chapter; my mother, Theresa, who always believed there would be a writer in the family; and to God, for giving me the imagination to create new worlds.

About the Author ⚬

Sarah Armstrong-Garner lives in Northern California with her husband and three children, and get this. Not only is she an author, screenwriter, and photographer, she also shoots indie films with her husband. Sinking is her debut novel.

You can visit **SarahArmstrongGarner.com** to learn more about her and her upcoming releases.

Reviews ⚛

Did you like this book? Authors treasure reviews! (And read them over and over and over…) If you enjoyed this book, would you consider leaving a review on Amazon, Barnes & Noble, Goodreads, or perhaps even your personal blog? Thank you so much!

Coming Soon from
Love2ReadLove2Write Publishing

Candace Marshall hates zombies. As in, loathes, abhors, detests — you
get the idea. She also refuses to watch horror movies. You can
imagine her complete and utter joy when her boyfriend surprises her
with advanced screening tickets to the latest gruesome zombie flick.
Annoyance flares into horror as the movie comes to life, and Candace
finds herself surrounded by real-life, honest-to-goodness zombies.
She learns how to shoot and scream with the best of them and
surprises herself with — courage? But, just when Candace thinks it
can't get worse than zombies, it does. Don't miss this lighthearted
adventure, Book One of the Candace Marshall Chronicles.

CPSIA information can be obtained
at www.ICGtesting.com
Printed in the USA
FFOW04n1206160316
22399FF

9 781943 788040